Melody Unbound

A through the portal coveted fairy romance

Coveted Prey
Book 17

L.V. Lane

Cover character art by Softdraws
Cover design by Three Spires Creative
Editing by Steph Tashkoff

 Created with Vellum

Contents

Prologue

Melody

"Melody, put on your boots," Bard chides.

I don't want to put on my boots. I want to dance. But I can tell from the look on his face that my guardian is not going to suffer my mischief today, so I try very hard not to pout.

Usually, Jasmine helps me with my boots. She is the bond-servant tasked with my care. In the mornings, she helps me dress and then gets my breakfast. After I break my fast she often lets me plait her hair. But she is late today, and I have dressed myself, except for my boots—I still struggle with laces.

Bard sighs and stoops down to help me.

He makes quick work of my boots and is rising with a grimace when the tent flap bursts open. I look over, wanting to tell Jasmine that I have got ready without her, and then I see who it is.

"Mama!"

I know that Winter is not my real mama, but I like to

1

pretend that she is. I can only *just* remember my mama's warm embrace and the way gold dust from her wings shimmered in the light, making me giggle when it landed on my nose. Winter is the only fairy I have seen since Bard helped me flee from my home, and it doesn't matter to me that she doesn't have wings.

"I'm taking her," Winter says to Bard.

His eyes widen in response to her statement and, a moment after, his shoulders sag. He nods.

Her? She means me. I'm sure about it. "Are we going on an adventure?" I've had many adventures in my life, and I'm not yet six years old. "Where are we going? I haven't had breakfast yet."

The tent flap opens, and Jasmine enters... but without my breakfast tray. A frown is etched into her pretty face as she looks first to Bard and Winter, and then to me.

"Something is happening in the bondservants' part of the camp," she says to Winter. "And your guards have gone."

"Are we going on a trip?" I ask, feeling impatient now.

"Get your cloak, Melody," Bard says.

"Yippee!"

"Help her with her cloak, Jasmine," Bard says in his firmest voice, usually reserved for my worst mischief.

We are about to have an adventure. I can barely contain my excitement. Jasmine tries to dress me in a cloak, which is difficult when I'm dancing about our tent.

Bard and Winter are talking.

A clamor rises beyond the tent walls. My brow furrows, for the sounds unsettle me. I hold still, so Jasmine can finish with my cloak. The noises outside remind me of the day the dark fae painted the Citadel's walls with blood, and a tremor runs through my body.

Bard crouches before me, his hand on my shoulder. His expression is serious, as it often is. "Winter is going to take you away from here, Melody. You must be a good girl for her and keep very quiet."

Beyond the tent, a rushing roaring swell of shouts and cries of alarm makes my tummy queasy.

"Are you coming?" I ask Bard, a little quiver in my voice.

His face softens and he shakes his head. "No, Melody, you must move swiftly, and I will only slow you down."

"Will I see you later? After the adventure?" Except, now, I no longer think I will like this adventure, and tears sting the back of my eyes.

When he shakes his head again, my tears begin to spill. Outside, the rushing roaring sounds draw ever closer.

His face is very solemn, and I know that this is a sign that the darkness is coming for me once more.

"You must be a brave girl for me, Melody, like you were the day the dark fae came, when your mother and father entrusted me with taking you to safety. You trusted me then, and you must trust me now. Winter will take you to Sanctum, and you will see all the wonders she has talked to you about. I pray that you will indeed see them. I pray that I shall never see you again, for it will mean you are safe."

I throw myself at Bard, the man who was once my bard but is now simply my protector. I have a terrible feeling that he is right—that this is the last time I will see him—and all my sadness spills out in great wracking sobs.

I cling to him. He holds me just as tightly.

"Your bard is old now, precious child. One day, I hope you will forgive me for some of the truths I have hidden from you. You are still too young to understand. When you are older, I pray that you will come to do so. But for now, you must be brave and go with Winter. She will take you to where you will be safe."

He stands, urging me with a gentle squeeze of my shoulder

to go to where Winter has her hand stretched out to me. My eyes are full of tears, and I can barely see. But I do as he asks, for I recognize that it is important that we go now. And so, although a part of my heart is being ripped away, I take Winter's hand.

Chapter One

Melody

When I was little, I had a lot of nightmares—the legacy of a dark fae attack. Then the Blighten came and rescue-captured me from the fae. I lived with them for several years, under the misconception that orcs were good.

Orcs are not good. They used me—and the gift I have to work with portals—to prey upon innocent worlds to support their ever-hungry quest for blood and war.

That time ended when Winter freed me from the orcs and brought me to Sanctum, where a sweet breeder omega named Shiloh became my third and final mama. Mated to a warrior, she had four young alphas when I came to live with her. Two were her birth sons, and two were the adopted sons of her heart. The boys were kind and protective of me, and when I had trouble sleeping, I would ask one of them to stroke my hair, and ears—which are highly sensitive—until I could drift off.

I was a child then, and their innocent touch comforted me.

Many years have passed since I suffered from a nightmare. I'm a woman now, nineteen, and I've started having trouble sleeping again.

Only something has changed. Having one of my adopted brothers play with my ears doesn't comfort me anymore. Now it feels a tingly kind of good. And the last two times Zeke stroked the tips of my ears, I came.

It was a very quiet kind of coming, I must admit, because I was too embarrassed to say anything to him, or to anyone else. Also, I'm sure he would be shocked and would stop straight away if he realized, for Zeke is very sweet-natured.

My heart does not care that my mooning over him, or the others, is inappropriate on a thousand different levels—a strange, restless compulsion is building inside me, which draws me toward all my brothers in a very unsisterly way.

I've become addicted to them petting my ears. It's all I think about all day as I listen to the portal scholar drone on about lore. I don't need to learn about portals. I know everything instinctively—I could open a portal now if I chose to. I admit that I sometimes open one if no one is around and I want to get somewhere quickly.

"We will begin the visualization again," the scholar calls. "Pair up."

We all groan—visualizations are the most tedious part of all. We must hold a carry stone and project an image to our partner's mind, which they verify or correct against pictures in the portal book.

Also, this is the time when the scholar finds important things to do in his study, which adjoins the classroom.

He is not doing important things. He is taking a nap. Today it takes all of five minutes for his snores to permeate the room.

Isabelle, my class partner, chuckles. "I think that was a

record." She is an imperial omega of lower rank because of her weak portal skills and low-potency blood.

She is also my best friend.

"Did I see Marcus sneaking out of your room this morning?" Juliet asks Athena at the table next to ours.

There are eight omegas in our class— thanks to Athena's mischief, all of them hate me except for Isabelle.

Sanctum is all about status and ranking. The Chosen— powerful beings—stand apart like gods at the very top of society. Below them is the king. Below the king are the imperial omegas with their powerful blood, and below them are the warriors. At the very bottom are the feeder and breeder omegas.

All fairies are omegas, just as all warriors are alphas.

Our class is for imperial omegas who will one day command warriors on important quests. I am one of the younger ones at nineteen, although our ages range from eighteen to twenty-one. My problem is that I feel like an imposter being here, and I am not alone in thinking that. There have been more than a few pointed comments from Athena that I'm not an imperial omega at all since my blood offers no special enhancements such as stamina or strength. It does not even provide healing like a feeder omega.

It offers nothing at all.

So here I am among imperial omegas, an interloper who can make portals without a keystone or a portal site, which is not a very useful skill in Sanctum, where all that matters is the potency of your blood.

Athena is a natural beauty whose blood is said to offer outstanding benefits to the warriors she gifts. She has hated me ever since the king mentioned me in a public address not long after I arrived and started portal lessons. Athena thinks she is better than me because of her 'superior' blood. So she is insanely jealous that it was me who was mentioned by the king, not her. In addition to being hateful to me, she is spiteful to my best friend, Isabelle, who is the sweetest omega you could meet.

Athena has put glue in my hair, sabotaged my books and homework, and has spread many lies about me, saying that warriors disdain me because of my weak blood and that I have delusions of grandeur for being noticed by the king.

I wish the king had never mentioned me, even though I felt prideful at the time when he said how my portal skills were exceptional and important to Sanctum. Not that they have proved exceptional or important so far. As for my weak blood, it is a sore point with me. It is well known that warriors, while only too eager for the lowly breeders and feeders, are much enamored by those imperial omegas with potent blood.

Worst of all, I am particularly small and weak, and I have heard the portal scholar talking to Celeste, my omega mentor, telling her I'm unsuitable for quests.

So, not only do I have defective blood, but I am too pitiful even to aid the cause against the Blighten. Shiloh was convinced I would suddenly grow—I didn't.

I'm effectively a lowly breeder omega with some small capabilities that are likely of little benefit beyond being a curiosity to the king.

There is nothing wrong with being a breeder. Shiloh, the mother of my heart, is a breeder, and she is a kind, joyful omega who took me in and showed me love. I will not hear a bad word said against breeders. I have already gotten into one fight with Athena as a result... which did not end well given that, in addition to being tiny, I have the constitution of wet parchment.

I tell myself I don't mind my lowliness; only that is a lie. I would not mind my lowliness were I given classes with other omegas who are the same. Instead, I am forced to endure waspish omegas who take joy in putting me down.

"Not only Marcus," Athena replies. "But Rodrick as well."
Juliet gasps.

A couple of the other omegas giggle as they listen in.

I admit, I am also listening in, as is Isabelle, who has been staring at the same picture on the portal book for long minutes and has yet to project a thing.

"Goodness, they are both strapping alphas," Juliet says, fanning herself with her hand. "But I have got my eye on Draven and Aengus. I have heard they, too, sometimes share."

With his midnight hair and bright green eyes, Draven is the definition of handsome. Then there is Aengus who is very much a barbarian in looks and ways with his blond hair shorn at the sides of his head and his rough beard. I know this is the way of things, that my brothers are desirable, accomplished warriors who catch the eyes of omegas of all ranks, but I don't have to like it. My fists clench, and a small growl escapes my lips.

Isabelle grimaces as if sensing the disaster about to unfold. Past experience has shown that drawing Athena's attention is a sure road to a pinched ear or a ruined course book.

Athena smirks as she turns to face me. "Fine warriors," she purrs. "They are highly sought by imperials for quests, as is Theron. I've heard their mistresses command them to take their bodies as they take their blood. Soon, I will be going on my first quest. Celeste said she will petition for me to have the warrior of my choice."

"You are so lucky that Celeste favors you," Juliet gushes, redirecting Athena's gaze. "There will be a trial soon, I heard, for a new alpha ascending to warrior rank. I have a friend who could sneak us into the warrior hall after. The celebrations that follow are wild, by all accounts. Imperial omegas would have their pick of the best warriors."

I feel sick that these witchy omegas set their sights on my

brothers. It is a small comfort that they have not lain with them yet.

"Hey." Isabelle rests her hand over mine, stirring me from the well-scripted fantasy where I spirit Athena through a portal to some desolate place where monsters eat fairies for fun. "They are talking nonsense. No way would they be allowed to attend."

"Unless a friend sneaks them in," I point out.

A blush stains Isabelle's cheeks, and defeat enters her eyes. She is sweet on a young warrior and, like me, would probably be reckless enough to sneak into the warrior hall for a chance to get closer to him.

Like me, she is also innocent. All we do is suffer Athena's tall tales whenever the scholar naps.

A particularly loud snore is followed by mumbled words. All eyes turn toward the scholar's open door. He often rouses himself when he snores loudly.

Footsteps follow, and we all pretend to be dutifully engaged in visualizations as he emerges into the classroom.

The rest of the day passes under tedium and the scholar's watchful eye.

I know what is coming, at least for everyone but me.

A few months ago, there were twelve in the class. Now there are eight. We are all nearing the end of our training, and soon the rest will complete their first quests, marking their passage into imperial omega ranks.

Only I don't know what will happen to me.

And I'm terrified that Athena, so pretty and capable, veins thrumming with her potent blood, will catch the eye of one of my brothers.

Melody Unbound

I am out of sorts when I return to my beautiful quarters at the end of the day, parting ways with Isabelle as Athena, Juliet, and the others babble excitedly about their plans to sneak into the warrior hall during the upcoming celebration.

There is a solution to my sadness; he has golden hair and a noble disposition. My youngest brother is only a few years older than me and already in training to be a warrior. Just as I have changed, so has he, steadily building muscle where he was once lean. Then there is his height... Goddess, he is twice the size of me. Sometimes I sneak into his room so he can pet my ears; just nestling down in front of him on his bed and feeling surrounded by his strength is enough to make me weak. Let alone what happens when he runs his fingers along the tips of my ears.

I shouldn't do this *again*. I have no excuse, no matter how sad I am. But before I can think about it too much, I slip from my bed so that, in the space before the window, I can call a portal to the deepest part of the Sanctum and home to the warrior caste.

The portal winks closed behind me. I am in the central living chamber with five doors leading off—one for each of my brothers' bedrooms and one for the corridor that leads into the lower chambers of Sanctum. Two long fur-covered bench seats brace two walls, with a huge oak table between them. There are no windows this deep inside Sanctum, so a stone fireplace, where a fire is lit but dying out, offers warmth and a little light.

The dark wooden floor is warm beneath my naked toes as I slip into Zeke's room.

I should not be here. The truth is, I would not venture to walk down the passages without an escort were I unable to use a portal to facilitate my arrival. The only omegas who venture down here are the breeders and feeders who come to spend the night with the warriors, where they engage in carnal pursuits.

Should a warrior find me walking through these passages, he might presume me to be as such, which would be very dangerous. All warriors are alphas and possess an allure that omegas of all kinds, save those who are older and skilled, find difficult to resist. Their pheromones are potent. I might easily find myself seduced. And I don't want to be seduced by just any alpha I come across. There are only four warriors in my heart.

Standing on the periphery of Zeke's bedchamber, I take in my fill of the resplendent alpha sprawled out on his belly in the middle of his bed. The room is dark save a shaft of light from the door behind me. But my eyesight is good, and I can see the beautiful lines of his body as he sleeps.

I fidget from foot to foot and nibble on my lower lip before I take a step. As I do so, I hit a loose board, and it creaks.

I freeze.

Zeke rolls over onto his back and stares over at me. "Melody?" He yawns and scratches absently at his chest before he rakes his fingers through his messy blond hair. It sets a whole range of muscles rippling in the most arresting way.

I take another step, not moving directly toward the bed but in a convoluted route that takes me around to the other side of the bedroom and then slowly closer to where he lies.

His lips tug up. "Melody, do you ever walk anywhere in a straight line?"

I giggle and skip the last three steps before I jump into the bed beside him. "I was restless." My eyes trail over his chest, sweeping lower, over ridged abdominals, to where the blanket has fallen away to expose the smattering of golden curls creeping up from his groin.

I swallow and snap my eyes up to meet his again.

"Was it a nightmare?" He cups my cheek, brushing his thumb across the skin.

Nightmare... It is only a small white lie. I grew out of the nightmares when I was little, and Zeke has not questioned why they suddenly started again. "Would you stroke my hair again... and maybe my ears?"

He sighs heavily. "Melody, you're a big girl now. All grown up."

"I know." My lips tremble, and a watery pressure builds behind my eyes. "But would you?"

"Of course," he says. "Don't be sad. I will comfort you until you can sleep, and then I will carry you back to your room."

"Okay." I nod and tuck straight down.

The mattress dips as he settles behind me, not quite touching, his huge body curving around mine.

I go to wriggle back, but his broad palm clamps over my hip, stilling me. "Ah, ah, Melody. You're not a little girl anymore."

"Fine," I squeak. When I glance at him over my shoulder, I find a stern look on his face and turn quickly back around.

"That's my good girl," he says. "Close your eyes. I want you to think happy thoughts. There are no nightmares here. Not while you are near me." He draws my long curls over my shoulder to expose my ear.

I shudder—he places his hand on my shoulder and gently squeezes. "There, you are trembling. Was it a very bad nightmare indeed?"

I nod and gulp. That is another white lie. I'm trembling because I'm close to him. In his bed and surrounded by his scent, feeling the heat from his body.

"It's over now," he says. "If it will ease you, I will let you snuggle against me just this once."

"Please." A small trill escapes me as I press my bottom back against him.

He grunts and chuckles. "You are very eager tonight. Are you sure it was a nightmare, and you were not just bored?"

Realizing I have been too bold, I force myself to lay very still. To have my ass pressed against his body, even though the way he curves around me means I cannot feel any impression of his cock, has me thrumming with excitement and brings a hitch to my breath that I must fight to hide.

He eases in a little closer, his chest butting up against my back before his fingers find my ear—I shudder again.

"It's okay, Melody," he says, misreading my reaction once again.

I try to think pure thoughts, to feel the caress of his fingers as they used to be when I was a child, and nothing more than comfort.

But that time has passed and now, as he traces his fingertips around the shell of my ear, it is like a golden thread is being drawn all the way down my body, stiffening my nipples to peaks before pulling deep into my womb. A needy clench rolls through to my pussy and kicks off a sweet, achy throb. My clit tingles with every gentle sweep of his fingers. Then he closes his finger and thumb over the lobe and rubs it between them.

I bite my lower lip, fighting to steady my breathing as each gentle tug coaxes me to an ever-higher state of arousal. The hot pulsing sensation deep inside my core consumes my thoughts, and my nipples tighten and bud further from the faintest abrasion of my nightdress.

"Good girl," he says. "Let yourself relax. There are no monsters here. Zeke will protect you."

The combination of his words, his tone a gentle growl beside my ear, and the caress of his fingers brings a now familiar unfurling sensation like petals opening on a rosebud.

I am lost to his touch, basking in his light, like I am laying in a summer meadow where waves of heat bathe my body, pulsing, pulling me, drawing me ever closer to that blissful edge.

My breath catches again, and then my body pitches over, and sweet clenching climactic waves pulse through my pussy. My small teeth bite my bottom lip so hard it throbs in tandem with my aroused body before the sensations peter out, and I relax.

"That's my good girl," he says, oblivious to what just transpired.

I let out a long sigh before taking a shallow breath, my body having been starved of air while I was wracked by sensation.

And then he presses his lips to the very tip of my ear. "That's it. Sleep now, sweet Melody. When you wake up, you will be in your own bed."

I drift to sleep almost instantly, and true to his words, when I wake I am back in my bed.

It is only now, however, after Zeke has roused me to a sweet climax for the third time, that I realize everything has changed.

Chapter Two

Melody

"You know you don't need to cover them anymore," Shiloh says. "You're a free fairy now and an adult. Your wings are so pretty. It is a shame to hide them as you do."

I shake my head as Shiloh applies the broad straps that keep my magical wings out of sight. "I feel more comfortable with them covered."

At first, I covered them because I was shy when I saw that no other fairies in Sanctum had wings. But as time went on, I didn't want another point of difference between me and the omegas in my class. Athena would be twice as waspish and find cruel ways to taunt me if she knew. Probably complain about the mess they make when they shed fairy dust, how it is unhygienic, or other nonsense.

Shiloh is the only person here to have seen them. When I was very little, Bard insisted I hide them, although I didn't understand fully why at the time. I used to get up to mischief whenever my wings were freed, dancing around and sending clouds of fairy dust all over the place until he would get cross with me and tell me to behave.

Bard. Even thinking of him being annoyed with me reminds me of how I miss him.

My memories of the fateful day we fled the Blighten camp are jumbled up in my mind. The adult in me acknowledges that Bard sacrificed himself for me, yet my heart hopes he escaped like me and lived out his remaining years in peace.

I am blessed to have had Bard in my life, just as I am blessed by the three fairy omegas that have claimed the position of my mama. The first was my real mama, then came Winter, the imperial omega, who helped me escape and still lives here with her warrior mate. Finally came Shiloh, the kind breeder with two natural-born sons and two more sons, who, like me, were orphans.

"You are a woman now, Melody," Shiloh says kindly. "When you're ready to take a lover, they shall get quite a surprise when they discover your wings."

I peep back at Shiloh. A former breeder whose only purpose was to bear children for the alpha warriors who gained the privilege through service and deed. Only she caught the eye and heart of a higher warrior and the father of her second-born son, Theron, who claimed her as his mate.

"I do not wish for a lover yet," I lie. Athena and Juliet are always talking about their lovers, how the warriors make their bodies sing, and how they purr and hold them after.

I turn away as Shiloh finishes placing the strap.

"Of course, my love. You will know when the time is right. Goodness knows, your brothers suffer no such reservations. I swear whenever I meet with young breeders and feeder omega, they nearly swoon when I mention my sons!"

I bristle at her comment, although I do my best to hide it. I understand well how the sweet breeder and feeders feel—and not only them, but also the witchy Athena and Juliet—when I feel it myself for Shiloh's four sons.

Draven, her firstborn, whose father died in battle.

Theron, her second born.

Aengus and Zeke, the adopted sons of her heart.

Four strapping alphas that every unmated omega within Sanctum swoons over.

All of them are my adopted brothers.

All of them care for me as the sister of their hearts.

They are protective. They are bossy. They are accomplished warriors—although Zeke is still in training.

My heart is ever doomed to want them as I do.

"Well, that was unexpected," Shiloh says. I realize belatedly that she has paused in her task and has gone very still.

"What?" I twist to look back at her. I was so busy mooning over my brothers, and now I wonder what she refers to.

She smiles gently. "I just noticed something in your aura, but it is gone now."

I blush furiously, feeling very exposed. Shiloh has skills in reading auras, as is common among breeders but rarely talked about. They are natural nurturers, seeing things deeper than the eye.

It is why she adopted Aengus, Zeke, and me, sensing our nature and emotions, perhaps also that we needed love.

"Are you sure there are no young warriors or omegas who have caught your eye?"

"No," I squeak, shaking my head swiftly, relieved that she misinterpreted my aura, less so that she read the lusty thoughts behind them with accuracy. Omegas are gregarious, highly sensual beings who embrace adulthood with the enthusiasm of a starving man presented with a feast. I must seem a very odd omega when I add, "There is none that I desire."

"You will know when you are ready," she replies, tucking the last strap into place.

"Did you know?" I ask earnestly, turning to face her.

She smiles and shrugs. "I'm a breeder omega who was offered her choice of attentive warrior males. Finding my next lover was the only and most important thing on my mind until I met Herald, and, well, no other would do for either of us, even though it was forbidden for him to take me as a mate. We caused quite a scandal at the time. I have no regrets."

I giggle because I have heard the story of their secret mating and the outrage that ensued. In Sanctum, breeders should be available to all warriors until they reach the end of their breeding time. The story brings me joy every time I hear it, for the love between her and Herald shines through their every interaction.

"Still, that you feel different is to be expected, given your nature. You are special, Melody, an omega who can create portals out of nothing. You may write your own destiny."

Her kind words tease me with hope I dare not feel, even as I accept that I'm not special. My weak blood and tiny stature surely render any portal skills I may have as null and void. I don't even care about being special. I would gladly be a lowly breeder if it would deliver me my heart's desire.

The pressure is building inside me. As my body changed to that of a woman, I saw my brothers in a different light.

What I want is unorthodox, possibly even considered taboo —I want four warriors, and all of them are forbidden. Sanctum is a fairy kingdom steeped in protocols that rarely move. All this notwithstanding, they might not care for me in the way I care for them.

I know it can never be.

They love me.

But they love me as a sister. I have already crossed the line with Zeke, letting him pet my ears until I climaxed.

The worst part is that I can't wait for him to do it again.

Chapter Three

Zeke

I stand, chest heaving, body bathed in blood and sweat. My muscles quiver from the many tests I have endured and completed in this vaulted undercroft arena, deep in the lower reaches of Sanctum. Around me are now silent spectators, warriors, and fairy nobles lining the viewing tiers, who came to witness my trial. The rite of passage is the most important part of every warrior's life. We must demonstrate our skills, undergo many and varied tests, and impress upon our masters that we have the disposition and determination to be all that is needed of our ilk.

To fail is to be relegated to other duties, such as that of a weaponsmith or builder, or other necessary work that alphas might undertake in service to the King.

There is no shame in such honest work. Those with dispositions better suited to other roles are often weeded out early on during the training, so that a warrior put forward for the trials will more often than not succeed.

As my breathing slowly evens out, the aches, pains, and sting of wounds make their presence known. The outcome was never certain for me in ways it is for other warriors. The youngest of four brothers, adopted as a child, I have ever been the runt following in the footsteps of warriors who breezed through the trails where I have fought every step of the way.

Old Cecil, the warrior master whose face is lined and ancient, does not give much away, but I sense his approval even before he turns to the noble warrior at his side. Cecil encouraged me to consider other options. I'm gifted with horses, and I could have apprenticed with the stable master helping in the breeding, rearing, and training of warrior steeds.

However, no other route was acceptable to me when I hoped to claim and mate the highest fairy living within Sanctum.

I need to be not only strong and capable but clever and true of heart.

Have I done enough? Could I have given more?

Whether I have done enough is out of my hands now. I gave everything; if I have failed, I must accept the bitter blow that my dreams are not meant to be.

But as my eyes shift to the towering warrior at Cecil's side, my hope dares to soar—I know this man well.

Sanctum is a strange world; one I came to as a four-year-old boy rescued from the human markets at Bleakness. The warrior who saved me was a former slave of orcs, going against orders and earning himself a whipping for his insubordination to free Aengus and me.

I am forever grateful he disobeyed orders.

My savior's name was Jacob, and it is he who is the proud warrior standing at Cecil's side. Now mated to an imperial omega, he has risen to be second only to the king. He has also mentored me since the day he liberated me.

Jacob turns to Cecil and gives a single nod.

I blink back the sting of tears as Cecil raises his right fist, and a great cheer engulfs the crowded undercroft.

I am not an apprentice anymore.

I am a fully-fledged warrior, albeit of the lowest rank.

I see a small smirk lifts the corner of Jacob's lips as I'm caught up in the swell of warriors who surge into the arena. They are thumping my shoulders and offering their congratulations. I will drink and enjoy revelry later, as is my dues. For now I can't get the fucking smile off my face as Theron grabs me in a bear hug. He is replaced by Aengus, then my oldest brother, Draven, who grins broadly as he slaps my back.

"I'm proud of you, Zeke," Draven says. "But you will always be a fucking runt."

I laugh, not even caring about the same playful insult I have endured all my life. I will always be their runt. I don't mind it. I'm a warrior who has passed arduous training and trials. Although every part of my body aches, and I have more cuts and bruises than can be easily counted, I barely notice them amid the euphoria that floods me at the realization of my dream.

The warrior life is not an easy life. We must be honed. We must be ready and alert. Warriors must be strong of body and purposeful of mind. There is no place among the warriors' ranks for weakness.

Of course, it helps that the blood flowing through the omegas of Sanctum holds power and gifts. The feeders of the lowest official blood rank offer healing when we take their blood. The breeders may be for pleasure, and breeding if you are chosen and deemed a worthy warrior by deed or virtue, but they also offer their blood freely, although it is no more than an aphrodisiac.

I've only ever lain with a breeder or a feeder... I will be

allowed a feeder tonight to heal my body. Of course, all omegas are highly sensual creatures, and it's a given that there will be rutting involved with whoever offers their blood.

"What first?" Draven asks, throwing his arm around my neck and pretending to strangle me—the annoying bastard knows I'm too weak right now to throw him off. "Do you need some blood? Or do you need a drink?"

"I need both," I say.

He chuckles, releasing me, and we are swept away by the crowd to the warrior hall, where drinks, food, and revelry of every kind soon ensue.

But as I gratefully accept a beer, and the pretty breeders and feeders come around and offer me their veins and more, my mind is elsewhere. I am thinking of the sweet young omega who holds my heart, but my mood is soured when I get a visit from Athena and Juliet.

They are always making eyes at Draven, not that he pays them any attention. He is more alpha than either of them can handle. Knowing they share a class with Melody, though, brings me out in cold sweat, and my eyes search the crowd. If Melody is here, she will be getting her bottom spanked and sent straight home.

And if any fucker is touching her, I will get into a damn fight, which would be a bad idea given I have barely taken any blood and am still exhausted from the trial.

"You are not old enough to be here." I alternate between scowling down at them and scanning the room. It is not unusual for the younger omegas to sneak into the warrior hall during events like this. "Is Melody with you?"

"Your sister?" Athena says, tone sharp. "No. Why would she be here?"

"She is innocent," Juliet adds, like this is a failing.

"Good." Thank fuck she is not here. She is by far the prettiest omega in Sanctum. The warriors would be fucking queuing to get their hands on her, to fog her mind with pheromones so they can... No, I am not going there. It is always an omega's choice, but I would not like her first time to be in the warrior hall, where she might be overwhelmed.

Not so for these two, who are seasoned at seduction.

"Is Draven around?" Athena asks.

"Or Aengus?" Juliet adds a hopeful note in her voice.

So, they only talk to me to get to my brothers. I should feel more pissed about their ill use of me, but I don't care.

And then I see red... or, rather, I see Melody, sneaking along the back between the tables with her friend, Isabelle, in tow. They are both pink-cheeked and nervous looking as they pass a warrior who has a breeder spread out on a table and is snacking on her cunt. "The fuck!"

"Zeke?" Juliet calls.

I don't look back, already slamming my way through the crowded hall seeking to cut the brats off. Isabelle is no more worldly than Melody! What were they thinking, sneaking down here?

As I home in, I spot Wes, a young alpha who gained his warrior status only a few months ahead of me. He sits staring into his ale as a pretty breeder rubs his shoulder. He looks as mournful as I was feeling when Athena and Juliet accosted me. "Wes!" His head snaps. I stab my finger in the direction of Melody and Isabelle.

His head swings. I can see the cogs turning slowly before he surges to his feet.

I am right behind him.

By the time we close in on our quarry, they have caught the attention of three warriors who, scenting fresh pussy and blood, cut off the two omegas.

29

"I'll take it from here," I say to them, sidestepping in between them and their chosen prey.

Wes is right beside me, shouldering them out of the way—he is nearly as big as Aengus and makes a good wingman all around.

"Fuck off," Wes growls when the alphas look like they might protest our cut-in.

He has gone for the less subtle approach and is radiating edgy menace. The three warriors shrug and move on to easier pickings.

"Zeke!" Melody looks guilty as fuck. Her face is bright pink, and her eyes land everywhere but me.

"What the fu—hell are you doing here?"

"We were invited," Melody says boldly, although she still does not meet my eyes.

"Oh? By whom?" My blood is up after the trial, and her sweet, familiar scent hits me like a punch to the gut.

"We snuck in," Isabelle blurts out. "We only wanted to see what all the fuss was about. Also, I was dared and have... issues with a dare."

"She cannot back down. It is ridiculous, really," Melody says, her shoulders slumping.

Wes grunts. I bite back a smirk, for this is no joking matter.

"Do you need some blood?" Isabelle asks, gesturing toward me.

I am dressed in naught but my boots and leather pants, having come straight from the trial.

Wes growls.

"I was only offering blood, not..." she stammers. "I thought since Melody's blood doesn't..."

Wes growls again before fisting her arm. "I'll deal with this brat." He nods his head at me. "Isabelle and I are going to be having a long chat about the dangers of entering the warrior hall unescorted."

"Is there a way to get an escort then?" Isabelle asks.

The lass clearly has no sense of danger or how close to his limit Wes is. He has been patiently waiting for her to be ready for her first quest. Plenty of omegas take an alpha to their bed long before quests. But if they don't, well, the first blood gift with a warrior can be highly charged. Perhaps sensing there would be blood on the floor if he didn't come through, Cecil must have presented a compelling case. It is all now agreed, although Isabelle is yet to learn.

If the adoration in Isabelle's eyes as she gazes up at the big warrior is any indication, she will be happy with the decision.

I chuckle as Wes tosses her over his shoulder and strides out of the room.

"Goodness," Melody says, alarmed.

I turn back to my sweet and very naughty charge. "Come on." I take her by the hand and shoulder my way through the throngs to the nearest exit. "I am taking you back to your room. If Draven finds you here, you will not sit for a week."

She makes a small whimpering sound and clings to my hand, which I take as an indication of compliance, and that she understands how serious this is.

It is a long fucking walk back to her part of Sanctum. Her cheeks remain flushed, likely from being in a hall full of lusty alphas, many of whom were rutting. I all but toss her into her quarters and slam the door shut, breathing a deep breath.

I shake my head, rousing myself from the stupor of her scent, and walk all the way back down to the warrior hall.

Wes is still absent, I note.

I sit down. Though I do not stay alone for long as I'm the hero of the night. So I accept with thanks the beer that is passed my way. And so it is that I find myself drinking with a feeder

31

omega in one arm and a breeder on the other side, lounging on the fur-covered benches that line the warrior hall, feeling strangely alone. A shadow falls over me, and I blink up, a little drunk on the ale and the sweet omega pheromones clogging the air.

"Time to move on, lasses," Draven says. "Our brother has been supping too liberally of the ale to meet the needs of a couple of lusty omegas. Go and find yourselves another warrior."

They pout prettily as they rise but send Draven a saucy grin. He spanks the nearest one's ass to get her moving as she sashays past him—she only giggles and then squeals as a passing warrior scoops her up into his arms.

I watch them leave, looking longingly after them, wishing I could and knowing I could not.

Draven flops down beside me and throws an arm around my shoulders. "Don't mind it, runt. Every warrior's cock fails him at some time or another."

I roll my eyes. "There is nothing wrong with my cock."

"No?" He raises a brow. "Most newly anointed warriors are balls deep in any willing pussy and with a belly full of blood."

"They are not what I want," I mutter sourly, reaching for my ale on the table.

"Life is rarely fair, and we don't always get what we want."

"That is very fucking philosophical," Aengus mutters as he throws himself down on the other side of me, jostling my ale and sending it splashing over my chest. "Did you not notice there is a celebration going on?"

Theron follows after, dropping down on the other side of Aengus. "What's up with the runt? Is his cock broken?"

"He is mooning over a certain fairy," Draven says, talking over me.

I take a gulp of ale. It does little to numb the pain radiating from the center of my chest. I should tell him about Melody, but I'm reluctant. She has already had a fright tonight. If Draven finds out, he will go on a fucking rampage.

"Ah, Melody," Theron says knowingly. Despite having a different father, he shares many similarities with Draven save he carries less brawn. "She has bloomed into a fine omega. We are not the only ones who notice. I put a thumping on Kline a few days ago after I caught him hedging with Cecil to be the one to accompany her first quest." He smirks. "I believe he withdrew his offer."

"What quest?" I sit up too fast, sending ale sloshing over Aengus, who curses and glares at me.

"She is past the age where omegas are expected to command warriors in their first quest," Draven says. "I wondered if she would be exempt, given how special she is." He shrugs. "Apparently not. The first few quests are usually simple, allowing them to get a feel for commanding a warrior. It is more about training them rather than them actually performing any service to the king."

"One of us should go with her," I say. My mind is racing. Cecil pulled the strings necessary for Wes; he can do the same for me.

"We offered," Aengus says. "Too experienced. They want someone malleable... new to the binding."

Binding. When a warrior takes an omega's blood, particularly those above breeder and feeder rank, they become subject to a magical binding. We are subservient to our omega mistresses and compelled to obey. That we take blood and enjoy their bodies is on their terms and, sometimes, at their command.

Some warriors are rankled by this. There have been increasing murmurs of discontent since the king released Jacob from the binding. The imperial omega, Winter, was stripped of her status and gifted to him after she refused to feed him when he was gravely injured. There are rumors that warriors were never meant to be subservient, and the binding might one day be gone for all.

I have known no other way, yet I have overheard Draven talking about it with Aengus and Theron—he believes the binding should be removed. Warriors should be free to feed whenever they need, and even for pleasure. Alphas were never meant to be subservient to omegas.

I do not mind it so much. I would embrace any role if it meant serving Melody.

Okay, I would assuredly rut her, given a choice, would spoil her pussy with attention, and use every alpha guile at my disposal to make her purr for me.

Perhaps it's for the best that the binding is in place.

"I'll do it," I say.

Three heads turn my way.

"I am newly anointed. It is my right to petition for a quest. They will want me to take her blood. It will strengthen the binding. Further, I am seen as lowly among alphas" —I grimace — "and compliant. I will appear to be the most obvious option."

Draven rubs his jaw slowly as he thinks this over.

"He is right," Theron says. "They will see him as malleable and the perfect choice for Melody."

"He is not fucking malleable," Draven says dryly. "But I believe the fools who make the decisions will be too stupid to notice. Were they to ask the sweet breeders and feeders about Zeke, they would suffer no delusions."

My chest puffs a little.

Aengus snorts. "Aye, the binding will be fucking broken by his deviant ass."

"It will not help him against the high ranking, of course," Draven points out. "And Melody is very high ranking. No one has taken her blood yet, but I've heard they tested her, and found it unique. How that might work, given she is our adopted sister, we cannot know. Still, I believe you should petition for the quest."

"I fucking hate the idea of any bastard sniffing around her," Theron says. "It was all I could do not to liberate Kline of his balls. The thought of anyone but us having her... taking her blood... or anything else..."

Draven puts his hand on Theron's shoulder.

I drain the last of my ale.

She was once the sister of our hearts, a young orphan that our mother and father took in, like they took in Aengus and me.

Then she matured into an imperial omega and a beauty, and everything changed.

"She came to me for comfort last night." I put my ale down, aware of their sudden absolute interest. I'm also hedging a little as I work up to telling them that she was here in the hall tonight. "She said she had nightmares and asked me to comfort her." I shrug. "She snuggled sweetly before me and fell asleep shortly after."

"Did she show any signs?" Draven demands.

"Are you asking me if she was aroused?" I say bluntly.

He nods.

I swiped a hand down my face. "How the fuck would I know? Just being near her gives me a raging hard-on. Her sweet scent was all up in my nose. It was all I could do to maintain a gap between us so she wouldn't notice my condition. I was not thinking clearly enough about anything beyond keeping my hands to myself."

"You had better keep it fucking innocent," Draven growls, taking me by the throat and slamming me against the back of the bench.

I raise both hands and decide to keep Melody sneaking in

here to myself for now. "I swear I did. I will not fucking touch her unless it is her desire! I simply touched her ear as I used to when she was little. Then, once she was asleep, I carried her back to her quarters."

"Peace, brother," Aengus mutters, placing his hand over Draven's wrist where he still fists my throat. "The runt will not rut her. I hold no such compulsion if the brat asks me to pet her ears. Best hope the binding is strong if she slips into my bed of a night."

Draven releases me as he scowls at Aengus, who, unbothered, only smirks.

"Do you think it's a good sign, though?" Theron asks. "That she has gone to Zeke? He is the closest to her age, and she probably considers him the gentler option."

Draven grunts. "He is a deviant bastard. Fuck knows how she does not sense it, although we all know he can play at being sweet when it suits him. I hope it's a good sign. It has been some years since she suffered nightmares. Perhaps she is drawn to us but does not yet know why. She is innocent, and she will stay that fucking way until she decides otherwise. But I agree that her visiting Zeke was a good sign. Let's hope for all our sakes, and for the sake of Zeke's dick, which is presently broken" —he smirks— "that she decides soon."

Chapter Four

Melody

Today is not a good day.

Last night was worse. Stupid Juliet dared Isabelle to sneak into the warrior hall. My best friend is usually meek and sweet in disposition and never misbehaves... unless someone dares her. Then she turns into a mule and will not listen to reason.

She has issues.

A few more since Wes tossed her over his shoulder. She could not sit still all through the portal class on account of her tender bottom.

I admit to being jealous that he gave her a spanking for her mischief. All Zeke did was escort me back to my room.

I have tried not to think about it, but I know that he would have returned to the hall, and I know what would follow after, for I saw plenty of it going on.

I am devastated after he held me so tenderly only two days ago, made me come, and carried me to my bed. In my mind, I had constructed an elaborate fantasy where he might see me as more than his sister, and want me. Now, I feel like such a fool.

And on top of everything, as if this were not enough to deal with, I am told I am going on a quest. Celeste, my omega mentor who has guided me since I arrived, explains what I must do. But I am not paying attention to any of it, for my mind has sunk into a catatonic state that can take in only that I must go upon a quest.

A real quest. Outside.

My mind has a lot of catching up to do.

The Chosen are immortal, and while all fairies are immortal in the eyes of humans, we are but a blip in the lives of the Chosen... I have never met them nor thought about them overly much, save they are higher than the king and guide Sanctum in the never-ending war against the Blighten.

It is strange how I presumed I was free and only now realize that I'm not. I have duties and a purpose—I have responsibilities to Sanctum and must play my part in protecting all.

And now I must leave. Not only that, but I will be responsible for the alpha warrior whom I must command.

Celeste carries on talking. But her words and consequences are slow to sink in. This is the way of our kind. Imperial omegas hold the power while warriors do our bidding. They are treated as little more than expendable brawn to keep the Blighten at bay and protect us during quests.

Command... What do I know about command? How will I, an omega, ever be comfortable ordering an alpha warrior to do my bidding?

This does not feel natural to me, although Celeste assures me that it is, and I will grow into command the more I wield it.

"The binding ensures their complete obedience," Celeste says.

My eyes shift to the young warrior who is as often as not in attendance on Celeste. They are not mated but, since taking her blood, Jonas has risen high for one so young. I don't like him very much, although he rarely speaks. There is something unnatural about him and his obedience, like his personality has been scoured away.

"Once the blood is gifted, which may be from the wrist if you prefer, you will feel the magic of the binding in a deeper, very personal way. Before the binding was initiated into our laws, we were pets for the alpha warriors and used without care —an omega, rutted, drained, and left for dead was the inciting incident for change."

I blink in horror at the image, and the room tilts around me.

Her blunt words leave wounds upon my innocent mind. I am horrified. I do not wish to believe her. Only I can find no reason why she might lie. My foundations are crumbling. I cannot imagine my brothers treating an omega this way, binding or not. I feel a little sick: that I don't know them, that they are monsters.

"Fear not, Melody. The binding holds firm and will protect you. But never forget you must control a savage beast. Treat them as such, and you will come into yourself and your power. As is usual for first quests, they have selected a young, newly anointed warrior to accompany you. Do not let the fact that he is your brother sway your purpose or deed."

"A-adopted brother." It feels important to point this out, even as my mind scrambles as I wonder which. Theron—It must be Theron, for Zeke is still in training.

"Zeke," she says. "He completed his trial yesterday. By all accounts, there was much revelry in the lower reaches of Sanctum—breeders and feeders were availed of by the warrior ranks." Her nose wrinkles as though thoroughly disgusted.

I know now what happens in the warrior hall, given I snuck in there last night.

"You will leave at first light."

Dismissed, I leave the room in a daze.

Too shattered to even be mischievous by making a portal, I wander the stone corridors until I find myself at a familiar door.

❧

Winter welcomes me with a smile and immediately calls for tea. Many years have passed since she brought me back to Sanctum. She is a mother now with a young alpha son already in warrior training.

I wring my hands as the kindly beta servant bustles in with a tray bearing honey cake and all the trappings.

I love honey cake, but I cannot eat a bite.

"Celeste said before the binding came into being that we were nothing more than playthings and magical nourishment to an alpha," I blurt out.

Winter's face softens. "Oh no, Melody. Please do not let them fill your head with such nonsense."

"It's not true, then? An omega was not rutted, drained, and left for dead by a warrior? That this event was not the catalyst for change?"

Her lips tighten, and something akin to rage suffuses her face. "That careless witch," she mutters with heat, shocking me. "I will have words with the king about this. Perhaps I'm not the only imperial in need of attitude correction."

I'm unsure what this means, but I'm convinced I've gotten Celeste into trouble. I ask myself how I feel about this, and the truth is I don't feel much guilt, given I'm being forced to go on a quest and further am expected to magically know how to command an alpha three times the size of me, who is more experienced in life, dangers, and quests.

"Melody, I tell you this because I care deeply about you

and want to undo the damage her careless words have caused... I'm old. One of the oldest of our blood here. Old enough to remember the time before the binding."

My eyes widen. I knew Winter was old but didn't realize she was *that* old. "What was it like... before?"

"Balanced," she says. "Surprisingly so. Alphas loved and respected the omegas they were allocated, whatever their blood rank, from breeders to imperials. Life was much as it is now, save that alphas fought because they chose to and not because they were compelled. And we were *not* drained and left for dead: save for one omega, that is. That part of Celeste's story is true."

"That omega was you," I say softly, looking at her wan expression.

She nods. "I was mated to a warrior. One I loved with all my heart. I lost him in the great battle that brought us to Sanctum. I was a shell, shattered by the events and the many deaths: the one that was personal to me and the wider losses that decimated our ranks. We were fighting for our lives and to survive for another day. There was no time to grieve. I was old, even then. The new warrior they paired me with was young. I gave my body and blood to him as freely as my wounded heart could. He was inexperienced and treated the war as a game and my gift as his right. I tried to explain to him that omegas need love and affection, that without it, I was dying as surely as those on the battlefield under Blighten axes... He did not heed me... We were desperate and losing the war. My emotional needs seemed of little consequence in the greater scheme of things. Perhaps, too, I wished for the relief of death when I was still grieving for the warrior I loved... I was found drained, fading into death, and that's when everything changed. That is when the binding was put in place."

I brush the tears from my cheeks, only now realizing I am crying.

Her hand encloses mine. "My sweet Melody. I tell you this not to make you sad but to explain why, so long ago, changes came. Leander was an anomaly. Even then, in such desperate times, warriors gave love to the omegas, who gifted them healing through blood and shared intimacy. But sometimes, the pendulum swings too far. We try to counter one wrong and end up creating a different one."

"Is that what *you* think?" I ask. "That the binding is wrong? Is that why the king released your mate from the magic?"

She shakes her head, and a flush creeps over her cheeks. "The binding was removed because I was a foolish, embittered omega." She shrugs one delicate shoulder. "I was afraid to give my blood, even after so long. And I nearly lost Jacob because of my fears. I was the pendulum at its most extreme and reckless. After, when they lifted the binding and I no longer commanded him, I only felt free."

Her smile is warm and speaks of her deep love for her mate.

"I don't want to command an alpha," I say. "It does not feel natural to me."

"The wheel of progress within Sanctum moves slowly. Jacob petitions for the binding removal among mated pairs. A few now have chosen to go that route. But you have not yet mated, Melody, and the binding cannot be switched off and on at a whim."

My cheeks heat.

Her lips twitch. "An alpha has caught your eye?"

I nod, blushing furiously. I've already determined my love for them is unrequited, and I need to move on, so why I admit this eludes me.

"You are young. Why not enjoy many before you worry about mating?"

My blush spreads down my throat and to the tips of my ears. This is a turn of conversation I was not expecting.

She raises a brow. "There is more than one?"

I nod.

"How many more?"

"Three more," I say, wringing my hands.

"Well, that's going to become complicated," she says dryly. "Alphas are naturally possessive and territorial over mates. Do they-ah-share well now?"

"I don't know." Goodness, why does the thought of them sharing well make me all tingly? Why does the thought of them *not* sharing well make the tingles worse? "I have not lain with any of them. I just want them all equally." This sounds ridiculous. I'm not sure why I feel compelled to offer this confession. Perhaps it's because I consider Winter one of my mothers, but it is slightly easier to talk to her about this because it is not her son's heart I pursue. "One of them is to be my warrior on the trip."

She nearly chokes on her tea. "Zeke?"

I wince and nod helplessly, relieved she does not ask about the other three. She is clever. I believe she is drawing conclusions now. There is no chance of my cheeks cooling anytime soon. I am slightly reassured that at least she does not appear disgusted by my confession, only amused, as she puts her tea down with a smile.

"Well then. This is your perfect opportunity to sound the matter out. Before you consider removing the binding, you must experience what it means for yourself. You have a quest and a purpose. You must give him your blood to complete the binding before you leave. Such acts hold intimacy. Wield your power well, Melody. For the duration of the quest, he is yours to command. Afterward, I believe you will better understand of both the binding and the alphas you seek to mate."

My belly takes a slow, fluttery tumble. I am broken that he celebrated his rise to warriorhood last night, drinking, rutting, and feeding on blood when he should have been thinking about me. I want to punish him for this, even though it makes no sense. My judgment of him is unreasonable. How could he know that his actions ripped my heart to shreds? I am nothing to him but a sister. He doesn't even know how I feel about him, and if he did, he would likely laugh, be horrified, or make things awkward.

He would never comfort me or pet my ears again.

I tell myself I don't want him to touch my ears or cuddle me if he ruts other omegas.

I know it is a lie.

I still want to make him pay, even if he doesn't know why. Maybe I will like this quest after all.

Chapter Five

Melody

I admit to being nervous as I approach the chamber where my first blood gift will occur, with the warrior master Cecil at my side. I wear one of my fancy gowns, a whimsical creation of lace and silk.

An omega's first quest represents her transition, much like a warrior's rite of passage but in a far more understated way. Still, maids were sent to tend to me in preparation, even as Celeste came to offer her final counseling on the matter.

I still seethe whenever I think about Zeke. Not that he achieved this goal, for I am proud of him and know it was everything he wanted to be, and he worked hard for his place. But what vexes me is the thought of him taking blood from a pretty breeder or feeder, of him touching them, kissing them, petting their ears, putting his cock inside them, and making them tremble with pleasure.

He is so sweet. I'm sure omegas of every rank must be eager for his attention.

So, I am determined this morning to show Zeke a new side of me. To present myself in the most favorable light, like this might show him what he was missing when he went back to rut the sweet lower omegas in the warrior hall after depositing me in my room.

Isabelle pointed out that we didn't actually see Zeke rutting a lass, and that I might be jumping to conclusions.

I will hear none of it. My vexation with him is all very pointless, yet I am set on this path. Worse, he barely glances at me when I enter the plush chamber, instead turning expectantly toward Cecil as though seeking direction.

Perhaps he is nervous?

My lips narrow. No, I believe Zeke is relaxed as he stands with broad shoulders back and to attention.

His eyes do not linger on my face and my perfectly curled hair, nor do they stray to my breasts, which are plumped up and displayed to perfection in my artfully crafted gown. The neckline is low to facilitate the taking of my blood, should I choose to let my quest warrior take it from my throat.

He performs a brief bow. "Mistress," he says formally. "It will be my pleasure to accompany you on this quest." Then he returns his focus to Cecil once again.

I feel my irritation rise. He's probably well-sated after expending his lust on sweet breeders and feeders who doubtless rewarded him for his efforts in completing his warrior trials.

"It is customary, my lady," Cecil says, "for blood to be gifted at this time. Did Celeste counsel you in this?"

"She did," I reply.

"The wrist is acceptable. The vein at the throat" —he clears his throat— "is more often preferred and lends itself to a deeper connection through the binding, but" —he clears his throat again— "the wrist will assuredly do."

He expects me to offer my wrist. I had considered offering my wrist and spent excessive time pondering exactly that. Only now, as I glance around the decadent quarters, do I recognize the potential for intimacy in the act. The room is small but finely furnished, with a chaise lounge to the right of the doorway facing a fire, presently lit and low. Subtle lamp lighting offers distinctly sensual undertones. Then there are the internal double doors, which stand open, through which I see a canopied bed.

As understanding blooms, it brings an instant tightening to my womb.

The wrist would be sensible, given my already libidinous state. To take my blood, even in that way, still holds intimacy.

Zeke's stance remains an alert kind of relaxed, and his attention is focused directly ahead so that he does not look at either Cecil or me. Maybe he is cross about me entering the warrior hall, interrupting his celebration so he could escort me back to my room?

I want him to look at me, to *see* me. Only I cannot predict how I will feel if he holds me while taking blood from my throat. No one has taken my blood, although I was tested when I first arrived, no more than the faintest prick of a blade to extract a few drops. I suppose my weak blood will work for the binding, even if it offers nothing else.

I feel hot and flushed suddenly, which worsens the longer I take to decide, blood pounding through my veins.

I become a little light-headed. My hand reaches out blindly, and Zeke is there, taking it, offering me support. Having his warm, calloused hand hold mine helps restore a marginal level of calm.

"Mistress."

He has never called me mistress before. I do not like it one bit. I am Melody.

"Perhaps a wrist would be plentiful this first time," Cecil counsels.

"She is flushed," Zeke says, voice harsh and bristling with insubordination. "Flushed with blood."

"I am aware of the pertinent facts," Cecil replies tersely.

Goodness, what is wrong with me? Why must I react like this?

"It is a natural reaction, my lady," Cecil says. "Omegas can flush with blood at the thought of offering it to an alpha for the first time. It is the same reaction you might have were the warrior injured... or seeking your blood in another way." He clears his throat again. "Once the blood gift has been completed, you will feel better. If I might encourage you to decide swiftly."

"It needs to be from the throat," Zeke says bluntly, "Look at her. She's trembling and extremely flushed."

My control is crumbling. This was not how I envisioned events playing out. In my mind, I was calm and collected, perhaps a little aloof, and it was Zeke who was spellbound as he took my blood. God, I was so sure of myself. I would show him how I could be in command and sophisticated like omegas are supposed to be.

And now, I'm clutching his hand like a lifeline.

"Tell me how you wish me to take your vein, mistress," Zeke says softly. "You're flushing, dangerously so."

This is not poised. This is nothing but a hot mess.

A whimper escapes my tightly clenched lips. Celeste warned me I might flush the first time I offered blood, but this is extreme. His rich scent is all up in my nose. I want his hands upon me. I want his...

"Clear the room," Zeke growls.

"She is untried," Cecil says. "I should call for Celeste."

"I am in control of myself." Zeke's voice is a low snarl. I've never heard him speak this way, and to the warrior master, no less. "Some privacy would be good at this point. I shall do nothing that she does not desire."

I sense Cecil's conflict even as another whimper escapes my lips.

With a final stiff nod, Cecil strides for the door.

As it clicks shut, one kind of tension eases, and a different, more sensual awareness blooms in its place.

"Melody," Zeke says gently, and there he is, my sweet brother, and the pounding in my throat eases a little. "That's my good girl, my Melody. Please tell me how you want me to take your blood, and I shall do it. It hurts me to see you suffering like this. You know I will take care of you. I will guide you through your first blood even as I will protect you in this quest, and lay down my life for you. But please. Tell me how to take your blood so I may ease your pain."

"My throat." The words come out in a croak. I cannot even look at him and turn my face to the side in an offering.

"Such a good girl," he croons, and I feel myself soften, leaning towards him. "May I hold you as I take your blood?"

Goodness, the formality in him. I wanted him to see me, but not in this weakened, desperate state. The flush spreads through my body, kicking off a pulse deep in my womb. The arousal is sharp and insistent, and almost electrical in nature.

"Please," I say, "I would prefer that, for my legs are a little weak."

"It's okay. I've got you, Melody." He steps into me and gently wraps his arm around my waist, drawing my small body flush against his, gathering my hand in his and pressing my palm against his chest in a smooth move that makes me feel utterly cherished.

All the sensations rush through me twice as fast. His

gentleness disarms my fears even as the intimacy overwhelms me.

It was supposed to be a small gift of blood, enough to strengthen the binding. I never expected it to be like this.

"I'm just going to move your hair out of the way," he says. His fingertips skim over my collarbone, brushing my hair over my shoulder and exposing the column of my throat. "You look lovely—such a pretty dress. I'm afraid, given how very flushed you are, there might be a little blood spilled on it. It can happen sometimes." As his eyes lower to my quivering breasts, I watch them darken. "I will not take much. Only as much as I need to make you feel more comfortable." His warm hand lightly collars the side of my throat.

I am trembling and must squeeze my thighs tightly together lest my rampant arousal trickles out. Alphas have an impressive sense of smell, and I seek not to linger on whether or not he might know.

"Please," I say. "I'm ready."

"Good girl," he says, brushing his thumb over my throat as though testing the throbbing pulse point there.

My body, softened by those words, relaxes in his hold. This is Zeke. I trust him.

"You'll feel a little sting, nothing more. And it should be pleasurable. Don't worry about your reaction. Many omegas become aroused when a warrior takes their blood."

Goodness, does he need to point that out? I'm horrified that he even mentions it, yet to my shame, it makes me even wetter, knowing he can tell.

"Such a beautiful fairy. I'm so proud of you, Melody. So proud of you for taking your very first quest." His lips lower to brush over that pounding pulse point.

Do I hear him groan?

Then he closes his mouth over the throbbing vein and

sucks. A sharp sting is followed by a blissful surge that has me swooning. The blood gushes out. I gasp as a climax rolls through my body, fisting my womb before setting off a chain reaction of spasms deep in my pussy. My nipples grow taunt and hard. My clit throbs. I whimper, clinging to him as a maelstrom rips through me.

I feel like a golden thread reaches into my heart.

I feel him as though he were inside me, his cock surging, filling me, offering me respite from this all-consuming ache.

I feel the binding like a leash wrapped around his neck.

His arms are the only thing holding me up as he swallows my blood. The sounds of his feeding make my pussy clench, and another sharp, sparkling orgasm crashes through me.

He rumbles a sweet purr between swallows, and I wonder how much he takes. My body spins out of control as I writhe in his arms seeking greater contact for a source of friction against my sensitive clit.

And still, he drinks.

His purr deepens. He gives a single vigorous suck that compels another rapturous climax and a needy whimper from my lip.

His lips pop off, and a wet trickle spills down my throat.

"Gods," he mutters. "You were very flushed. I didn't expect to take that much."

I sink into a state of blind panic as I take in the way I cling to him, thrusting my hips against his thigh, and a different kind of flush passes over my hot cheeks.

Still supporting me with an arm at my waist, he puts his fingers under my chin.

My pussy is still sparking through the aftershocks, and I must steel myself to meet his eyes.

"It is over now, Melody. Are you well? How do you feel?" His gazes lower to my heaving breasts before they return to hold mine. "There is only a little blood on your pretty gown, and your color is better."

I blink, trying to gather my scattered wits and steady my ragged breathing.

"Speak to me, Melody. Tell me what you need."

His scent seems so much more potent with the binding in place, like his presence is inside me. My pussy quakes... it is almost like I can feel him there. Is this what it is like for all omegas, I wonder? Celeste's words, which confused me then, now make sense, as does the bed. When an omega gives her blood to a warrior, it can spark lust.

I can see easily how that might happen because it would take only the lightest encouragement for me to spread my legs for him, to take him inside me, fully, and in a way I know would feel even better than what has already transpired.

I want him to. Caution dictates I do not.

"I am well, thank you. I'm sorry. The moment overcame me in ways I did not expect."

His lips tug up in a disarming smile. "Well, mistress, that is only natural. I hope I was not too forward in holding you like this. I feared you might collapse. When you are ready, I will release you."

Goodness! His mouth appears to be magnetically drawn toward offering commentary on my most shameful acts. I did not expect to be this aroused. I did not expect him to be so gentle and sweet.

Draven is so much more dominant and commanding. What would happen if he were here? Would he have rutted me? Then I consider if it were my wicked Aengus or stern Theron. I imagine Theron being very proper. But Aengus... I can imagine him spreading me out on the plush rug, uncaring of my untried state, and rutting me roughly.

"You're looking a little flushed again," Zeke points out,

brushing his fingers across my cheek. "Are you sure you wish me to let you go?"

I take a deep breath and search for calm. "Yes, I'm fine, thank you."

His mischievous side shines through, and a smirk lights his lips as he slowly releases me and steps back.

It takes me several stretched moments to compose myself. I glance down, seeing the blood stain against the neckline of my beautiful gown. That shocking evidence tells me that I have given my first blood, as does the rushing sensation that courses through me connecting me to Zeke in otherworldly ways. The binding is strange and abhorrent to me. I hate the way it presents in my mind as a leash.

I press my hand over my heart.

"The binding is strong," he says, and without apparent shame, lowers his hand to his crotch to adjust the thick bulge straining his leather pants. "Don't mind it, mistress. The taste of omega blood can have predictable effects on alphas. We are lowly creatures. It is for the best that the binding is in place lest we succumb to our instincts and spread a sweet omega out and rut her with all our savagery."

Goodness! He's not helping me to calm myself with his blunt, uncivilized words.

"I'm yours, mistress, yours to command. Of course"—he winks— "some omegas make very naughty commands. It is the highest pleasure to tend an omega however she desires."

And I thought Aengus was the wicked one. My nostrils flare. He is toying with me, telling me what other omegas have done with him. I feel the power of the binding but also the play. Although I hold the leash, I do not have absolute control.

Zeke reminds me with those few words that while alphas, through the binding, are under our command, they are not beasts. They are powerful men, compelled to obey only because of magic.

Alphas are not mindless savages, not that I ever presumed them to be, despite the words that spilled from Celeste's mouth. I soon come to understand that the binding only goes so far.

§&

I have practiced visualizing locations since I was a little girl. The dark fae captured me from my home for my ability, and then the Blighten snatched me from the dark fae, using my skills with ruthless intent. I remember standing in the portal scholar's workshop in Kung, and how he instructed me to review reference points in a book and visualize the place.

I was young. It didn't always work.

It was only later that I understood those portals I created had sometimes sent orcs to their death.

And sometimes, they opened up new worlds and people for the orcs to conquer and enslave.

The Blighten is a war machine, and their king, ever hungry for more, bought my compliance through treats he instructed his kitchens to craft.

It is a terrible awakening when you understand the part you played in wicked games by wicked people. I do not hate all orcs, for many of them are kind. Edwin, the general whose home we stayed in, made me feel unexpectedly safe. Then there was Doug, Jasmine's mate, a pure white half-orc who turned into a monstrous beast the day we were freed. He never once spoke, yet his ways and gentleness reflected his soul.

So I understand that sometimes people, whatever race they might be, find themselves doing things they shouldn't, that they wouldn't otherwise, if they were given a choice. I feel a lot of guilt for the part I played in the Blighten war and, although I was a young child and none of it was my fault, it does not lessen the burden I carry.

As I stand in Sanctum's portal room, ready to mount my horse with Zeke at my side, I feel the weight of all that I am, all that I was, and all that I might be. The good I can do now might go some way to counterbalancing my past misdeeds. I have been caught up in my head, lusting after inappropriate alphas and not concentrating enough on my scholarly tuition.

Though I find it boring, I recognize that there is a method, a purpose in iteration when doing so helps prevent mistakes. It is only now, as the newly anointed alpha warrior comes to stand beside me—his rich pheromones tickling my nose while he assists me into the saddle—that I acknowledge I am a work in progress, that virtue is not a straight line that holds true, but one that undulates.

I accept the importance of taking my very first quest. I must do this right and put matters of my heart aside, lest they distract me. This is the beginning of my new adult life.

I can make a difference, perhaps finally recover the stolen portal keystone I held as a child but never saw again.

Danger lurks ahead of me. Perhaps not today nor tomorrow, but soon it will come. There will be times when I must make choices and, should I make the wrong one, the people I love, the people of Sanctum, and those of other worlds, might suffer the consequences.

I clamber in an ungainly heap up into the saddle, and Zeke passes me the reins. His head is down, intent on placing them perfectly before checking my saddle for the last time.

I appreciate his attention, for I am a passing average horse rider, not needing to use one often, given my command over portals.

Zeke's blond tousled head is down, but as he finishes his

task and lifts his sky blue eyes to meet mine, I'm reminded of his beauty.

His smile is like sunlight bathing the darkened chamber.

"It will be all right," he says. "I have completed many patrols with experienced warriors during my many years of training. Like you, this will be my first quest without a guide. My first as a warrior. I am charged by a strong desire to serve you well and not fu—mess up."

"You won't, Zeke. I know you won't. I believe in you." And I do. He's still young, just a few years older than me. Of all my adopted brothers, he has a natural athletic build. He's not as bulky as some alphas. Aengus is the biggest alpha I have ever met, with thick meaty shoulders and hands the size of shovels. Draven does not have Aengus' brawn but is unquestionably the first alpha and leader among my brothers. And then there is Theron with his cat-like grace and stern disposition. They are all highly capable, even Zeke, my playful golden warrior who petted my ears and then carried me back to my room.

I lower my lashes. I should not be thinking about that. I need to hold on to what I am, and my purpose. I need to remember, for all we shared blood and intimacy, he was also bedding feeders and breeders a short time ago. The pain I experience knowing he loved other omegas after comforting me is like a lance to my chest. It helps me firm my resolve and remember I'm an omega, that I command him, and not vice versa. "Are you not a little tired?" I mutter a little waspishly. "After the celebration in the warrior hall?"

When I look down, he is smirking at me.

"What does a sweet innocent omega know of the warrior hall, Melody? Were you gossiping with the breeders before you snuck down? You're lucky it was me who spotted you and not Draven."

My tummy takes a slow dip at the word *breeder* like a caress passing over my skin. How I envy the sweet breeders that they caught his eyes and felt his lust. The binding does not hold between the warriors and the breeders or feeders as it does for me. He would rut them because he chooses to, not because it was a command.

"I do not gossip." This is a bold lie, for I gossip with Isabelle every day and listen in on many conversations I should not. My cheeks heat. What makes me mention this now, such a loaded subject, so soon after the intimacy we shared as he took my blood?

"That was a bit of revelry," he says, grinning broadly now. "As I'm sure you noticed. You know it is not only the breeders and feeders who come to the warrior hall. Sometimes the imperials like to play at being a breeder for the night. I still need to find out who let you in so I can give him a good thumping."

Heat pools in my lower belly, and the binding pulls tight between us like he is yanking on the leash. "Ready your horse. It's time that we left."

"Yes, mistress," he says. His words are formal, but I catch the smirk playing on his lips. I do not recognize this version of Zeke. The wicked alpha is playing at being subservient, making me question if I am doing this right, if I am deficient in some way or, worse, if my emotional attachment to him leaves me vulnerable.

Maybe he simply senses that I am uncomfortable in command. As Celeste pointed out, I will grow into my power. I'm suddenly glad it is Zeke who accompanies me. Goodness knows what a mess I might be were Draven here in his place.... or all of them.

"I'm ready, mistress," he says, gathering the reins to his horse.

Mistress, how I already hate that word. How does the male offer insult even as he is deferent toward me? Is it a skill unique to Zeke, or one all warriors have, to ride that line between courtesy and disrespect?

No matter. He is my warrior. We have a quest to complete. I focus my awareness on the portal before me. I do not even need to be at the portal site. I could conjure one out of nothing. But this first time, and likely many times in the immediate future, I will use the portal like other omegas do... mostly. I refuse to hold the keystone at my throat. It is an insult that Celeste insisted I even bring it.

I chant the incantation, feeling the power surge and crackle in the air. The dormant portal explodes into life, and the surface ripples like water, shooting sparks out into the air.

"You did not use a keystone?"

When I glance across, I find Zeke staring at my hands where they rest against the pommel. His brows draw together.

"Why would I need a keystone? I do not even need a portal site. Did you think I could only travel inside Sanctum?" I feel a little smug as his jaw hangs slack. "I can go anywhere, anytime. I can go to another world in a blink of an eye." My lips tug up, and I lift my nose in the air. "The keystone is for ordinary omegas. I am not ordinary."

I press my heels to my horse's flank, and we walk into the portal.

I hear a soft curse as Zeke follows me.

Chapter Six

Melody

We emerge into a snowy forest and ride for half a day to an outpost, where we spend the rest of the day observing movements in and out.

It is very boring.

It is freezing.

"First quests are often uneventful, mistress," Zeke cheerfully informs me as I contemplate which toe I will lose first to frostbite.

Zeke calls me mistress all day, and it really gets on my nerves: *Yes, mistress, no mistress, what are your orders now, mistress?*

I am ready to box his ears by the time the sun sinks when, as per our orders, I open a portal, and we return home, where Celeste questions me in laborious detail.

Zeke snickers when I admit to missing a patrol arriving because I was emptying my bladder.

Apparently, we were sent specifically to see this patrol, and I missed it because I needed to *go*.

Finally, when Celeste has wrung me dry, I am given leave to return to my quarters.

Zeke is looking bright and perky, whistling as he mentions enjoying an ale in the warrior hall while I am ready to collapse from exhaustion and convinced I suffer frostbite on my toes.

Worse, I shall have another 'quest' next week, and this time Theron will accompany me.

I return to my quarters, seething that Zeke is likely rutting a sweet breeder while I am thawing my extremities in a hot bath.

My mind does not linger long on my cold toes, which are fine, nor the tedium of the day. All I can think about is the blood gift with Zeke and the blissful climax that tore through me.

Will it always be that way? Will I fall into a similar lusty daze when I must give my blood to Theron? Maybe I should offer my wrist? Only I have a strong suspicion the mere thought of him taking my blood will drive me to flush, and he will have no choice but to drink deeply from the vein in my throat.

I want him to.

I also want to box Zeke's ears and scratch the eyes out of the breeder that he is likely rutting right now.

Donning a simple nightgown, I take to my bed. Only my sleep is fitful, and I can barely keep my eyes open through lore lessons the next day.

I tell myself I won't go to their quarters again, that I can resist, that it's time I move past these ridiculous fantasies and find a more appropriate object for my lustful musings. I manage one night and then two. And then, I overhear a conversation in the corridor as I exit the portal lore class. Two sweet breeders pass by, they giggle about how they plan to catch Draven's eye, how he has a reputation for his skill in rutting two lasses at once.

Two of them.

"Oh," Isabelle says, inadequately, at my side. Isabelle, who is over the moon because she is going on a quest with Wes. "I'm sure it was just talk."

"It's fine," I say, although it does not feel fine inside.

My heart sinks, and I feel a little sick. Zeke is the only one who has touched me so far, yet my jealousy ignites at the thought of Draven rutting those sweet breeders and making their bodies sing.

Then the sickness abates, and in its place is a blinding rage. I stomp along the corridors, not even bothering to find a quiet place to open a portal to my quarters. The walk soothes me. It allows me the opportunity for my rage to manifest fully. How dare Draven rut the breeders?!

My thoughts spiral as I pace back and forth before the giant window of my room, gazing out across Sanctum from the lofty vantage point. Few rooms here have windows, yet I would give it all up and live in the depths of Sanctum if I could be with my brothers in the way I desire.

I'm getting ahead of myself, wishing for things that can never be. I fluctuate between deep despair, outrage, and desperate longing. How would I be enough for him when he's a warrior who must have two breeders and, further, expect him to share me with three other alphas?

My thoughts are chaotic. My mental state is dangerously unstable. I know I should find myself a lover and purge this nonsense once and for all. Yet the thought of submitting to any other but one of *them* makes my soul want to wither and crawl into a corner.

I go to bed but am too restless for even fitful sleep. Rising, I stand again before the great window. The sky beyond is dark, save for the moonlight. If I were in Zeke's arms, I would feel better and could forget what I want is impossible.

Before I consider the foolishness of my actions, I open a portal.

It's only when a surprised Aengus blinks at me that I recognize the recklessness of my act.

"That's a neat trick you've got there, brat," he says, nodding at the portal that winks out behind me. He is standing beside the fire, dressed in the leather armor all warriors wear. On the table rests a pack, as though he has only recently returned.

Where Zeke is sweet, Aengus is dark. When I'm with Zeke, my heart lifts. He's kind and gentle with me... well, at least he used to be before I gifted him my blood, and he started calling me mistress. When I was little, he would pick me up and rub my scraped knees. With Aengus, his stormy blue eyes hold a mocking innocence that belies the danger that lurks beneath the surface. He is also a barbarian, taken from the eastern clans by the Blighten before he was rescued and joined the warrior ranks.

"I came to see Zeke." I tip my chin in the air and take a meandering route toward the fireplace, aware of my questionable attire, being in my nightgown and nothing more. I glance surreptitiously at Aengus under my lashes.

"Is that so?" he says, unbuckling his belt and removing his sword and scabbard before placing them with a clank on the table. His dark blond hair, a little too long, is shaved close at the sides but at the back it curls around the edges of his collar, and his beard is neatly plaited to keep it close to his face. He is a huge alpha and a sinful kind of handsome. "Well, Zeke is out on patrol and can't help you. Draven and Theron are similarly engaged. So, there's just me, Melody."

I tell myself that this is Aengus, and I will need a different approach than I might take with Zeke, who is never suspicious of my motives.

"I was not having a good night." My lips tremble, for this is the truth. "And I could not sleep."

His face softens in a way rare in Aengus. "Was it the nightmares again? It's been years since you had any."

I nod, aware I'm going down a dangerous route. Aengus always saw through my mischief when I was little. Will he see through me now?

Maybe it won't feel the same when he touches my ears, anyway, and even if it does, I know how to hide it. What I am doing is wrong, I recognize this, but I'm so empty inside and would take any risk just for him to hold me.

"I cannot sleep," I say.

He steps closer, not seeming so wicked when his face softens with genuine concern. And this soothes the hurt I experienced listening to those breeders talking about Draven. It's not only Draven who the Sanctum omegas coo over. Aengus's wicked disposition and barbarian facade have never deterred their interest when he is a handsome, capable warrior.

His black armor is as intimidating as the alpha within it. As he draws closer, I feel very much an omega prey caught in a hunter's sights.

"Would you"—I feel as though I balance upon a precipice below which is a great fall— "comfort me as you used to?"

He stops no more than a pace away and rubs his jaw with his thumb. I can hear the faint scrape of his nail across the bristly stubble. "You want me to pet your ear?"

I nod, my heart beating furiously.

"And this will comfort you?" He sounds skeptical.

I nod again.

"Fine, then." He turns and sits on a nearby fur-covered

bench, drapes one arm across the back, and taps his lap with the other hand.

My eyes dart from his lap to his face, and color heats my cheeks. I presumed he would take me to his bed as Zeke does, but somehow this seems more intimate to nestle fully clothed upon his lap. Well, he is fully clothed. I, on the other hand, wear only a nightgown.

His face is one of feigned innocence like he is daring me. "You seem to be shy suddenly, Melody. Do you not wish to sit upon my lap, like you used to when you were little?" He smirks. "Well, you are still little. Still my naughty little girl."

My tummy takes a slow dip as I remember he has a playful side. Why does Aengus calling me his naughty little girl make me all aflutter?

There is danger here, yet I can't resist and want to be cuddled, even if he plays with me. I expect him to chuckle and tell me I'm a fool.

I'm prepared to take the risk. There's a lightness to my steps as I move around to the front of the seat, shifting from foot to foot and nibbling on my lower lip. Not quite ready.

He raises both brows. "I don't have all night, Melody. I have patrols in the morning. Come on, up you get. Then, once you are settled, I will take you back to your bed.

A small trill escapes me as I take the last step and climb nimbly onto his lap. I tremble as I nestle in his arms like I belong.

"There," he says. "Is that better? Is that what you needed?"

I nod, lashes lowering. I cannot meet his eyes. He wraps one arm around me, drawing me closer to his chest. The leather of his armor is soft and supple under my cheek.

"You know you shouldn't be using the portal," he says. The stern edge to his voice makes me try to get up. He clasps his arm tightly around my waist. "Uh, uh. I like you right here so I can watch your face while you try to lie to me."

I gulp, and my eyes lift to clash with his.

"You should not be using the portal, should you, Melody? Not without a portal scholar on hand."

I am trapped. He has trapped me on his lap. Not to comfort me but for interrogation, it would seem.

He smirks, and his eyes shift to my ear as he carefully tucks my long hair behind it.

I shudder as his thumb brushes over the shell.

"Some omegas," he says conversationally as he begins petting my ear. "Especially imperials" —he rims my ear with his fingertips— "have sensitive ears."

My breathing turns choppy, and my heart rate climbs.

"How many times has Zeke done this?" —he caresses my ear with a light, skilled touch that has me panting even as I squirm under his damning words— "How many times have you gone to Zeke through your portal and asked him to pet your ears?"

His eyes shift from my ear to mine as he tugs roughly on the lobe.

A little moan escapes me. God, my entire pussy throbs as arousal pools in my core.

His head lowers until his lips hover over mine, almost touching them. "What a filthy little omega."

I swallow. "I-I don't know what you're talking about." I grasp his wrist to tug his fingers from my ear—he is strong as an ox, and they do not budge.

His smile is predatory as he doubles down his torment and sweeps his thumb all the way to the tip.

My thighs squeeze together, and I must bite my lip lest I come.

"Are your ears sensitive, Melody? Does this feel good

L.V. Lane

when I do this? And when Zeke does it? Does my sweet younger brother even know what a naughty little omega you are?"

Goddess help me. I am terrified on one level and deeply aroused on another.

He knows I like this in ways more than comfort. My face is hot and flushed—I am panting with arousal. A skilled lover, as Aengus surely is, reads all the signs.

His voice drops to a growl as he issues the damning words, "Is your naughty little pussy creaming?"

He is as scandalous as I am shameless. No one has ever spoken to me like this. No one would dare. Except Aengus is not like other males. He is as bold as he is wicked. He is also a barbarian and, while he has lived here for many years, I believe his uncivilized nature flows through his blood. Knowing he is toying with me, playing with my body and cataloging my reactions, twisting them up, and making me crave his touch to teach me a lesson, does not lessen my reaction or curb my aroused response.

He cups my chin and turns my head to the side before swiping the tip of his nose across my cheek until it brushes against my ear. I shiver. And then his lips close over the lobe, and he gently sucks.

Soon he will laugh and set me away, yet I still arch up.

His lips pop off, and his hot breath bathes the sensitive shell. "What a naughty, filthy little girl," he rumbles. "How many times has Zeke made you come without even realizing it?"

His tongue rims the shell of my ear—I'm delirious with pleasure.

"How many times?" he growls.

His big, rough hand, calloused from sword use, slips under the hem of my nightgown to rest over my knee, where he brushes his thumb back and forth across the skin as he sucks on my earlobe.

"If I lift this scandalous nightgown, will I find your pussy wet? Are you getting off on your brother petting your sensitive fairy ear?"

"No!" The denial slips from my lips.

"I don't believe you, brat. Perhaps I need to check for myself?"

I'm lost to his words and actions. This has already gone far beyond what I did with Zeke, where I could fool myself it was an accidental reaction to his innocent touch. There is no place to hide in this. It is front and center when Aengus handles me like a lover.

I want him to check. I want him to see the evidence of my desire.

"Open your pretty thighs," he says, "and lift your gown."

"I-I can't!" Now the moment is upon me, the one I dreamed of, I'm consumed by conflict and fears.

"Right now, Melody," he barks.

His command rips through me.

I'm so close to coming; I can't think straight. My hands are moving, my thighs are parting, and I'm pulling up the gown. I can feel how slick I am there. I'm ashamed. But Aengus is purring his approval now, and the sweet sound consumes my focus.

I'm mortified that I have done as he commands, put myself on display. An alpha bark delivers a compulsion. I've heard breeders whisper about how they can be compelled to come with nothing but a word. I always thought it would not affect me, given I am high and subject to the binding. Only, perhaps my nutrient-poor blood renders me little more than a breeder?

I'm still reeling from all of this when he makes a tutting noise. "That's my filthy girl. Is your sweet cunt creaming because I petted your ear?" He follows up his comment by caressing my ear, making me shudder and tremble. "Look at what you are doing, making a mess all over my armor." His voice drops to a purr. "Are you going to come for me?"

I shake my head. I can't, not like this. This is too exposed, too vulnerable.

"I think you can. I think it shall be our little secret. Or you can put your nightgown back down and, in the morning when my brothers return, I'll tell them all about your naughty ways. How you tricked the noble Zeke into making you come."

His words are my doom. He is manipulating me, knowing I'm too far gone, that I'd sooner die than lower my gown and stop his devastating caress.

He might tell the others anyway. This is Aengus, after all. Oh, why did I ever think this was a good idea? I should have winked straight out of the portal when I found he was here. Only I didn't. And then I climbed willingly onto his lap. And now I'm spread out upon it, and I'm so close to the cliff and terrified of the fall.

"Come, Melody, right now."

I do, my body splintering, pussy spasming, and head tipped back as I emit a tormented cry of pleasure. My hips jerk forward, and my legs spread further apart as a great gush of slick pours out and saturates my gown.

"That's my good girl," he croons. "Now, it's only fair I have a little taste."

I blink my eyes open, chest heaving as I suck in a breath. His thick fingers slide up my thigh until they meet where the slick spreads across the top... then he lifts his glistening fingertips to his lips and laps it up with a groan.

Chapter Seven

Theron

I am to accompany Melody on a quest, and I gather in the warrior hall for a debrief with my brothers before I go for the obligatory blood gift tomorrow.

I'm still not sure how they allocated it to me. I mean, Zeke, I can see how they might have gotten away with it, given he was newly anointed. "I heard they were going to give it to Derek," I say before taking a deep drink of my beer.

"I put a thumping on him," Aengus explains, "during the training session. I told him to back off. He refused." He shrugs casually.

I take another gulp of beer. Aengus is a barbarian. An orphan like Zeke, he was taken in by my mother, who loved him as her own. Despite living with us since he was young, he is a barbarian in appearance and ways. As the saying goes, you can take the barbarian out of the clan, but you can't take the barbarian out of the man. They do things differently in his world.

Not that I'm any better when I want to rip out the throat of any man who so much as glances Melody's way.

"Good work," Draven says, nodding approvingly. "We don't want any other bastards sniffing around. Especially given how she reacted."

My head swings towards Zeke. I have not heard anything about how she reacted. I have been on patrol for a whole week and returned a short time ago, to be rounded up by Draven no sooner did I finish stabling my horse for this discussion on the new development. "How did she react?"

"Strongly," Zeke says, reaching for his beer.

"Fuck."

"Exactly," Aengus says. "We don't want that bastard Derek anywhere near her."

Derek is not, in fact, a bastard. He's just a typical lusty warrior.

"How strongly?" I ask, yanking on my collar, which suddenly feels too tight.

"She came," Zeke says. "More than once, at least twice, maybe as much as three times."

I swallow thickly.

Draven reaches for his beer resting on the sturdy oak table between us and drinks deeply. "She is close," he says, wiping off the beer from his beard as he puts the tankard back down.

"Close to what?"

"The frenzy," Aengus says.

"Fuck!" I snatch up my beer and drain it before slamming the empty tankard down. A serving lass is prompt to arrive with another round for all of us.

"We can't afford another alpha to touch her at such a delicate time. We don't want them clogging her mind with their pheromones," Aengus continues.

"Do you really think we can keep her for us?" I ask the

burning question. "She is important and will soon be expected to engage in real quests. How can we swing this so she's always with one of us?"

"I've got it covered," Aengus says, cracking his knuckles.

"We can't solve everything with our fists!"

Zeke chuckles. "I'm pretty sure Aengus can."

I sigh heavily. This is a mess. "We need to claim her."

"I'm fucking working on it," Draven says.

Gods, there's not enough beer in Sanctum's cellar for a discussion of this kind. We have tiptoed around this matter for a long time. I've not been able to rut anyone since the night of Zeke's broken cock. It's like the knowledge that she went to him and let him pet her ear has broken me too. I want Melody and only Melody.

"This is unorthodox," Zeke says.

"Like we don't already fucking know?" Draven mutters darkly. "No omega has ever been claimed by four mates."

"No omega has ever opened portals at will," Aengus says. "So, she is special all around."

"Not quite at will, though, is it?" Draven asks, confused. "I thought her skills lay in the discovery of new worlds?"

"It is at will," Zeke confirms.

"How do you know?" Draven's eyes narrow on the younger warrior.

Zeke shrugs, and a little color enters his cheeks. "We went through the portal, and she didn't need to hold the stone. And then, when we were returning, she said a few words under her breath, and a portal opened up right next to us."

As he brings his ramble to a stop, I notice Aengus has buried his nose in his beer. "What did you know about this?" I ask Aengus, remembering that he was the first to mention this.

"Fuck all," he says, glaring at me. "I'm just here to thump any bastard who goes near her."

"We all need to do our part," Draven says.

"And what exactly is my part? What if she... What if matters escalate?"

"You mean she wants you to rut her?" Aengus says bluntly.

"It happens," I say, feeling defensive when I only asked a pertinent fucking question.

"You don't rut her," Draven says. "You take her blood. And nothing more. If she comes, she comes."

"Well, it's all fucking right for you to sit there and say if she comes, she comes. You're not the one feeding while she is making cute little moans and begging sweetly for cock!"

"Zeke managed to restrain himself. So can you." Draven tosses the words out like a personal challenge... which it is.

We are all very competitive with one another and have always been so. I share a mother with Draven while Zeke and Aengus are adopted. But we have been close all our lives. Perhaps our mother sensed that we belonged together, the four of us. Now it feels like the world is pulling us in a direction. *Destiny.* Or maybe we are writing our own story.

"It doesn't matter whether it's heard of for four warriors to claim an omega. Melody is special. She is an imperial who can open portals at will, as we have just discovered" —I still want to know how Aengus knows this when only Zeke was with her, but that is a different matter— "Most omegas offer their wrist for the first blood gift and are so fucking nervous you barely get more than a taste sufficient for the binding, but certainly not enough to come two or three times."

"I think it might have been four," Zeke says. "It was hard to tell. She didn't stop coming once she started, and they sort of blended."

Aengus grunts and, without a hint of subtlety, leans back to adjust his cock.

"They do not flush like that," I say, returning to the matter. "It sounds like she was already primed."

Draven suddenly glares at Zeke. "She has been coming to you for comfort. Was it anything to do with that?"

Zeke scowls back at Draven as though deeply affronted. "What are you suggesting?"

"I also think he might have been secretly priming her," Aengus says bluntly. "Perhaps getting her off while you were petting her ears."

"She was not fucking getting off! Do you think I would not know?"

Draven raises both brows. "You've already admitted you were hard when she came to you for comfort last time, and how her scent was all up in your nose, how you were not thinking clearly and struggling to keep your hands to yourself." He stabs a finger in the direction of Zeke's crotch. "Your fucking cock has been broken ever since."

"It is not only *his* cock," I venture to admit. "Mine has likewise been broken ever since he mentioned the ear petting."

"Mine too," Aengus agrees sourly.

"She did not get off when I was petting her ear," Zeke says, making a slicing motion with his hand. "She *did* get off when I took her blood." The bastard smirks at me. "Perhaps her coming to me to pet her ears indicated that she is already bonding with me. Perhaps she will not react to you in the same way."

I go to launch myself across the table at him and put a thumping on the cocky bastard.

"Woah!" Aengus shoves me back into my seat.

"Enough," Draven says, cutting through our mischief. "You'll just have to see how things play out when you get there. If she's very flushed, it's understood you will need to take it from her throat. You may hold her while she comes, but you are not, under any circumstances, to put your dick in her, no matter how sweetly she begs."

"I believe she will beg." Zeke shrugs. "I was being a dick before. She was all but begging with me, and it was her first fucking time. I believe the second time will be even more intense for her."

I reach for my beer, taking a deep gulp and draining half of it. "Fine, I will do this. I will take her blood. I will see how it goes. I will not put my fucking dick in her. Even if she begs me." I'm yet to be convinced I can abstain if she begs very sweetly, but I shall try and further understand that if we are to claim her, we must do it together. "What after the quest? Will you petition for Aengus to take her out next time?"

"We'll see," Draven says. "They may start to get suspicious if warriors end up out of commission every time they put their name forward."

"We need a plan," Zeke says.

"We do need a plan," Aengus says, looking toward Draven.

"Do not look at me. I do not have a fucking plan!"

"You are first alpha," I say. "It is your responsibility to have a plan."

"Fine. I will think of a fucking plan. But do your part. And then report back."

Chapter Eight

Melody

I am going on a quest again. Hopefully, this one is not as boring and does not involve the potential for frostbite on my toes. Also, I am determined not to drink anything lest I need to relieve myself at an inopportune moment.

Busy worrying about the embarrassment of potentially needing to empty my bladder, frostbite, cold, snow, and utter boredom, I forget about the first step involved in a quest: the gift of blood.

It is only when a guard arrives and escorts me to the same room, the rutting chamber as I have now named it, for it is clear what it is about, that it dawns upon me what is about to happen. By then, the door is closing again, and I find myself trapped and alone.

My heart rate explodes in my chest. Goodness, I can't do that again. It was bad enough in front of Zeke. Theron is older and wiser—he's an experienced warrior. What will he think of me, swaying in his arms, coming like some rampant hussy?

I pace before the fire, which is banked low and offers enough heat to take the chill off the room. The double doors lay open, exposing the bedchamber. This is what goes on every time an omega goes on a quest, how they give their blood to a warrior. The blood, combined with intimacy, cements their relationship and deepens the binding. I feel my inexperience like a weight upon my shoulders. I tell myself that because he is an experienced warrior, he has doubtless done this with many young omegas, confused and overwhelmed, as they give blood for the first time.

I tell myself he will not laugh at me, that he will be respectful and kind because, really, I can imagine no warrior here treating an omega with anything but courtesy, however needy they may be.

Goodness, my cheeks grow hot, my hands are shaking and my nipples are taut. My clit throbs and that compelling achy need for something kicks off deep in my pussy... along with the pounding blood at my throat.

I am growing flush. I growl in my frustration and search for my inner calm.

There is no inner calm. I'm a hot, writhing mess. I feel a little faint. And then the door swings open and closes again, and I know it is too late.

My head snaps around to find Theron standing there. His dark hair spills over his forehead, and his hazel eyes blaze. If Zeke is my sweet golden noble and Aengus is my blond barbarian warrior, then Theron is my stern knight.

"Fuck!" he mutters gruffly as he strides toward me. There is no preamble. He wraps an arm around me and yanks my body flush against his. The effect is overwhelming—his mastery of me, his rich scent, work together to smother me.

I swoon.

"Tell me how to take your blood."

A needy whimper is all that escapes my lips. God, my hips are rolling. "Oh, please!"

He cups my cheek, forcing me to meet his eyes when I'm in a writhing mess of omega need. "I will kill the hapless bastards to leave you alone like this. I should have been waiting for you, not the other way around."

I only whimper. His aggression toward those who carelessly left me here further sparks my arousal.

"Melody, tell me how to take your blood. You're flushing. This is dangerous for a young omega."

I turn my head to the side in the offering.

He turns it right back. "The words, Melody. Give me your fucking permission."

"My throat. Please, I need you to take it from my throat." I quiver with anticipation, stealing myself for the sting and knowing what comes after. I feel like I am on the cusp of climax, just being in his arms.

"I have got you," he says. "I will take care of you, now and always." And then he carefully draws my hair back from my throat and presses his lips against my skin in a feather kiss.

A shiver ripples through me as he gently kisses me again.

"Try to relax, Melody. You have nothing to fear. All these are natural reactions. You do not need to feel shame. Just trust in me. I will take care of you—it will all be okay."

His words, whispered against my throat, make my skin tingle. "Please, Theron."

He closes his mouth over the throbbing vein, and a sharp pinch is followed by pure, condensed bliss as the blood rushes out. I cling to him as he swallows down my blood, climactic explosions rippling through my body—I'm coming, my pussy spasming, body dancing and twitching as though subject to an electric shock.

He holds me still, one hand on my waist, the other hand

87

fisting my hair that I took so much care with. My gown of pale blue silk will once more bear the blood stain.

I arch up into him, mumbling nonsense. I want him: I want his cock. Innocent, I know not what I ask for. "I need you. Theron, please."

He sucks deeper, a sharp, insistent pull, like a thread directly to my clit. The climax is breathtaking. My body turns rigid as I twitch and writhe in his arms. This is worse than last time. I feel like I'm falling and shall never hit the ground. My only anchor is his hands upon me and a steady pull at my throat.

I fumble between us, seeking his belt, and I gasp with joy as it gives enough for me to thrust my hand inside his pants and close my fingers over hot, hard flesh.

He growls a deep, aggressive sound that sets all the little hairs on my body alight and sparks another breathtaking climax.

"Fuck!" he mutters gruffly, wrenching his mouth from my throat.

I feel the trickle of blood. The bite point throbs in time with the pulse in my pussy as it sparks through the lingering climax.

He plucks my hand from inside his pants and pins both my wrists to my lower back. "That was very naughty, Melody."

I blink, turning away, mortified by my actions. I just put my hand on Theron's cock. Oh, what must he think? "I'm sorry," I say. "I don't know what came over me. I am better now."

"Hmm," he says.

I peek up at him through my lashes. His face is very stern. He is so handsome. So much larger and more powerful than me. I love everything about this, being pressed against him, feeling his power and yet how gentle he is, how he shackles my wrists in an unbreakable bond, and yet how light that touch is.

Instinctively I pull against him, groaning at finding myself thoroughly trapped.

A spark lights his eyes, and his nostrils flare.

And then he emits a deep rumbly purr, and all my tension implodes.

"That is cheating," I whisper, softening, submitting.

His lips tug up. "It is not cheating, Melody. We shall never go on this fucking quest if I let you at my cock again."

I blush, trying not to think about how it felt, how soft and silky the skin was over the incredibly hard flesh, how thick it was under my fingers, how it might feel if it was inside me...

"You are flushing again. Try to clear your mind. Focus on my purr." Releasing my wrists, he draws my body into his, pressing my cheek to his chest.

He is cuddling me, a sweet cuddle that disarms all the tension in my body. I breathe. Letting myself be in the moment. I have missed him. I have missed the simple comfort of an embrace. I have missed being cuddled.

"There," he says, stroking gently through my hair. "Have you calmed down now?"

"Yes," I say, my awareness belatedly centering on the pulsing binding between us. I hate that it is like a leash, twisted and unnatural. I wish it weren't there. No, that is not quite right. I wish it were a different binding. One that was equal on both ends. I swallow and seek to compose myself. We have a quest. There are things we must do.

"Will it be cold?" I ask, lifting my head.

He grins. "I don't know what it is about these quests, but they are all fucking cold. Best wrap up, mistress."

And there it is, that word, *mistress*. I am no longer Melody to him. The binding is in place. The formality returns, just like it did with Zeke. I do not want to be his mistress. I do not want to command him. I want to leave Sanctum with him at my side as an equal. I want to let him guide me, for his experience is greater than mine. "I don't understand the binding," I say. "It makes me feel cold."

His face softens as he strokes my hair back from my cheek, his eyes lowering to where he bit. He brushes the pad of his thumb over the flesh, and the light touch is enough to have me quivering once again.

He sighs and takes his thumb away before his eyes meet mine. "No warrior likes the binding, mistress. But I understand why it was put in place."

"You are not a savage—I know you."

"And I know you, imp. But the binding is what it is, and we have a quest."

Chapter Nine

Melody

We emerge from the portal without incident on a snowy outcrop at the edges of a forest. The air is sharp and frosty and turns my breath into a cloud.

I draw my fur cloak tighter around me and share a look with Theron.

"This way, mistress," he says, and turning his horse to the left, picks his way between the trees and emerges on a path. It is wide enough that we can ride side by side. The forest is quiet, and the snow is not as thick as the other day. I think we might be further south.

"What are these quests about?" I ask. "Are they just nonsense to freeze my toes?"

He chuckles softly. "You know there is more to it than that."

"It is about me leaving Sanctum and commanding a warrior."

L.V. Lane

He cuts a glance my way. "And do you feel like you're learning to command a warrior?"

I think that he is teasing me. "Yes," I say confidently.

He chuckles again. "Then it's working, mistress."

"I do not like it when you call me mistress."

"And I do not like a leash around my throat," Theron replies dryly, "yet it is there."

Although his tone is not harsh, I sense deep, dark emotion behind his words.

"The quest is about far more than mere experiences when you are so special, Melody."

My name, the real one on his lips, is like a balm soothing a wound. "I don't feel special." I feel like an imposter doing these quests when I don't even have powerful blood.

He shrugs. "You do not have a fucking choice... And we are here because the lost portal keystone is here. Or it will be. And they wish you to be near it so you can familiarize yourself with its tone, or however fairies sense them."

My brows draw together. "The patrol that passed when I was with Zeke. They had it, didn't they?"

He nods. "Yes, mistress."

"But where are they now? Who tracks them? How do you know we shall meet them today?"

"We have many warriors in these lands, and they track all kinds of things and people, one of which is the keystone. We lose it sometimes. Most high-ranking imperials can sense the keystone. You should be aware of it once you have been in its presence. At least, that is what I'm told."

I touched it as a child. Is that why the king mentioned me? Does he think I have some special affinity to it because I put my hands upon it? "Winter used to track it, didn't she?"

"She did," he agrees. "And she still does on occasion. She is a mother now... and after the binding was stripped from Jacob

94

and her, they do not like her to go on quests. As if Jacob would ever harm her."

"Is that what the binding is about? Stopping you from harming me?"

"You had better ask Winter about it," his tone is unusually sharp. "She knows more than most."

"I've already spoken to Winter about it. I know what happened to her and how it came about. I wondered about your side. If you might feel different, had it never been in place? If it was in place, would you change after it was taken away?"

"These are complex questions, mistress. And no warrior can answer how it might have changed him, save we understand it has. Do you really think I could harm you with or without the binding?"

"No," I say quickly, feeling foolish to have even voiced such a thought and fearful that I have hurt him. "I don't understand why it is still there."

"What did Winter say?"

"She said that change was slow in Sanctum but that some bonded alphas and omegas had chosen to be released from it.

"Half a dozen," he says bitterly. "There are thousands of warriors and fairies within Sanctum, tens of thousands, all subject to the binding."

"If I had a mate, I would release him from the binding," I say.

Theron comes to an abrupt stop. My horse takes a few more steps before it stops, and I turn to face him.

He's staring at me, frowning. "You are young, Melody, and that is a big decision."

I lift my nose a little. "So I am Melody when I say something you consider foolish."

His lips tug in a smile, and the tension between us eases. "My mistress is wise beyond her years. Your mates will appreciate you releasing them from this curse." He nudges his horse into a walk.

I follow, but my heart is pounding furiously because he said, *mates*. I glance across at him surreptitiously, trying to gauge whether it was a slip of the tongue or something else—daring to wonder, to hope. No omega has multiple mates. Well, I think a few might have more than one, but I have never met them. It was a very unusual choice of word.

I'm about to question him when he suddenly lifts his arm and stills. I bring my horse to a stop. He's staring straight ahead.

"Fuck." He wheels his horse around, his face a picture of stern determination. "They are not supposed to be in this area. They said that it was clear!"

"What?" Panic grips me. "What is happening?"

"Off the path, now! Call a portal if you can." He spins his horse into the trees. "Quickly. There is no time to linger."

His tension snatches at the binding, making it lash and undulate. I am in command here, yet I do not hesitate to obey.

We plunge into the forest to the side of the path. The ground is thick with snow and falls away into a steep slope that has me clinging to my horse's neck. I begin the chant. The horse stumbles on the uneven ground, nearly pitching me from the saddle, and I lose my place in the spell.

"Keep moving!"

My vision is coming through a tunnel, terror beating down on me. Something or someone comes for us, dark and evil.

A horn sounds.

The call is familiar to me—the Blighten, their battle cry, the one they use to rouse for violence.

A sob tears from my throat as I urge my horse down the steep slope. Staying in the saddle takes all my concentration.

"We shall meet another path soon," Theron calls. "We

cannot move fast through this forest, but we can move faster than orcs."

I hear crashing from behind, but I dare not turn and look, engaged in clinging to my horse as it skids and navigates the slippery ground and hidden dips.

A small outcropping breaks the slope, and we move onto a narrow path.

Theron spins around, his horse dancing, perhaps sensing the danger as we do. "Keep moving. Open a portal, and do not look back. I will hold them off."

The horn sounds again, closer.

Too close.

He told me not to look, but I do—Orcs, five of them. FIVE.

I go to protest. "Ride!" he snarls, face as a savage mask as he slaps his palm against my horse's hindquarters, and the terrified beast takes off at a canter.

A sob erupts from my chest. He is going to hold them off—he's going to die doing so. My mind sinks into a catatonic state. The orcs are bearing down upon him, charging him. He told me to ride, yet I disobey him, fighting with the horse for control and to stop the mad flight. I feel the binding lashing between us like Theron is pulling on it, trying to exert his power and failing.

I begin to chant.

Only I do not create a portal to escape.

Theron's head swings back to me. "I told you to fucking ride! Make a fucking portal!"

He turns away, and his horse kicks off as he meets the first orc, swinging the blade low and sending a spray of blood arching up. But the others are closing in.

My chant stops—a portal opens ahead of Theron, and two orcs plunge through before it winks out.

I have tossed two orcs into an innocent world. I don't even

know where it has gone, only that it is gone. The other two orcs are upon Theron. My horse dances, terrorized, and I must use all my concentration and skills.

"Melody, for fuck's sake, ride! Open a portal!"

A terrible screaming sound follows. His horse goes down. He stumbles to his feet, staggering backward under the savage assault of the nearest orc.

"Theron!"

I begin the chant, calling the portal for Sanctum, praying that he might break free and prevail, still fighting to control my horse.

Then the second orc rounds on Theron, sweeping his feet from under him.

The portal pops and sparks into existence.

My horse rears, and I am flung from it straight into the void.

I land on my knees, where I heave up bile. The horse is not with me. The portal behind me winks out. For a moment, I'm confused. Surrounded by a snowy forest, it feels like I'm still on the same path.

I feel the first prickling of unease as I note that the sun is higher in the sky, and the air feels slightly warmer. The snow is not as deep, breaking up in patches to reveal tufts of coarse grass.

I stare around me, confused, and then I hear the thunder of horses. I need to get off the path. I need to get back to Theron, only I don't have a clear picture of where he was, and I question whether I can get back. I stumble into the nearby trees, beginning to call a portal, but tripping and falling over and breaking the spell. I half crawl, half fall down the slope. As the thunder of horses near, I throw myself behind a tree, trying to gather my wits and breath, trying to will away the stupid tears that spill down my cheeks so that I can think.

Desperation is like a creeping disease under my skin. Somewhere else, Theron is battling orcs.

"Please pass, please pass."

They do not pass. The horses come to a thunderous stop, and shouting ensues.

I need to open a portal. I need to get to Theron. Yet I dare not open the portal while others are so close lest I bring greater trouble to him.

More horses are approaching. A great roar goes up, followed by the clash of steel meeting steel—they are fighting no more than twenty paces from me.

Heart pounding wildly, I peer back. A dozen men on each side clash, horses screaming as they scatter from the path.

Two uniforms. One is that of Sanctum. One that of the Blighten, but the human soldiers, those who have shunned their own race and now follow the Blighten cause.

I am lost, staring at the battle. I should go, try to slip away, yet I dare not draw attention to myself.

And then they are falling, men on both sides, sinking to the ground bloody and beaten.

I have never seen a man die before, only fairies when the dark fae came and painted the walls of Estoria with blood. Those distant memories clash with the new ones and incapacitate me. I am a young girl again, crouching in the corner of the throne room, watching the dark fae decimate my home. The soldiers' blood is my blood covering the snow. It is a symphony of death.

Fear has me in a stranglehold. I know not what to do. Elsewhere Theron is battling with orcs. Perhaps his blood, too, paints the snow red.

I need to go to him, but my mind is at sea. I am a young girl again, cowering, watching her parents die.

And then the fog clears, and I see clearly, only now I wish I did not, as a helm is knocked aside to reveal golden hair that I have touched on occasion, beneath which is a face I am just as familiar with.

It is a face I hold dear.

Zeke!

I collapse to my knees, my arm reaching out. My mouth opens in a silent scream as he engages with one warrior, and another comes behind him.

My chest compresses as the blade sinks into him from behind—his body jerks, and then his blood splatters over the muddy battle-churned snow.

"No!" The word is screamed, torn from my lips. It is a cry for understanding.

It is disbelief.

It is grief.

As he crashes to the forest floor, lifeless, all eyes turn my way.

Someone snarls an order.

Gods, they are coming for me. My eyes are ripped from Zeke to the danger bearing down upon me.

I'm desolate. Tears stream down my face. I don't know how to live without Zeke.

They are coming for me, but I don't care. I will gladly go with him to the afterlife. Perhaps Theron is already waiting for me there.

Only something pulls at me: instinct, a drive to survive, the Goddess herself, perhaps. I stumble to my feet, staggering blindly, chanting the words that will bring the portal.

I sense they are closing in, hear the tread of heavy footfall, the ragged breaths, grunts, and curses.

The portal winks open, and I collapse through it to my knees.

Again.

Melody Unbound

It is quiet. A single arm, severed by the portal closure, drops to the snowy forest floor behind me.

"Thank fuck!" A bloody Theron staggers from where he kneels over a fallen orc. He crashes into me, cleaving me to him before he sets me away again and commences a feverish inspection.

"Where the fuck did you go? Why are you not in Sanctum?"

I try to speak, but gibberish comes out. He holds me to him, purring manically. Only I'm shaking up a storm, nothing can calm me.

"We need to get back," he says. "We need to get back now. Can you open a portal, Melody? Can you open a portal, my love?"

I cannot see through the tears streaming down my cheeks. It takes me long, valuable moments to calm myself enough to speak. "Z-Z-Z-Zeke. I saw Zeke."

"You could not," he says, brows drawing together. "It is his rest day. He is not even on a local patrol."

I shake my head.

"Open the portal, Melody. Take us home."

Somehow, I do. Only not to the portal room. Instead, it opens in my brothers' quarters...

Chapter Ten

Melody

They are all there: Draven, Aengus... and Zeke sitting at the table.

Everyone surges up, talking at once. I don't hear anything, busy clinging to Zeke as Draven and Aengus attempt to search me for imaginary damage with the same manic intent that Theron did. Once satisfied, they round on Theron like this might be his fault.

Zeke holds me tightly, purring for me as Draven, Aengus, and Theron argue. Theron is bleeding heavily from a gash to the temple, but he pays it little mind as he and Draven roar at one another.

Aengus thrusts his way between them.

"Betrayed," Theron snarls.

"Fuck!" Draven growls.

Everything happens in a blur. Draven carries me from the room in his arms. His scent washes over me, and his warmth, his fierce yet gentle presence, soothes my battered soul. Of all my adopted brothers, he is unquestionably the most handsome. With midnight hair and bright, brooding eyes, his beautiful, rugged looks have been the source of breeder and feeder gossip for years.

Zeke walks at his side, eyes on me, full of concern. Theron and Aengus walk ahead, talking, voices sharp. Theron is still bleeding. I hope we're going somewhere that he might be treated.

We enter a vaulted chamber, and then Winter is there, rushing over to me, instructing Draven to put me down on the long couch.

"Shiloh is on the way," she says, brushing the hair back from my forehead. "Herald has already been called in."

A grand double door to the right opens, and my brothers, except Zeke, who remains at my side, accompany Winter's mate, Jacob, into the inner room.

"Where are we?" I ask.

"The king's audience chamber," Winter says.

I have no time to ask further, for the main entrance opens again to admit the warrior master Cecil. He strides past and is shown directly into the inner chamber. As the door opens, I hear heated voices before it shuts again.

"Hush, it's okay now, Melody," Zeke says, drawing me closer to his side, and then, although it is against protocol, he lifts me onto his lap, pressing my cheek against his chest and offering me a purr.

I cling, sobbing, holding Winter's hand as she watches on in concern.

I have just seen Zeke die. Yet he is here. I don't understand what happened, but it felt real. Only how could it be?

Melody Unbound

Portals were once a source of wonder. Now they frighten me.

Raised voices continue in the other room. I can hear Theron, Draven, and Aengus as well, and a deeper timbre I presume to be the king. They are talking boldly, given who they are with, and I'm frightened for them all over again.

Chapter Eleven

Draven

"What happened out there?" The king demands of Theron. We stand to attention in his stateroom, forming a semicircle on the other side of the mahogany desk at which the king sits. Dark wavy hair falls to his shoulders from a widow's peak. His beard is worn short and neat. I have seen him on occasion in his ceremonial armor. Today he wears a forest green tunic with intricate silver stitching at the collar and cuffs.

The room is as stately as one might expect, with a thick carpet under our boots and broad leaded windows to the left offering views across Sanctum rarely witnessed by lowly warriors.

Theron has a nasty gash on his forehead. His right arm hangs loose like it has taken a savage blow. Bruises and cuts cover his face, and his armor is battered and slashed in several places that bear the distinct stain of blood. He fought with everything to protect the sweet omega we all hold dear.

"Orcs. Five of them," Theron says. "I don't know what they were doing in the area. It should have been cleared."

I put my hand on his good shoulder, seeking to temper the aggression riding him. He winces—maybe this shoulder is not so good, either. He needs to see a healer. Yet he's a warrior, as is everybody in this room, and his needs will wait.

"Teams were sent to pass the region this morning, sire," Cecil says. "They had not returned and reported as they should have. I did not approve of Theron and Melody leaving."

"Bullshit!" Theron snaps.

"My orders were for you to wait," Cecil replies, unruffled. The warrior master has lived long and seen his share of warrior outbursts of every kind.

"A miscommunication?" the king asks, turning to Theron.

Tension ripens the air. I was there when Theron received the note. If he read it in error, there will be consequences, given the danger it presented to Melody.

Theron looks down at himself grimly, thrusts his fingers into a sticky patch at his chest, and extracts the note. He cuts a glare at Cecil and, without bothering to read the note, passes it to the king.

Ballsy. I would have given the note a cursory glance even were I supremely confident of the contents.

The king unfolds the note, reads it, then passes it to Cecil.

He has not ordered Theron to the cells, which is a positive sign.

"This is not your writing, Cecil." He turns back to Theron. "Who brought you the note?"

"One of the servant lads who does Cecil's bidding. I don't know his name, but I would know him by sight."

The king nods, expression grave.

"The facts do not add up well," Herald ventures to offer. My step-father is an experienced warrior with many years of service. He has been working with Jacob as part of a special team for several years. His position is high with the king, and his opinion carries weight beyond his parental role. "My son does not make mistakes concerning his sister's safety."

I stiffen a little. My brothers and I agree that Melody is not our adopted sister anymore.

"Perhaps the delivery lad got notes mixed up." Jacob shrugs. "Although the handwriting is concerning, and I cannot quickly think of how we might explain this."

"Have your patrols subsequently returned?" the king asks Cecil.

Cecil shakes his head. "No, sire. They should have been back some time ago. That they are still absent is troubling"

"Explain what happened," the king asks, turning to Theron.

Theron tells us the story, keeping events succinct as he explains their flight from the five orcs. "I told her to make a portal and return to Sanctum. When she hesitated, I slapped her horse to get it moving. She defied me, pulled up her horse, and opened a portal. But not to Sanctum. She created one right before the charging orcs, and two disappeared through it before it winked out. She defied me and put herself in danger as a result."

I feel his fury and fear as though it is my own. A single alpha against five orcs is impossible odds. Three isn't much better.

Jacob's chuckle is dark and lacks humor. "Just another reason we should finally remove the cursed binding."

"This is not the time to pitch for the binding removal," the king says firmly.

Jacob shrugs. He may be young, but he is one of the few

warriors bold enough to be forthright with the king. "This would not have happened were she properly controlled."

Melody is also young and naïve, headstrong, and of an age where omegas of all castes seek to test.

"Do not speak to me about the fucking binding," the king barks.

To a man, we freeze, feeling the force of his power as an order.

"One does not simply remove the binding from all. As for Melody, she is unmated and lacks the maturity or years to know what she is giving up in order to make an informed decision. The option is available for all once they have experience from which to decide."

"She could have died," Theron pitches back, riding the line of insubordination. "She disobeyed me. Put herself at risk." His voice softens. "She also saved me. She opened the portal and winked two orcs out. I still don't know how I defeated three—I would not have defeated five."

Herald steps closer and puts his hand on the back of Theron's neck.

The king nods, expression bleak.

"Theron might have died today protecting Melody," Aengus says.

"If I lost her, I wouldn't want to live," Theron says quietly, words raw with emotion.

A warrior protects his bound mistress with everything. But Theron is not talking as a mere warrior bound for a quest, but as a man who would claim an omega as his mate.

Cecil clears his throat.

The king's brows draw together. He pins Theron with a look before his eyes shift to me, Aengus, and then back to me.

He huffs out a breath before his face smooths out. "You are set upon her, the three of you?"

"Four," I shrug, realizing we have given ourselves away. "There is Zeke, too."

Herald looks between us before his lips curl up the smallest amount. "My mate did say something about this. She has some skills in reading aura and noted the change."

"She did?" The king raises both eyebrows, then leans heavily in his fine chair. "For the love of all that is holy, will somebody send for a damn healer before Theron leaves blood stains that cannot be easily removed from my priceless rug."

"I will see no healer," Theron all but snarls.

"I believe it unwise for him to take blood from another omega at this point," Jacob says.

The king rubs his brow tiredly. "Four of you with one omega. This is preposterous."

"It is fate," Theron says boldly.

I believe he gets away with his insubordination because he has single-handedly defeated three orcs and brought Melody back home safely. Were he not bleeding all over the place, someone would have thumped him by now.

"We need to get to the bottom of this," the king says. "Someone sent you false instructions. We will need to track down this lad."

"Celeste has been pushing Melody to begin her quests," Herald says. "I offered my opinion that she had experienced great trauma as a child. I questioned if my judgment was biased. I have talked at length with both my mate and Winter about it. We relented on the understanding that one of her" — he pauses to look between Theron, Aengus, and me— "that our sons would accompany her, and the first quests suitably vetted."

"She is valuable," the king says.

"And she will one day be our fucking mate," I say, before I

can better think about it. I am not injured, nor have I recently defeated three orcs, so this is forward and foolhardy.

"You will mind your place," the king bites back. "Or you will be mating no one."

I lower my eyes, feeling the full force of a stronger, unbound alpha subjecting me to his considerable will.

"We understand she is valuable," the king continues. "And if you had allowed me to finish, I would have explained that I have no desire to put her at risk. She does not leave Sanctum again until we get to the bottom of this."

"We have been infiltrated," Jacob says. "Someone has been bought, maybe someone old and embittered, maybe someone new. Who knows."

"For now, she will need to be closely watched," the king decides.

"We will do it," I say.

"You will continue with your fucking duties," he barks, alpha force ripping into me. "It is reasonable for us to keep her inside after such an event. Whoever is behind this will not be suspicious of this course of action. But it will draw suspicions if the four of you suddenly start shadowing her every move. We do not want them to go into hiding for a century or two, because that has happened before. Time passes, fears fade, and that is when the enemy will strike. No. I want this resolved. I want the culprits found and dealt with. The keystone has been gone too long from our hands.... You will continue your patrols on rotation so that one of you is always here."

"She has been visiting Zeke," I say. "She goes to him at night often enough."

The king nods. "No one will interfere. But you will do nothing more until she voices her side and acknowledges you are her mates. It is always an omega's choice."

Jacob dares to chuckle.

The king shoots him a glare, then emits a small huff. His smile is brief. "I believe Winter was very much in agreement with the way matters transpired. She would have chosen you even then."

Enemies to lovers, to enemies again... And finally, to mates. The story of Winter and Jacob is tumultuous, to say the least. They are happily mated with a young alpha who is in training now. Jacob's position was elevated after he was released from the binding and given unfettered access to the blood of his omega mate.

"I will watch over her," Jacob says. "In whatever way I can."

Jacob has made it his life mission to free bondservants held by orcs. He is clear of purpose. I would trust Jacob with my life. Now I must trust him with Melody's, even though I wish the four of us could claim that right.

The people in this room are wise. They also take this threat seriously. Yet something bigger than us is at stake.

The king turns to me. "It is not unusual for you to meet with Jacob, and it is not unusual for Jacob to meet with me, so he will bring me any news. Cecil, you may contact me directly if anything draws your suspicion. Now, I would like to speak to Melody. And if Theron will not go to an omega healer, you best get somebody else to stitch him up. And, perhaps, return his shoulder to a more natural place."

We bow and turn to leave the room.

"They have acknowledged our claim," Theron says quietly.

Aengus smirks. "So they have. Pity we did not think to have you beaten half to death before."

Chapter Twelve

Melody

"The king will need to speak to you, Melody," Winter coaches, her sensitive eyes on mine.

I nod, mind scrambling over events and worried I might get Theron in trouble.

"Speak only the truth, Melody," Winter says, her eyes searching mine like she can read my thoughts. "You will not be in trouble."

"You don't know that." My lip quivers.

"This was only your second quest, love," Shiloh says. She sits beside me, having arrived not long ago. "The king will not be hard on you. And if he does, then he will see the fierce side of me."

"The area would have been scouted before you were sent," Winter adds. "These early quests are to build confidence, not shatter it. There will be questions as to why you came under attack. The king does not accept risk to any fairy, but especially not to one such as yourself."

There it is again, that determination that I am special.

But I have no time to ask more, for the door is flung open, and the king, whom I have only seen from a distance, strides out, accompanied by my brothers, Herald and Jacob. He is a large, intimidating alpha with a thick dark beard and a little white at his temples. His face softens as he takes me in.

I try to sit up straight and scramble from Zeke's lap, but the king holds up a hand and surprises me by crouching before me.

"Can you tell me what happened, Melody?"

I swallow. My tongue feels large and clumsy in my mouth.

"Orcs. F-five orcs... Blood... Z-Zeke."

"She is fucking traumatized," Draven growls, seeming to forget he is speaking to the king.

The king turns and narrows his eyes upon Draven, who dares to glare right back.

My breath catches, and tension thickens the air.

The king turns back to me and nods once. "Rest now, Melody. When you are ready, we shall talk again."

"Let's get her back to her quarters," Shiloh says. She may be a breeder and lowly, but she is first and foremost a mother, and her words carry authority.

Zeke carries me back to my quarters, where Shiloh fusses over me, calling for a warm bath and some honeyed wine. My brothers leave, and I'm offered privacy into which I fall apart. Shiloh, ever attentive, stays with me, and although she does not ask what happened, I see the questions in her eyes.

Later, when I go to bed, I hear her talking quietly to Winter in the day room.

I feign sleep when she opens the door a crack to check on me.

She comes over because this is Shiloh, and she knows me well. The bed gives a little as she sits down beside me and brushes the hair from my cheeks. "How are you feeling?"

"I am fine," I lie. What I want is Zeke... and to see Theron, who was injured and still bleeding last I saw. "Can I see Theron? Is he well?"

Her smile is full of tenderness. "He was still walking, and, short of missing an arm or a leg, well, warriors are tough," she says dryly. "But I dare say he went to a feeder."

The rage that suffuses me momentarily robs me of thought.

"Not all blood gifts carry emotional attachment, Melody. Sometimes, it is just that, the giving of healing."

My lips tremble. She has seen right through me; I don't know what to make of that. My volatile emotional state is a living entity and one I cannot control.

"You love them," she says softly. "I have known it for a while."

I am exposed, vulnerable, and unable to shield all I feel. I have loved them all my life, so her saying this should not feel significant, yet her choice of wording does. I have so many questions that I don't know where to start. It is a lot to take in. Is this her accepting that the kind of love I feel for them is different now? She is the most loving person I have ever met and has always offered unconditional support without judgment and nurtured all her children, whether they were hers by blood or adopted.

She leans down to kiss my forehead. "Do you wish me to stay with you, love?"

"No. I-I really am fine. But exhausted and—" I don't have the words for the quagmire that consumes my brain.

"You need to let all the thoughts rest," Shiloh says. "You have been through much and on top of that you are awakening. I will stay in the day room. If you need me, call. When you are ready and, if you wish, I am a good listener. Now, rest, my love."

She rises, drawing the blanket up to my chin, before turning down the lamp.

Then she is sweeping out of my bedroom, taking her soothing breeder scent with her.

❧

I am far beyond exhausted, but I do not sleep. Despite my determination to let the thoughts rest, they have me in a stranglehold.

I don't stop to consider what I do. Compelled, I open a portal directly into Zeke's bedroom.

He lays sprawled out amid messy covers like he is restless, but wakes with a jolt. "Melody! What are you doing? Are you well? What's happened?"

"Nothing," I say, feeling foolish now that I'm here.

He scrambles up off the bed and joins me. He has always been tall and of a lanky build. But as I see him in his sleep pants, I see a honed warrior. I swallow as he takes my hands in his. His touch is gentle, his eyes earnest as they hold mine.

"Talk to me, Melody. Tell me what you need." His gaze turns toward his bedroom door, which unusually for Zeke, is shut. "Do you want me to get the others? Let Draven know?"

I shake my head. I swallow. "Would you... Would you hold me? I don't want you to pet my ears. But just to lay beside you." I cannot tell him what has happened, that I have watched him die. How can I? I don't know what I saw. Perhaps I conjured it all up out of my terrified mind after seeing Theron with the orcs. "Please."

He nods and, taking my hand, guides me to the bed.

I blush furiously, recalling Shiloh's words. Except too much is happening at once. I cannot process any of it when, every time I close my eyes, I see Zeke dying.

If I am with Zeke now and can feel him touching me, I will know he is alive.

I climb in and scoot over. The bed dips as he settles behind me. "Will you hold my hand?"

"Of course," he says, pressing right behind me, his warm body curving around my back before his arm settles around me, sliding up until his hand encloses mine.

It is a broad, strong hand, and as it curls around my smaller one it eases the terrible ache in my heart.

He is here. He is alive. He is not slain upon a bleak forest path.

As I listen to his steady purr, I convince myself it was nothing more than a manifestation of my terror and not real at all. Exhaustion finally comes for me. His purr, the warmth of his body, the connection of where we touch, and the feeling of my small hand within his take me under.

When I wake, the room is empty. The bed beside me is cold. He is gone. I do not know what the time is. In the depths of Sanctum, there is no such thing as day and night. But the lamp has burned low, indicating I have slept for many hours.

There is a temptation to linger here, but I force myself to rise. Shiloh will likely check on me and would be worried if she finds I'm not there. I stand at the bottom of the bed for some time, wondering what to do. There is a strange reluctance inside me to open a portal.

I tell myself I'm being silly when I have made portals many times, that the horrible waking nightmare needs to be put aside. After experiencing danger for the first time in many years, watching Theron battle orcs, and having flashbacks to the tragedy of my childhood, it is little wonder that I hesitate.

This sounds rational as I stand wringing my hands and still not opening a portal.

But the strange prickling awareness at the back of my neck, the way my hands shake, tell me I have a way to go before I can put this aside.

I could walk back to my quarters, but that would take me through the long warren belonging to the warriors before I ascend many steps to the servants' quarters, and then the serving areas, the kitchens, washrooms and, after that, the chambers of the lesser omega, and all the way to the top, where the higher blood and the king and the chosen all reside.

I will not get all that way without being seen. My toes are naked, and I wear only my nightgown. I do not want to see people—I am not ready to see people in any state of dress, but especially undressed.

No alternatives present themselves. I need to be brave and make a portal.

The calling words spill from my lips, and the portal winks into existence, a familiar undulating black surface that sparks light into the room. The submersion will be brief for such a short trip. I will soon be in my room.

But the moment I enter the portal, I sense something is wrong.

The journey is long, and the oily blackness swallows me up. I wonder for a terrifying moment if I have miscalculated somehow. My mouth opens to scream, but there is no sound inside the portal, only nothingness.

I am spat out the other end, not in my chamber but onto a forest path.

The sun is high in the sky, and light snow dusts the ground with patches for scrubby grass to poke through.

Realization is like a slow creeping awareness as I lift my head and rise from my knees.

"No." I say the word that might make this untrue.

"No!" It is a plea for help.

As I turn and look behind me, I feel the steady drum under the soles of my feet where they contact the frozen ground. The icy chill seeps into me and a great, bone-wracking tremble tears through me.

Horses are coming, many horses, from both directions.

A familiar compulsion drives me from the path, my naked feet burned and scratched as they slip and slide over the rough, snowy ground. I sob as I run, hearing first the horn, then the clang of metal clashing as I throw myself behind a thick tree trunk.

Not again. I close my eyes, clamp my hands over my ears, willing the terrible sounds away.

I'm not here. I cannot be here. How can I be here? Where is here?

The answers to these questions elude me. They have eluded me before. I don't want to look. I don't want to hear. I don't want it to be true. Yet I must know.

Drawing my hands from my ears, and with dread churning in my belly, I turn to peer around the tree.

Zeke's body jack-knifes as a blade thrusts deep and is yanked out.

"No!" The scream is torn from my lips.

All heads swing my way. A roar goes up.

"No," I sob, even as I turn and flee, stumbling down the slope, calling the portal, and praying it will take me home.

I'm ejected into my chamber, where I collapse and heave up bile over the polished wooden floor.

The door is flung open, and Shiloh rushes in.

"Goodness!" She sinks to her knees beside me, drawing the hair back from my face. "You are frozen! Emily!" She calls for the maid. "Please bring a blanket and draw her a bath quickly.

She's chilled to the bone. Oh, your gown is sodden. Where have you been?!"

"Z-Zeke," is as much as I can get out.

The maid brings a blanket, and Shiloh wraps me in it and draws me into her arms. The maids dash about to draw a bath while shivers wrack my body, and I babble nonsense.

For the second time, I have watched Zeke die.

Is this a premonition of the future? Is it an alternate reality? What use is it to me if I don't know what to do with it?

"Zeke," I sob. I cannot be without him. I love him.

My tears are endless. My bath is warm. But it takes me a long time before I can calm down.

"What has happened, love?" Shiloh asks.

"I don't know," I say honestly. "I wish I did."

Chapter Thirteen

Melody

A week passes, and then two. I don't leave Sanctum. Nor do I go to my brothers, although they have stopped by occasionally when I visit Shiloh.

We are never alone.

I wish we were alone.

I almost wish for a quest so I might have an excuse to be with them, to gift my blood, and all that follows. Oh, how I crave what follows, to be in Zeke or Theron's arms, to come apart while they hold me, and to see and feel the evidence of their response to me.

Only, as Zeke so bluntly pointed out, alphas cannot help but react to omega blood... any omega blood. It is nothing more than an instinctive response on their part. I feel desolate thinking about them going on quests without me, taking from another omega, and tending them because they are commanded to do so. They would not have a choice. Not that they would care when, as Zeke said, it is no hardship.

It feels like a wall has been built between us, one that can only be breached should I finally overcome my fears and make a portal.

I know I need to gain confidence again. So much has happened in my short life, and I have always picked myself up and refused to let my past define me. This strange desire to wallow is new and confounding.

My portal classes resume, although most of us have been on at least one quest, and already another two omegas have completed their mandatory training quests and been deemed sufficiently experienced to leave the class.

As soon as the portal scholar issues us with reading and goes to his office for his unofficial nap, Juliet is quick to divulge the details when another girl asks where Athena is.

"She has a quest today. She petitioned for Draven, but he has been taken off quest rotation, and no one knows why. They allocated her to Kain. Everyone knows he is a fearsome, experienced warrior and twice her age," Juliet says, with a definite note of relish.

My ears perk up. I share a look with Isabelle. I confessed my infatuation to her last week. She only smiled and said she already knew. She is on my side and fully committed to aiding me in any way she can.

"It was her own fault," Juliet continues, voice ripe with censure as she turns on her former friend. The two girls got into trouble when they sneaked into the warrior hall during Zeke's rite to warriorhood and have barely spoken to one another since. "She had to persuade Celeste that she needed a more mature alpha so that she could ask for Draven. Now, instead of getting a younger alpha as we all do, they decided upon Kain."

"She was very confident of herself," another girl says diplomatically.

Juliet peeks in the direction of the scholar's office, from

which steady snores emerge, before her voice lowers to a whisper that I must strain to hear. "I overheard the scholar talking to the warrior master, Cecil. He made it clear that Athena was willful and should be subject to a firm hand."

"What does that mean?" Isabelle blurts out.

Juliet turns to look at us and, for once, there is no malice in her eyes. "You have both been on quests. What do you think?" Her lips tug up. "The binding only goes so far. It is different when you lay with an alpha for pleasure compared to how they behave on a quest. Apparently, Kain is skilled at riding the line of subservience to his quest mistress. Then there are the rumors that the king is considering releasing some of the higher-ranking warriors from the binding like he did with Jacob."

Someone giggles. "She ruined my homework last year. I'm not sorry if she suffers a little now."

No one disagrees.

I wish I had the energy to gloat.

I do still gloat a little.

Life is changing.

We are all maturing.

The snores rise to a crescendo before coming to an abrupt stop, and the portal scholar emerges, bringing an end to our chatter.

My longing for my brothers is like an unstoppable force rushing through me. I'm going to do something foolish soon... like blurting out that I love them while Shiloh is sitting right there.

Only how can I love them when they do not also love me? Love is not a one-sided thing. Both parties must be equally involved. Unrequited love is not love at all. It is an echo.

I do not want an echo. I want the moon and stars. I want the sweet and dark passion, the wickedness of Aengus, the blissful gentleness of Zeke, the stern power of Theron, and the dominance I have only glimpsed in Draven.

To my shame, I want to go on quests not because I want to do good for Sanctum but because they will need to take my blood. How I crave the blissful rush as the blood leaves me as I tremble in their arms. Before me lies an uncertain future. The scholar spoke to me in private when I first returned after the fateful orc attack. By order of the king, I am not to go on a quest. Unless I go on a quest, I cannot complete my training.

I also cannot break my cycle of fear in creating a portal without a quest to force it.

I feel trapped and tearful.

Yet time does soften the fears. The terrible vision of Zeke dying that haunts me so brutally at first fades and becomes less tangible. I persuade myself I did not see it, that it was some strange manifestation of my terror, all caught up in the child-hood tragedy.

Zeke is still here, very much alive, golden of hair, and beautiful. When he came to have tea with Shiloh two days ago, he talked about his patrols and shamelessly teased Shiloh about her honey cake, saying it is not quite as good as the one the cook makes in the warrior halls. We all know it for a lie. I loved his conversation, seeing him full of vitality. I feasted my eyes on him, and every interaction helps to crush that prior, darker memory where I saw him fall.

I miss him, being in his presence, but not in the way I wish. I dream of him holding me as he did when I returned from that ill-fated quest, purring and pressing my cheek to his chest.

Everything changed the day Zeke petted my ears, and I came. But it changed more the day Theron battled orcs. The fear that I might have lost Theron and Zeke makes all else feel inconsequential.

I crave them, all of them, crave a level of intimacy I worry may never be mine. I remind myself that unrequited love is not love but a pale echo, yet it consumes me.

Time passes.

No one asks me to make a portal.

I wonder about my purpose, living in these beautiful chambers, whether I will be relegated to breeder or feeder when I do not even participate in quests by order of the king.

I question myself. I question whether I am broken.

How could I not be?

If one of them would hold me in his arms, illusive wholeness might be mine.

The pressure is building. I need to do something, anything. Even if the outcome is not good. It's like a driving force behind my every move. So, whenever I go to visit Shiloh for tea, I don my prettiest gowns just in case one of my brothers should pay a visit.

"That is a lovely dress," Shiloh says, smiling as she prepares a tray with the tea.

It is Thursday afternoon, and Theron came this time last week.

"Thank you," I say, carrying the prepared tray access to the occasional table of her lounge, around which sit two beautiful ornate couches. The quarters are fine for a former breeder omega and reflect her status as a mate to a highly regarded warrior.

"Is it new?" she asks.

I blush, wondering if Shiloh can see through my actions. *"You love them,"* she said. *"I have known it for a while."*

My heart skips a beat as I am taken back to the morning when she said those words. The very last time I called a portal... the second time that I saw Zeke die, how my gown was sodden, and my body chilled like I was really there.

No one has asked me about it, and nor have I volunteered,

the memory too sharp and painful, as though my talking about it might make it real.

A deep, pervasive sense of malaise crawls under my skin. "I have had some adjustments made," I say brightly, determined to push the memory aside. Likely it is a false one, like all of it.

"Well, the color and cut are very fetching."

It is scandalous; the décolletage is better suited for pre-quest blood gift than tea with Shiloh and it showcases my small breasts to perfection. I've worked on it every evening for a week after finishing my portal lore lessons. An unaccomplished seamstress, I've punctured my fingers more times than I can count.

Shiloh smiles. "And I noticed the little slits carefully worked into the back. Are you considering showing your wings?"

Did I make them more obvious than I intended? "I'm not ready yet. Do you think anyone will notice my changes to the gown?" I question why I did such a thing when I have so long hidden my wings.

"No, not at all. I expect I only noticed because I know you have wings." She leans forward to stir the teapot, and my eyes shift toward the door. I have looked at it twenty times already and have only been here for five minutes.

Shiloh smiles, catching me in the act. "They might not come today, my love. They are very busy, from what I understand. The king remains concerned after the orc attack."

I suck a breath as we dance around a matter we have not spoken about properly.

"I want them," I blurt out. "But I don't know how to make it happen. I don't know if they want me."

Her smile is far too knowing and holds no surprise.

She pours the tea into two cups, then adds some cream and honey before passing one to me.

I don't want tea. I want Zeke. I want Theron. I want Aengus, even if he will taunt me insensible, and Draven—I still dream about him carrying me to the king's chambers.

"It is not something talked about often, but breeders can often sense emotions as colors. It is like an aura around a person; depending on the depth and type of emotion, the color will change." Her expression holds no judgment. "Your color changed in their presence a little while ago. When I saw my sons the day of the orc attack, it had changed for them. I have only witnessed the like before in fated mates. The ways of the Goddess are not for the likes of breeder omegas to understand, nor even kings. Their love for you is no longer that of a sister but that of a mate."

Their color has changed.

So too, has mine.

Fated mates?

Dare I hope?

"You need to speak plainly, Melody." She sips on her tea like this is an ordinary conversation, like I am not a hot mess on the inside and adjusting with painful slowness to this news.

"They seem so busy," I finally say.

"They are warriors in the service of Sanctum. They will always be busy. Just as omegas are always busy."

I swallow. I want to tell her about my brokenness. That I cannot make a portal anymore, well, I can, but I'm choosing not to. Only that wound feels raw, and I'm reluctant to poke at it.

"You need to tell them, not me. It is always an omega's choice—it has always been an omega's choice. No warrior would ever dare to press the matter lest they suffer the king's wrath."

Is she saying only I can do this? That I must be the one to take the risk? To put my heart on the line? What if she has read it all wrong? Colors can change depending on the light. What if she mistook the signs? It was a very charged time, ripe with emotion and upset.

Before I can ask, the door opens, and Aengus enters. His armor is clean, and his hair is a little damp like he has recently bathed; beneath the clean scent, his pheromones are rich and potent. My thoughts scatter at his arrival so soon after that charged conversation.

His eyes hold mischief as his gaze lowers to the tray between us.

"Is that honey cake?"

Shiloh chuckles. "I swear, as a boy, you could smell baking from the other side of Sanctum. It's good to see you, Aengus."

"You too, mother of my heart." He nods to me before taking the seat beside me. His eyes are on the honey cake. "Are we going to eat it or just look at it," he says bluntly.

"Do they not feed warriors?" Shiloh asks as she takes a plate and the knife. She cuts a small slice and passes it to me before placing the knife to cut another.

Aengus clears his throat.

With a raised brow, she moves the knife so it will cut a bigger slice before checking with Aengus.

"Go on. No point in wasting it. Two tiny fairies will never get through that slab."

She moves the knife even further along until Aengus finally nods. "You will make yourself ill." She still cuts it anyway, lips twitching like she is only amused. "I'm so glad I'm no longer responsible for your meals."

He pats his stomach. It sounds solid and distracts me from my cake. It has been years since I saw Aengus without his shirt on, but from the way he fills out his armor, I believe he will be impressive. My eyes shift to his hand, that huge, capable hand, and I get a little tingle inside. He is a barbarian. No one could ever doubt his heritage when he looks so... uncivilized... despite living in Sanctum and dressing as all warriors do. There is just a presence to him, an edge, a roughness in manner and speech that never changed. And his ways. Goddess, I am much enamored with his ways.

Shiloh chuckles as she hands the giant slice of cake over.

He doesn't even bother with a fork, just takes a cake in his meaty hand and stuffs half of it into his mouth.

He groans.

I swallow and blush furiously, failing to drag my gaze away from his blissed expression. He is unquestionably handsome, with dark blond hair longer on top and cropped short at the sides. His shoulders are thick and round, and his arms bunch most arrestingly as he polishes off the last of his cake.

His head turns, catching me in the act of staring, my own cake untouched. "You are jealous, brat."

"I..." What am I jealous of? I blush. "I'm not jealous."

"You wish you could eat this much cake, but your small fairy body would explode."

Shiloh chuckles again. "You know Melody could eat you under the table in honey cake. Fairies have an infinite capacity when it comes to sweet treats. It is the way to an omega's heart."

"Is that so?" Aengus says. "I shall keep that in mind should I need to woo an omega."

"You will not woo an omega," I say, tone sharp, and before I can think better about how that might come across.

Smirking, he shoves the last of the cake in his mouth and puts his empty plate on the table. He slowly chews, staring at me the whole time.

I stare back. Why is the way his throat works and that hungry gleam in his eye making it so difficult to breathe?

My cheeks grow hotter as I recall how I sprawled out on his lap, how he made me lift my nightgown so he could check the mess I had made...

"Any specific omega? Or omegas in general?" he asks.

"Why don't I get some fresh tea," Shiloh says brightly, gathering the pot and leaving before either of us says a word.

I cannot drag my eyes from Aengus, who is now staring at my lips.

"Any omegas," I clarify in a whisper.

His eyes turn positively predatory as he leans casually against the couch, which is fancy, with plush seats and gold scrollwork across the top. He is a warrior covered in dark leather armor and looks ridiculous sitting on it.

It reminds me that he is an alpha, whereas I am a tiny omega. We should not fit well together, yet we do.

"Not even you?" He smirks. "Do I sense possessiveness, Melody? Do you want to keep me all for yourself? Are you sorry that there has been no quest where I might have a turn taking your blood? My brothers and I have talked in some detail about your lustiness. Zeke swore you came two or three times, maybe even four. Theron claimed that you did not stop fucking coming while begging sweetly for his cock. They believe it to be only the effect of the blood-taking, but we know better, don't we, Melody?"

My chest heaves. I feel both exposed and trapped. "*Speak plainly*," Shiloh said. But now, when I have the opportunity to do just that, to admit, as Aengus points out, that I came in the arms of Zeke and Theron, just as I did for him, not because of the blood gift, although it certainly heightened things, but because, fundamentally, on every level, I am besotted with my brothers.

My mouth might as well be sewn shut, for no words come out.

Why is it so very hard to speak plainly when it comes to love?

I am scared. That is the bottom line. That is the unavoidable truth.

Does he tease me? Taunt me? What would happen if I did confess? Would he throw his head back and laugh?

Or would it be the catalyst for all I desire?

The door opens, and Shiloh returns.

"Well, I'd best be getting on," Aengus says gruffly. "I have a late patrol today."

He kisses Shiloh's cheek, nods to me, and then leaves, striding out the door.

Shiloh pours me another cup of tea, adds three spoons of honey, and passes it to me without a word.

Chapter Fourteen

Aengus

"She is close," I say as I meet up with the others in the warrior hall for ale.

We have seen little of each other recently, and it's near unheard of for all four of us to be together. Local patrols are constant and on high alert in the face of the mysterious attack. The lad who brought Theron the note was found dead, the poor bastard's throat slit before he was tossed into the sewage drain.

Of course, few know about this beyond our inner circle.

"Good," Draven says, drinking deeply of his ale and leaning forward on the table. "What happened?"

Zeke and Theron similarly sit forward in their seats. Around us, the warrior hall has succumbed to the usual revelry that happens every night.

For warriors, life is brutal, and every day brings danger. The orc bastards test our defenses regularly. We must patrol the forests around Sanctum lest we find them at our doors.

There are also several large towns and many villages that supply us with food and goods in exchange for our protection. All must be patrolled and, when necessary, defended. Between the patrols, there are many and varied quests. When warriors hang up their weapons, they often come to the hall to eat, drink, and find a breeder or feeder to share comfort among the furs with... Well, *I* have furs on my bed, for I'm still a barbarian at heart, and that will never change. The rest of the soft bastards have blankets on their beds... while omegas love soft things, and nests, which every alpha of every race is openly obsessed with.

Not that any of us have gone on quests or partaken of omega companionship when we are all suffering from broken cocks.

"It was my turn to visit while Melody was with Shiloh, as we agreed. She stared at me like she wanted to eat me instead of the honey cake. If I'd lifted that scandalous and very pretty dress she wore, I would have found her pussy creaming."

"Fuck!" Zeke says roughly before burying his nose in his beer. The lad is hiding something. I have a nose for such things... probably because I am also hiding something.

"She's taken to wearing low-cut gowns," Theron mutters. "I swear it is a fucking test to keep my thoughts pure while Shiloh is in the room."

"She left," I say. All heads swing my way.

"Who?" Draven asks.

"Shiloh," I explain. "That has never happened before. She left to refresh the pot of tea, but I'm certain it was already full, given she held it in two hands."

"And?" Zeke demands. "What happened while she was out of the room? How long was she gone? I swear it is like getting blood from a stone getting information out of you."

I take a deep drink of my beer before returning it to the table.

Theron rolls his eyes.

"Nothing fucking happened." I wish something had.

"Why did Shiloh suddenly leave the room?" Draven asks, tone sharp with suspicion.

"How the fuck would I know?" I scowl at Draven and reach for my ale, not liking the note of accusation in his voice.

"She has never left the room before while any of us have been in there," Draven points out, narrowing his eyes on me before pinning Zeke and Theron with a look—they both shake their heads.

There has always been conflict between Draven and me. We're not far apart in age, and, well, I'm a barbarian, a big bastard, and I don't back down from much. He is the first alpha, but I give him a hard time and make him work for it. If he's going to be the one in charge, the one who sets the rules and the boundaries, he must fucking earn the place. He has always been the first alpha, but not because he is older or a better fighter. He has a few months on me, and I have fifty pounds of brawn on him. I could be first alpha if it were down to strength alone, but I'm not, because Draven has always been, and always will be, the natural leader among us brothers. Also, I have some questionable personality traits, not suited well to the position... such as lifting the nightgown of a naughty omega to check on the condition of her pussy.

I should have told him about that—I will at some point and when I'm ready.

They are all fucking blind where the brat is concerned. It is always an omega's choice here, and while I am congenial to this, I see no reason why an alpha cannot help matters along.

"She said I was not to woo another omega." I smirk and take another drink of ale.

Draven narrows his eyes on me like he is thinking about thumping me.

"Fuck!" Zeke mutters—the lad curses a lot.

"The details," Draven says in his no-nonsense leader's voice. I decide not to test him. He looks fit to bust me open if I'm not forthcoming with the goods.

"We were discussing honey cake, and Shiloh mentioned it was the perfect treat for wooing omegas, given they have such a sweet tooth. I said I would have to remember that next time I needed to woo an omega... Melody took exception and said I was *not* to woo an omega—any omega. That's when Shiloh left the room."

"What the fuck happened next?" Draven demands.

I shrug as casually as I can. "I might have riled the lass up about her enthusiasm during her blood gift with Zeke and Theron."

"You were not fucking there!" Zeke says, face turning an unhealthy shade of red. "She will know we must have told you!"

I shrug again. "She flushed a pretty shade of pink, and I damn near got wood. I had to think about dead bodies lest my dick go off. I didn't want to be thinking about dead bodies right then. I'd much rather have been thinking about bending her over that fancy couch and—"

Draven slugs me. My chair crashes back, sending me sprawling across the floor.

A cheer goes up as warriors around us raise their tankards in approval.

Theron is holding Draven back as I roll to my feet, straighten my chair, and test my jaw. I was half expecting it... I was riling Zeke up and thought he might have launched himself across the table at me first... Zeke does not hit as hard.

"You have told her we were discussing her!" Draven snarls.

He must be really pissed to be repeating what Zeke has already said. "I thought it might speed matters up." The fight goes out of Draven. I cautiously take my seat. He sometimes goes at me again if I'm being particularly challenging.

"It's getting harder to remain rational," Theron says.

"What is she waiting for?" Zeke sounds like a man seeking divine guidance.

"She's a very strange omega," I say bluntly. "They are not usually hesitant when it comes to matters of lust. They are demanding little things, asking for cock and to be tended. It's all a warrior can do to keep up with them. You must peel the saucy imps off half the time, so you don't get whipped for missing a patrol."

"It is unusual," Draven says, reaching for his ale but only staring into it, "for one omega to claim four mates."

"Unheard of," Theron offers. "And she might also be shaken from what happened with the orcs."

The mood shifts to pensive. I snatch up my beer and take a deep drink, only to realize I'm at the bottom of the cup. I hail a serving lass who brings over another round and gathers our empties.

She offers us a pretty smile.

None of us give her more than a glance. We are all pussy whipped, as the saying goes, set upon one particular omega, and now no omega or lass of any kind will do. Fuck knows what will happen to us if she never declares... No, she will admit it eventually, somehow. "The business with the orcs troubles me," I say. "But what happened after feels worse."

We share a look. We are all equally troubled.

"Where do you think she went?" Zeke asks. "It can't have been a good place if she came back soaking wet and shaking."

Draven shrugs. "She told Shiloh that she remembered nothing except that it was cold."

"I wish I'd carried her back to her room," Zeke says. "I don't know why I didn't."

Theron puts his hand on Zeke's shoulder. "You cannot blame yourself for this. She's an omega with mastery of portals. At least she visited you. She has yet to visit me at night for comfort."

"She has not come to me, either," Draven adds before fixing me with an enquiring look.

"Nor has she visited me," I offer. It is a small white lie. Technically, she was not visiting me when she nestled upon my lap and soaked her nightgown as I petted her ear.

Draven turns to Zeke. "Has she visited you again, runt?"

Zeke scowls back, reaches for his fresh beer, and defiantly takes a deep drink before putting the tankard back down. "You know she has not. I would tell you if she did. We are all in this together now." He glares at me. "Well, other than Aengus, who does whatever the fuck he wants."

"What the fuck does that mean?" I slam my ale down.

"You did fuck Zeke and me over," Theron points out. "She knows we have been discussing her lustiness. She will not fucking trust us again!"

"Aengus will not fuck up again." Draven cuts in. "He will toe the fucking line."

I pick up my beer, feeling Draven's eyes on me. I boldly meet them. I promised Melody I would keep what happened between us our little secret. At some point, I will need to confess to Draven if the brat does not mention it first.

I smirk as the memory plays back in my mind.

"What have you done?" Draven asks, tone ripe with suspicion.

"I have done nothing. Shiloh was out of the room for all of a minute," I hedge for a distraction from what I was really thinking about. "Why she decided to leave is a mystery to me. Maybe she thought to urge matters along. Maybe the tea did need refreshing. I didn't even kiss Melody's cheek when I left!"

I am protesting this a little stringently. He will fuck me up when he finds out I willfully petted her ears and watched her come.

"Good," Draven says. "We will put our hands on her together, or we will not put our hands on her at all."

"What if she comes to my room again?" Zeke asks, sounding hopeful.

Draven appears to mull this over. "You will act normally, and we will discuss it the next day. Unless she shows signs of arousal, in which case, you must notify whoever of us is around straight away."

"This is all a lot of nonsense if you ask me," I say, wondering where Sanctum alphas keep their fucking balls.

They all glare at me.

"Barbarians do things differently. We are not afraid to woo a woman."

"You were a boy when you left the barbarian tribes," Draven points out. "How the fuck would you know?"

"I was eleven years old and fully matured, so I noticed a lot of fucking things. You want a lass; you woo a lass. You present her gifts such as flowers. Perhaps you make something for her with wood if you have skills. When the lass is an omega, competition is fierce, and you would want to acquire the best nesting material to offer as a gift."

"Maybe we should gift her some honey cake," Zeke offers.

"We're not sending her any fucking honey cake." Draven makes a slicing notion with his hand like Zeke is an imbecile for even suggesting as much. "That is a ridiculous suggestion."

Personally, I think it was a sound suggestion.

"Where would you even get a honey cake from?" Draven mutters, as though for all his protestation, he is considering it.

"We could ask Shiloh to make it," Zeke says, his young face flushing.

"That is not much of a wooing gift if someone makes it for you," I say. "None of you have a fucking clue."

"None of us will be wooing her," Draven says, getting all surly first alpha bastard mode. "Until she gives a clear indication that this is what she wants. Then we shall spoil her with a mind to claiming her as a mate."

"And her pussy," Zeke says.

Draven finally cracks a smile. "And her pussy," he agrees. His smile shifts to a predatory sort of smirk. "I believe she might be one of those omegas that take well to a little discipline. She disobeyed you, Theron, and put herself in danger. That has yet to be addressed."

Zeke swallows audibly. "How does that, ah, work? Fairies, especially imperials, command us. It is one thing to administer a playful spank to a breeder when she is in the moment, but this is..."

"What exactly are you proposing?" Theron asks bluntly. "A firm chastisement with the palm or something more impressionable, like a strap?"

My dick swells painfully behind my leather pants. I suspect we are all similarly afflicted after Draven's mention of discipline and Theron's mention of the strap.

"She will ask for it." Draven's grin is all teeth. "Might even beg."

My nostrils flare. I can admit that this is why he makes the best first alpha. "I believe she will beg," I say thickly, reaching for my beer.

Chapter Fifteen

Melody

T do a lot of thinking after I leave Shiloh's quarters. Her indication that we are destined to be mates ignites a flame into a fire. Fears are pushed to the back of my mind as I pace before the window of my quarters, watching the sunset. I keep having flashbacks to the night I sprawled out on Aengus' lap. How I came while he watched.

He keeps my secret still.

Only the craving is like a living entity under my skin.

I need to go to them.

I need this to be resolved.

Aengus will be away on patrol, having mentioned it when leaving Shiloh's quarters. Not that I do not wish to see him. No, it is more that I want to see him too much and fear what madness might consume me in his presence. I'm not quite ready to speak the words and confess what I feel, but I believe if I can see Zeke, who has always been the gentlest of my brothers, I can better judge the matter.

As I stand poised to open the portal, I convince myself that I need this. Not only to purge the terror of my last portal use but to have comfort and be held. I can handle laying with Zeke. I will not succumb to the fever and can let him pet my ear to a gentle climax before he carries me to bed.

Then I shall be able to think straight again.

However, when I emerge from the portal into my brothers' quarters, the door to my right opens, and a sleepy Theron walks out. He stops abruptly and blinks across at me. He wears naught but loose sleep pants and yawns as he rubs absently at the thick ridges of abdominal muscle.

I am thrown back to the day he took my blood, and a blush creeps over my cheeks. My shame does not deter me. I crave his touch, his fingers petting my ear... and at the sight of him I desperately need to come. He is not sweet like Zeke, but he is not wicked like Aengus either, and either way, I'm here now.

"Will you pet my ears until I fall asleep?" I ask as casually as I can.

His eyes bug in his head in a way that might be comical were this a less fraught moment.

"Are you having trouble sleeping, Melody?" He glances around before his eyes narrow. "How the fuck did you get here?" He closes in on me, a towering wall of muscle that makes my knees weak. "You can't wander around the corridors in your nightgown. This is the warriors' section. What if someone mistakes you for a breeder or a feeder? I will fucking kill any man who puts his hands upon you, whether I call him a friend or not."

A tingly thrill rushes through me at his possessive undertones. His words soothe me even though he is intimidatingly close and bristling with rage. His rich scent saturates the air, made potent as his protective instincts are roused by my state of dress and the perceived risk I took in getting here.

"I used a portal," I squeak. I blame my addled mental state and his potent pheromones for this slip.

He stops an inch away from me. "That was very naughty, Melody. I shall need to discuss this with our brothers."

Gods, no! This is not good.

His eyes narrow suddenly. "Does Zeke know you use a portal to get to his room?"

I shake my head vigorously, even though Zeke does know I use the portal. "Can you pet my ears? Please. I shall never sleep unless you do."

He sighs heavily. "Fine. Go and get in my bed. I will comfort you until you fall asleep, then *carry* you back to your room."

I all but fly into his room, eager for his touch.

Inside, I find the ambience dark and imposing, with stone walls and a sturdy-looking oak bed centering the opposite wall. The covers lay open, a little rumpled from where he was sleeping. A nightstand to the right holds a lamp set low. It illuminates the bed but leaves the rest of the room in shadows.

A tiny trill bubbles up as I slip between the sheets where I am enveloped in his scent and the residual warmth from where he lay.

It's only now, as he follows me in, shutting the door firmly, which Zeke does not do, that I realize where I am. This is the first time I have entered Theron's room since he left home and the first time he has petted my ear since I was a child.

My heart thumps about inside the cage of my ribs as he stalks over and rounds to the other side of his bed. He climbs in behind me and tugs me closer until my back is flush with his chest.

I squeak—he rumbles a purr. "Settle down, Melody. It's late, and I have a long day of training tomorrow. If you want me to pet your ears, this is how it shall be done."

My heart rate climbs to a gallop as he curls his arm under mine, nestling his forearm right between my small breasts until he can reach my ear while I'm all tucked up in his arm.

Only he is not as gentle as Zeke and tugs the sensitive lobe in a way that has me instantly stifling a groan. Goddess! I'm already certain this was a bad idea. Zeke coaxed me to a gentle climax, and I was able to keep my breathing steady so that he did not know. But Theron's gentle rub, followed by a rough tug, has me twitching and biting back moans.

Then he swipes a thick thumb all the way to the pointed tip and tugs there.

I groan.

He stills.

I swallow and bury my face in the pillow. Did he notice?

"Melody?"

Does his voice sound a little strained?

"Yes," I whisper.

His big warm hand cups my cheek turning me to face him. "Look at me," he commands.

Goddess, he has such a stern voice, and I cannot help but obey. As my eyes lock with his, and I'm forced to hold his gaze, he swipes his thumb all the way to the sensitive tip and tugs again.

Heat floods my cheeks, and I must bite my lip to stifle the groan.

His eyes lower to my lips. He is still holding the tip of my ear, petting it between finger and thumb, tugging it rhythmically as his gaze roams over my face, then lower to where my nipples are peaked against the sheer material of my nightgown.

Oh, I'm going to... I'm going to...

He stops and throws himself off the bed.

"What? Why?" I pant, disoriented that he stopped.

"Melody. That was very naughty," he says, pacing and

throwing a stern look my way that makes my pussy throb in tandem with my ear, which is so heated from his touch that it feels like he is still tugging it.

He stops pacing abruptly. Staring down at me through narrowed eyes, he plants his fists on his hips.

"When Zeke comforts you, do you come?"

"I—" I shake my head, wondering how I could have messed up so badly.

"Think very carefully before you lie, Melody. You are already in a lot of trouble."

I swallow. "I-I might do... Zeke does not do it as roughly as you, and it just sort of happened the one time, and I liked it very much. Then the next time, it happened again. He didn't even realize." My shame is absolute. I knew this was wrong, and I did it anyway. My feelings toward my adopted brothers have devolved beyond all control.

"That was very naughty, Melody. Bad enough when I thought you were wandering corridors. Then I discover you are using a portal. Now, I learn you're getting off on my brother petting your ear. I believe this is one of those punishment times Draven spoke about."

"Oh! No, I'm sure it is not." My denial is stringent. I have no idea what this punishment time is, only that I can infer they have been discussing it, and *me*—Aengus was very blunt in pointing out how I came for Zeke and Theron during the blood gift. Now they are discussing me with a mind to punishment like I'm an errant fairy child.

"It most definitely is. Given that you deceived Zeke, I believe he should be the one to hold you while I take the strap to your bottom."

"No!"

"Yes," he says.

Common sense dictates I be fearful under this threat, yet

his stern voice and the prospect of having my bottom chastised in such a way has me near faint with arousal.

I believe I am irrevocably broken.

I believe I like being broken just fine, for I would have any of my adopted brothers' hands upon me in any way I can.

His nostrils flare, and his eyes lower to the apex of my thighs, hidden from his view by my thin nightgown. "Melody, is your pussy making a little mess?"

"It is not!" I say, indignant that he should ask me this, and more so because it definitely is.

"Melody," he warns, voice lowering to a soft purr that makes my pussy clench and leak yet more mess.

"Yes," I sob. "Yes, it is. Oh, please don't punish me, thus. I should be mortified for you to see me like this."

He folds his arms. "You have deceived us. That is unacceptable. Given the severity of the matter, Draven and Aengus will need to witness your punishment too."

"But I thought Aengus was out on patrol," I whisper, horrified to learn that all my brothers are here. Worse, had I timed things better, I might have experienced a blissful gentle climax with Zeke, and no one else would have known. Only it was hard to mask my reaction before I gifted my blood, the little voice inside my head mocks, and *Aengus already knows.*

"Speak plainly," Shiloh coached.

I believe I have skipped this vital step. My mind sinks into panicked denial as Theron strides for the door without waiting for my answer. I rise to my knees on the bed and wring my hands as I wait, my chest heaving and pussy making a terrible mess in anticipation of the strap. My ear continues to throb from his touch, producing a confused swell of emotion. If Aengus confesses that he already knew about my mischief, my punishment will surely be even worse.

I'm about to create a portal and flee when the door opens

again, and all four of my brothers stride inside, filling the small space with their imposing warrior bodies, every one of them in a state of sleepy semi-dress and clogging the air with their rich pheromones.

Theron turns the lamp up on his nightstand, making me feel even more exposed.

"What's this about?" Draven demands. "We all have an early patrol come the morning..." He trails off as his dark gaze sweeps over me, and his nostrils flare. If Theron is stern, Draven is the epitome of dominance. As the oldest of my brothers, he is the leader among them in all things.

"Tell them," Theron says, nodding his head at me.

"Me?" Goddess, he is holding the strap!

His eyes narrow when I don't immediately answer.

"I—it feels, um, nice when, um, Zeke pets my ear," I admit, face heating with shame. I glance toward Aengus to see if he is about to betray me. My barbarian alpha only smirks.

"She is getting off when you pet her ear," Theron says bluntly. Reaching down, he casually adjusts his cock, tenting his pants.

"Fuck!" Zeke says. The youngest of my adopted brothers has never sworn before, and that filthy word coming from his mouth makes me all hot.

"Are you sure?" Aengus says, rubbing his jaw and eyeing me with fake speculation. I glare at the male. "Such an innocent little omega could surely never have these lusty thoughts. Are you saying our sweet little sister is getting off—*coming*—when one of us pets her ears? That her pussy is creaming like a filthy, naughty little girl when she is pretending to be good?"

"I am," Theron says. "Look at her flushed face, at the way her nipples are hard. Her pussy is gushing, and I barely touched her."

"Is that the sweet scent?" Zeke asks.

"It is," Theron confirms. Leaning down, he takes the tip of my ear between his finger and thumb and gives a gentle tug."

"Oh!"

"Fuck!" Draven says gruffly. "She really likes that."

"She does," Theron agrees, tugging it over again, making me squirm. "See how her nipples become even harder, poking out of her nightgown. And were we to lift her gown and check, I'm confident we would find her drenched."

He stops—much to my frustration. As my eyes dart between them, my legs twitch, and like a pack of honed predators, all eyes lower to the juncture of my thighs.

"She needs to be punished," Aengus says ominously. Oh, the wicked beast.

"Agreed," Zeke says. "I cannot believe she would have me touch her and get her off like this."

"You cannot mean to punish me," I say, shocked.

They stop their discussion and turn to me as one. Zeke folds his arms. Theron adjusts his cock again. Aengus is smirking, and Draven is looking fierce. Goodness, they are intimidating individually, and worse when they present this united front.

"Fine," Draven drawls. "Melody, you may return to your quarters." He turns to his brothers. "Best we get back to bed and rest up."

"Do you want me to escort you to your room?" Theron asks politely, like he does not have a hard cock, or hold a strap he was about to apply to my bottom.

"I—" I have no idea what is happening here, but I don't like it one bit. "I don't wish to return to my room."

My guilt is fast and compelling. I have deceived them—lied to them. I can see now how wrong that was.

"It is always an omega's choice," Draven says ominously. "You may return to your room or stay here and be punished."

I gulp. He wants to punish me. He wants Theron to apply the strap to my naughty bottom. To discipline me for my deceit. He believes I deserve it. I believe that too. But it is my choice. I sense this is important, that my submission to their needs is the first step of many. And I want this, to be freed from the guilt, for the air to be clear between us, and whatever happens after, I want that too.

It is my time to speak my truth. My future rests in my own hands. It could rest in theirs if only I could trust them.

Trust. It is such a little word, but it reaches far and wide. It is the opening of a door.

It is already theirs—I trust them to discipline me, just as I trust them to protect me, to care for me, and, dare I hope it, love.

"I would like to accept my discipline," I say, finally finding my voice.

Draven nods. "And anything else we desire."

My pussy clenches, and my chin lifts. "You are bold."

"I am an alpha, and I will have your full submission and all that means, or you will return to your room."

The low growl of his voice is like an electric current sweeping through my body. I did not know. I did not understand it would be like this when an omega chooses. He promises everything I hoped for and more. "Anything," I agree willingly, my eyes resting on each of them. "Anything you desire."

"Agreed," they say in unison.

Then it is like a heavy spell has been broken, and they are all business again.

"I think you should hold her while I administer her punishment," Theron says, turning to his younger brother.

"Should it be against her naked bottom?" Zeke asks, shocking a startled gasp from me.

L.V. Lane

They ignore me, intent on discussing how my punishment will be done. I cannot believe Zeke is endorsing this. I was sure he would suggest something gentler. What has happened to my sweet brother? Who is this strapping warrior who curses and requests I be punished against my naked bottom?

"It will help to focus her mind on the stern punishment," Draven says. "Also, it will allow us to judge her response better if we can see her pussy at the time.

"You make excellent points," Aengus agrees. "Let's get her into position. Zeke, you should be the one to lift her nightgown so we can see her bottom and pussy."

I glare at him, then squeak and dive for the other side of the bed as Zeke strides for me. "Uff!" I am captured by a strong arm around the waist and tossed over the side of the bed, where my nightgown is thrust up.

Zeke lands a firm spank on my upturned bottom cheek. "Legs apart," he says gruffly.

"Oh!"

"You may tell us to stop at any time, Melody, and trust that we shall. Are you telling us to stop?"

I bite my lower lip, certain that telling them to stop is not a good idea and further that they will escort me back to my room in a flash.

"No. I do not wish you to stop," I say. "I trust you."

"Good girl," Zeke says approvingly, making me melt a little before his voice drops to a growl. "Now open your pretty thighs lest we decide you are too naughty for us to make you feel good once the punishment is done."

Another sharp spank, and my legs shoot apart.

"She is drenched," Theron says thickly.

"Did you only touch her ear?" Aengus asks casually.

"I did," Theron confirms. "As soon as I realized she was getting off, I came and fetched you all. I knew it was time for

156

her to be punished like a big girl, which she now is... Pull her ass cheeks apart, Zeke, so we can better see the mess she has made."

"Oh! Please!"

"Quiet, Melody," Zeke says. "You are already in enough trouble. I'm very disappointed in you for not telling me what was happening. I love you well, but you know your actions were unacceptable." He lands another sharp spank when I wriggle. "Do not make this matter worse by mischief now."

Shame at my deception brings a sniffle, and I take a deep breath and force myself to submit to Zeke and my punishment, which I understand I need and deserve. This is Zeke, my sweet brother, and I need to trust him, as I have trusted him all my life... I trust all my brothers, well, except Aengus, who is wicked to the core.

"Good girl," Draven says approvingly, and I feel my heart swell that I'm finally doing this right.

Taking a firm hold of my bottom cheeks, Zeke gently pulls the cheeks up and apart.

Someone makes a tutting noise.

"We will need to clean her up after," Theron says.

"I will do it," Aengus purrs.

"I will fucking do it," Zeke says, and to my shame, his blunt cursing makes my pussy clench again. "It was me she tricked into petting her ears so she could get off."

"He makes a valid point," Draven says. "Although technically, she also tried to trick Theron, he was just more astute and realized her game. Still, I believe she will need this daily from now on, so we shall all have a turn."

Chapter Sixteen

Zeke

"We are all agreed. This first time shall be Zeke," Theron says.

My hands are shaking as I hold Melody open for inspection. I sense the changes coming—ones I have been waiting for, as we all have.

"Can we take her nightgown off? I want to see how hard her nipples are." The words tumble from my lips before I can better consider the personal challenge this represents. My cock is hard and throbbing behind my sleep pants. I'm ready to spill my load just touching her. It will be much worse if she is naked.

There is a long pause before Draven says, "Okay."

Fuck! This is happening. She is ready to be our big girl.

"What? No!" Melody stutters.

"Melody," Draven's growl is a warning. "You may ask us to stop at any time. But if I might suggest you don't use the no word unless you mean it to avoid any misunderstanding."

159

"It just pops out sometimes," she squeaks. "When I get a little tense. Please do not stop."

"Would you like a safe word?" Draven asks.

She peeks back over her shoulder at him. "S-safe word?"

"Yes," he explains. "A word you can say if you want us to stop. Something obvious and easy to remember. That way, we can be sure you are not—just a little tense—and truly want us to stop."

"Like honey cake," she says.

"That is two words." His lips tug up. "But honey cake is fine. Do you think you will remember that if you need us to stop?"

She nods. "Yes."

Draven turns to me and nods.

I don't give her any opportunity for further mischief. "Theron, can you help me, please."

"My pleasure."

I hear the strain in his voice. It is echoed inside me. Melody was still a child when I moved from our family quarters five years ago and threw myself into warrior training. Making it my duty to play a part in the endless battle against the Blighten, which often take us away as we patrol the lands around Sanctum to keep them safe.

When she came for comfort, all grown up, I dared to hope that it might mean something more... that she was ready.

Only now it has come around—that it's happening—I'm ready to blow my fucking load like a green whelp.

Her nightgown is drawn all the way off, with Theron's help, for the brat is now wriggling and protesting, though she does not mention honey cake. Only as her nightgown is finally liberated and tossed to the floor with a whoosh, we both still.

"Melody?" I cup her chin and turn her face toward me. "What is this about? Why are you bound thus? Are you... are you injured? Why did you not tell us so we might be gentle with you?"

Her pretty eyes, such an unusual whirling silver, pool with tears, and I bite back a curse trying to work out what this is about, and sick that I might have treated her too roughly.

"When I first arrived, I was so excited to see other fairies, for I thought it would be like my home before the dark fae came. Only it's not. There are strange rules here, and the fairies don't have wings," she says, her eyes shifting from me to each of my brothers.

My gut clenches. She rarely talks about what happened in her young life, but we are all aware of it, how she watched her parents slaughtered by the dark fae, how the Blighten captured her from the fae, how she escaped the Blighten with Winter and Jacob, how the nightmares have haunted her ever since. She is a complex person with many facets, a playful fairy, who, at times, is deeply troubled, and who has an agile mind that works portals with the ease a skilled carpenter might work a chisel through a piece of wood. I want to hold her and protect her from monsters past, present, and future. I want to love her through her darkness and her light.

But I am also battling a creeping dread that she cut her fairy wings away, that under the band we shall find some terrible evidence of her mutilation—the bands are wide but tight, and you could not hide much beneath.

I want to hold and comfort her, explain that I love her and her scars, yet I am not first alpha and turn toward Draven in askance.

He nods to Theron and me, and we step aside so he can gather Melody into his arms, where she nestles sweetly. She is so tiny and precious. I have not seen her like this before, naked, save for the binding around her chest and back, the lovely form

L.V. Lane

of her body evident and in contrast to Draven's immense alpha bulk.

"Know that there is no part of you we shall not love," Draven says. "Will you trust us, Melody? Trust us with your secret?"

Secret? I'm trying to work out what this secret might be. Aengus and Theron look similarly confused.

There is a long pause before she finally nods. "Okay. But I should warn you. They make a lot of mess."

Mess?

Draven smiles, and I see all the tenderness there. He is our leader, our first alpha, the one we look to for guidance on patrol and in matters pertaining to the omega we hope to claim. Setting her to her feet before him, he reaches for the thick cream-colored band wrapped around her upper body and begins to unravel it.

She trembles a little as Draven works to loosen the band, and it falls away, forming coils upon the floor. As the last loop slips away, a shower of golden dust and two resplendent—and enormous—wings spring free.

"Oops," she says, blushing furiously as they waft and send clouds of golden dust all over the room and us.

I am spellbound.

I have never seen such a beautiful creature in all my life, from her tiny pink toes to her luscious ass, to her small high breasts, tipped with rosy buds, to the riot of red-gold hair that cascades over her shoulders, to her cute little pointed ears, so very sensitive. Melody is gorgeous... with her wings, high and proud, slowly wafting; she is otherworldly in her beauty.

"Where the fuck did they fit?" I mutter.

Aengus cuffs me and mutters, "Runt?"

I glare at him. "What? It is a pertinent fucking question."

"They can shrink," she says, her cheeks a rosy shade of

pink. "They are made with magic."

Magic. She is a true fairy, a throwback, from a different, more ancient race of fairy who still have wings.

I want to fall to my knees and pray to her. Before this night is over, I shall, and in doing so, be the first one to taste her body's offering as I clean her all up.

"Beautiful," Draven murmurs, taking her by the hips and turning her this way and that so he can see her from every angle. "Thank you, Melody, for entrusting us. We accept this precious gift with all due reverence it deserves. Now" —his voice drops to the stern one that we have all suffered at one point in our lives— "It is time for your punishment."

Melody

"P-punishment," I stammer. With the revealing of my wings, I thought this might not happen.

Draven smiles. It is decidedly predatory and makes me a little tingly inside for reasons that escape me. "Did you think we were distracted, love?"

I shake my head, but his growing smile tells me he sees right through me. His hands are on my naked hips, big capable hands that make me feel very small.

"Just a little taste," he murmurs before his eyes lower to my breasts as he draws me forward. He stops with his lips an inch from my right breast. "May I?"

I gulp. "Please!" His mouth encloses one engorged tip—and he gently sucks.

My hands go to his broad shoulders, needing something to anchor me. I arch into him as the sweet tugging sensation pulls all the way to my clit. My pussy clenches, and I squeeze my thighs together as I feel a little trickle of slick. His arm wraps around my waist, pulling me flush as his mouth opens wider, sucking more of my breast into his mouth, pulling on it harder, making it ache. A needy urgency blooms with a speed I have never experienced before. He rumbles a purr, nuzzling the side of my breast before moving over to the other. This time he flicks the hard nub with his tongue before sucking it deeply into his hot mouth.

"Oh, I'm going to—"

He stops abruptly, and I sway a little.

"She is very fucking sensitive," Theron says gruffly.

"I know," Aengus agrees.

All heads swing his way. Draven rises and hands me over to Zeke before stalking Aengus. "Oh? And what would you know about this?"

Aengus shrugs. "She came to me once when Zeke was away."

Draven slugs Aengus in the face. Aengus crashes into the wall. I gasp. Zeke snatches me from the bed and thrusts me behind him as Draven punches Aengus again.

"Asshole. We agreed to discuss it if she showed any signs of arousal," Draven roars.

"You did?" I ask, trying to peer around Zeke.

"Don't mind it," Theron says, standing beside Zeke and making a wall between me and what is happening on the other side of the room.

The meaty thuds, scuffling sounds, and rough grunts make me anxious. The growls and flood of pheromones are making me wet. It is confusing all around.

I peek around just as Draven slams his fist into Aengus' stomach.

Aengus huffs out a breath and holds up a hand. "Fuck! Fine, I fucked up. I could not fucking help myself. She got on my lap for supposed comfort from a nightmare, but as soon as I touched her ear, she was twitching and panting. Her pussy creamed clear through her naughty little nightgown and all over my leather pants! The little brat was coming to see Zeke. Only the fuckwit didn't know what she was up to."

"I'm right here!" Zeke growls.

"You are a fuckwit," Theron says. "We can agree on that point, at least. How could you not notice?"

"He is very gentle," I say, charged to come to Zeke's defense, for none of this is his fault. "Theron and Aengus are rougher about it, and keeping my pleasure sounds inside is hard."

Aengus smirks and puffs out his chest as he wipes the blood trickling from his nose with the back of his hand. "Looks like Theron and I have sharper wooing skills."

Draven's fist jabs in an uppercut so swift I barely see the movement save for Aengus' grunt as he staggers back. "Fuck's sake!"

"There is nothing wrong with Zeke's skills," I say, cross now. My wings are wafting with agitation, and gold dust is everywhere.

"Enough," Draven barks. "Zeke, Theron, see to her punishment. Aengus, you will be getting your dick wet last."

"He will?" Before I can ask more, I'm taken firmly by the arm and bent over the side of the bed, ass vulnerable for whatever they might do. "What does this mean?" I try to twist back.

Zeke brushes the hair back from my hot cheeks and tips my chin until I meet his eyes. "It means Aengus will get to fuck you last," he says bluntly. "That his dick will be the last to rut your needy little omega cunt, that we shall all knot you, hear you scream with pleasure for us, perhaps more than once before Aengus may have a turn. It means we are claiming you, Melody. We are all claiming you as our mate."

Chapter Seventeen

Theron

S he thinks Zeke is sweet. It is a misconception many a lass has when they first meet the gallant young warrior, perhaps dismissing those rumors about him because, surely, they could not be true.

They are true. Zeke has a mile-wide deviant streak and likes nothing more than edging sweet breeders and feeders, taking them in ways they fear they cannot endure yet come to crave. If he has been gentle with Melody thus far, it was only because he was awaiting her decision.

We all felt she was the one and hoped and prayed she would come to us when the time was right.

Now here we are, with her trust, and nothing shall hold us back.

Her body quivers as Zeke's words sink in. I palm her ass and squeeze, getting my first feel of her soft, plump flesh, imagining the rosy glow that will soon bloom as I apply the strap for the very first time.

I will keep the strokes light. This is more about stoking her arousal and mastering her than punishment. It's true. She has been deceitful. Had she spoken to us, we would have taken a gentler approach.

Yet everything about this feels right.

When she was snuggled before me on the bed, letting me pet her ear, the sweet needy whimper and the aroused scent that bloomed blew my fucking mind. Only I had to be sure. As I continued to pet her there, her body betrayed her, face contorting with pleasure, nipples growing hard and ripe.

She was aroused—for me.

She had already come for Zeke, probably Aengus too. Otherwise, she is innocent.

That is about to change.

"Good girl," I say.

Zeke gathers her hair from her hot cheeks and draws it over her shoulder so we can see her pretty face.

"The strap is going to sting a good deal," I explain as I continue to indulge in the opportunity to pet her plump ass. Putting my hands on her like this, feeling her tremble, sensing her arousal, is everything I ever dreamed—everything we hoped for.

She is ours now. Looking back, this was inevitable. The wondering is over. Soon, she will be perfect for us.

"I think perhaps a pillow under her hips," Draven says.

I glance back. He has placed himself in a position where he can see clearly what I do. Aengus stands beside him, nose puffy and red but equally riveted.

I take a pillow. "Lift your ass, Melody, so that I can put this pillow underneath."

She lifts, and I slip the pillow beneath her hips. When I check with Draven, he nods approvingly.

With her ass raised, I can see clearly how drenched she is.

My mouth waters, although Zeke will have that honor first. Knowing Zeke, he is sure to torment her, maybe not even allow her to come as he cleans her all up.

Zeke gathers her wrists and presses them against the bed lest she interferes.

"Ten," Draven says. "Enough to bring a pretty blush to her ass. Then Zeke may clean her up."

I squeezed my cock through my pants to ease the throbbing. It's no use. I doubt I will be down for weeks.

It's time.

I draw my hand back, and the strap lands against her ass with a *crack.*

She gasps and throws a look back at me.

"Good girl," Zeke says approvingly. "That is one."

I don't draw this out; the next three come swiftly. The brat clamps her legs shut and tries to twist away.

"Uh-uh," Zeke says, brushing his thumb over her cheek. "Nice and still. Open your legs again."

"Oh, I can't!"

"You can, and you will, for us."

She exhales a little puff and then pushes her legs apart.

Her pussy has creamed nicely, I notice, slick trickling down her inner thighs.

I share a look with Draven—he nods again—the next three quickly follow.

Her ass has taken on a pretty blush, and I pause to pet it. She twitches. I spank her once. "Keep still, Melody, while I check on you." Her little pussy hole clenches and relaxes as I skim my hand over her hot ass. Gods, I want to rip my pants down and thrust my cock into her, to feel her heat lovingly envelop me, to sink balls deep, and slam in and out until my knot blooms and locks us together. To flood her pussy with cum, and to watch my brothers take her one after another, using her, filling her all up.

She is an omega and fairy; this is what she needs.

I finish the last few quickly, and she breaks into a sob with the last one.

Zeke gathers her into his arms, where she hiccups, whines, and reaches back to rub her flushed ass.

I cup her cheek and lean down to press my lips to hers. Just the lightest touch, but she opens and groans into my mouth. That fast, my body surges with arousal, and it is all I can do to drag my lips away.

So, it has begun.

Draven

We are all close to our limit by the time Theron finishes with her discipline. The air is clogged with pheromones, hers and ours, yet I barely notice ours when that sweet tendril belonging to our mate calls to me.

Sometimes, among our kind, an impression is made between an alpha and an omega that cannot be denied. Admittedly, it is not often four alphas who take on the role of protector that later blooms into something more.

We bided our time and allowed her to choose. As we receive her acceptance, the time spent waiting for her to be ready is of no consequence.

Melody is unique in ways we are only beginning to understand.

No one has taken her blood yet save for the binding blood gift with Zeke and Theron, for no one would dare. She's neither a feeder nor a breeder and stands above and apart. We are lucky bastards.

We understand as much now, as the moment is upon us. I find patience as I watch Theron kiss her. He is breathing heavily by the time he pulls away, his touch gentle. She nestles in Zeke's arms, her beautiful wings wafting slowly and casting golden dust all over the room. I never imagined she might have wings when no omega in Sanctum does—how such magnificence would hide under a small band of cloth.

I can't take my eyes off them... or her. I wonder, are her wings as sensitive as her ears? I want to touch her very badly. I want to spread her thighs, plow, knot, bite, and claim her. But Aengus has pissed me off, and I have some rage to work through first.

Besides, two alphas, such as Zeke and Theron, with one omega are likely already overwhelming to her innocent mind.

So I control myself as I walk over and share a sweet, lusty, but brief kiss with her, closing my hands over her silken hair and feeling her trembling beneath my fingers.

"You will stay with Zeke and Theron tonight. Tomorrow, we have duties, but I will speak to the warrior master so they can be allocated to other alphas." I brush my thumb across her plump lower lip. "You are close to your frenzy. You understand that, don't you, Melody?" She nods, her silver eyes wide and bright. "It is our duty to tend to you, now and for the rest of your life. There is no going back from this."

She nods again. "I understand. I do want this—for a long time." She glances across at Aengus, and a blush stains her cheeks. "I didn't go about it in the best of ways... I was uncertain."

"Only natural," I say. "But now, I must clear our schedules so that we are uninterrupted for you. I will leave you with Zeke and Theron."

L.V. Lane

I release her reluctantly, forcing myself to release her and rise. When I turn, Acngus dares to step forward like he might kiss her as well.

My palm plants in the center of his chest. "Don't even think about it. We need to have *words,* brother. And you will touch her last."

His nostrils flare. "You've already had a fucking go at me."

Aengus and I are close to one another, which has also lent itself to competition. We have both lost a father. Aengus lost a lot more, being only eleven when Jacob freed him from an orc prison. Alphas do not make good bondservants and are often used for crude entertainment, made to fight for food scraps. He was already a big bastard when he came to us, and although he does not talk about it often, I know he had killed fellow prisoners for the entertainment of orcs and to survive.

He had much to work through when he arrived, but my mother, Shiloh, recognized a child worthy of love and saving and took him in.

We fought—a lot.

He is a tough bastard and violent toward anyone who wrongs him.

But he is also focused and loyal to Sanctum, and Jacob, who saved him. He accepted Shiloh as the mother of his heart and learned to channel his aggression toward good.

He hated Melody when she first arrived, which pleased me. Then he grew out of it, which didn't.

I was a possessive prick and competitive—I have done some growing of my own.

But I'm also aware of the darkness inside Aengus, that he was never destined to be first among us, even though he can kick my ass in a fight. He likes to test me. He wants me to prove that although he has several inches and weight measured in brawn over me, I can hold my own and, more importantly, keep him in check.

Because he needs that before he can let go.

He rarely took breeders or feeders to his bed without me there. At first, I didn't think much about it. Alphas can be possessive but are less so with breeders and when roused by post-battle lust. Then, he confessed one drunken night that he got off on fucking when under my direction, and it was the catalyst for change between us.

As we lock gazes, the fire in his eyes rises. He nods once. He understands that he needs this, to be reminded that I will be there for him.

It does not hurt that I get off on dominating him and controlling a more powerful alpha.

I consider it a win-win.

"We shall be back later," I say, taking a last longing look at the bed, knowing what will happen when Aengus and I are gone. "You may touch her. You may make her come. But you do not put your dicks in her anywhere. Understood?"

Melody gapes. Theron heaves a breath and nods once.

"Understood," Zeke says. He is smirking, the deviant bastard. I have every reason to believe he will torment the poor omega who has willingly entered our den and chosen to submit to us.

But so be it. It will stoke her arousal and lead her deeper into the frenzy. If we are to bond her, she must learn to take an alpha's ways.

Chapter Eighteen

Melody

As the door clicks shut on Aengus and Draven, one tension fades, and another rises in its place. I nestle on Zeke's lap, his arms lightly around me, my wings wafting slowly, covering both men and the bed in a shower of dust. It highlights their skin, creating a golden shimmer on their naked upper bodies. They are beautiful alphas, *stunning*, and now they shall be mine.

Only where I was bold in presenting myself and demanding they pet my ears, now I am a little shy. Zeke is not what I expected him to be. He is different. I admit to being nervous, in the butterflies-in-the-belly kind of way. Then there is Theron, who is everything I anticipated him to be and more.

This is really happening. I'm about to be claimed by four.

"Why don't you hold her?" Zeke says. "So she's more comfortable while I clean her all up."

"It will be my pleasure," Theron says. Plucking me from Zeke's arms, he climbs onto the center of the bed with his back to the headboard and sits me between his spread legs. My wings flutter wildly, sending more of the gold dust.

"Would it hurt your wings to lay back against me?" Theron asks.

"No," I squeak.

With his palm cupping the back of my neck, he lowers me until our skin presses flush together. He still wears his sleep pants, but I can feel the thick ridge of his cock pressing against my lower back, and it becomes a source of acute interest to me.

"How did these wings ever fit underneath those bindings?" he asks.

"They are magical," I explain, "and can fold up very small."

"They are beautiful," Zeke says, expression deeply admiring as he crawls onto the bed and kneels before me.

"Open your thighs, Melody. That way, I can see to your little mess." He encloses my ankles in his warm palms and draws them up and apart.

I gulp, and a shiver ripples through me when Theron gently traces his fingertips along the upper ridge of my right wing. "Oh!"

"Fuck," Zeke groans. "Are your wings sensitive as well?"

"Yes, very."

He swallows hard. "If you keep petting her wings, I think she'll be making a mess all night. It might take me quite a while before I am done."

"That's no problem," Theron says. "Draven will likely be some time as he asserts his place over Aengus."

I twist my head to look back and find Theron smirking.

"You are to be our mate, Melody. We cared for you as protectors when you were little because that was what you needed, but now things are different. Either way, there has ever been a rivalry between Aengus and Draven. Draven is our leader, the first alpha, but sometimes Aengus needs to be reminded of his place, just as Draven needs to be reminded of his responsibility."

Zeke's chuckle is wicked and draws my attention back to him. "It's their fucking loss," he says.

Goodness, I never heard him curse before tonight, and now he does not seem to stop. He stares at my pussy as his hands slide up my thighs. "Spread nice and wide, Melody. Put your legs outside Theron's, and it will help you be good."

He slips one leg and then the other outside of Theron's, spreading me lewdly, holding me wide open. My cheeks become very hot as I think about where he stares.

Theron cups my breast from behind. "Are you going to let her come?" He squeezes the weight and then begins to pluck absently at my nipple.

My tummy takes a slow dip. Oh, that feels even better than my ears.

"I might do." Zeke smirks in a way that makes me all fluttery inside as he sprawls out on his belly. He turns his head to the side and licks my upper thigh where all the slick is smeared. He groans, and his lashes lower as he laps up the stickiness.

When they mentioned cleaning me up, this was not what I had in mind.

I try to wriggle. Zeke's hands enclose my upper thighs and clamp tightly.

"Ah, ah, Melody," Theron says, still tormenting my breasts. "Keep nice and still." He moves his skilled attention to the other breast and squeezes before circling his fingertips around the distended nipple.

I want to come, want their fingers on my pussy, where it will feel best of all. But I'm caught between them. Zeke noisily lapping, Theron making a light, rumbly purr as he pinches and pets my nipples until they flush with arousal.

My body rises toward that anticipated peak. Only Zeke

gentles his touch... over and over again. By the time he uses his thumbs to spread my pussy, exposing me to his lustful gaze, I'm near insensible with need.

"How does she look?" Theron asks.

"Slick and pretty," Zeke replies. "She tastes so fucking good." Then he takes a long, slow lick of the length of my pussy before swirling his tongue around the sensitive little bud.

I arch up and moan as his tongue plunges into my pussy.

Theron kisses my temple and lightens this touch upon my breasts, fingertips tickling as he circles each areole.

I begin to worry this will never end.

My body coils with tension.

My skin grows damp.

My pussy weeps ever more slick.

Each time I feel myself rise, the wicked alphas lighten the touch. The moment I settle, they seek out the most sensitive places until I climb. I beg, nonsense pouring from my lips between needy groans.

My body is lit by a fire that rages from the inside out, burning ever hotter until I fear I might spontaneously combust.

Theron

Our mate lays between us, a twitching, shimmering mess that we have created. My heart thuds, a steady beat in my chest. I'm thinking about what comes next, about how we will share her between us, rut her through her frenzy, and then soon after, the time will come, and she will go into heat.

Her gold dust is scattered over the bed and me. Where it touches my skin, it lights a fire of arousal. My dick is hard, throbbing against her lower back, leaking pre-cum, in anticipation of more. I barely acknowledge my own needs as Melody consumes all my focus. I'm aware of what Zeke does, just as I sense he is mindful of me. Melody is the link that will bring the four of us together, two blood brothers and two adopted brothers, who will form a pack.

Pack? I like the sound of that.

We have never shared a woman before, Zeke and I, although Draven and Aengus often have, yet it feels instinctive.

She is a virgin. Untouched. We know because we have kept an eye on such things. Maybe that makes us bastards. I don't much care. If we sensed she wanted another, we would have stepped aside reluctantly... *probably.*

But she didn't, did she?

No, she came to Zeke, then Aengus, and finally to me, seeking comfort deep in the night.

I trail kisses up the side of her throat, thinking about the hot blood that pounds through her vein, wondering if she will taste different if I take her vein as I take her body. Distracted by the anticipation of taking her blood again, I notice too late that Zeke has stripped from his sleep pants and now kneels between her thighs with his cock in his hand.

I freeze, and more blood tries to pound into my dick. "What the fuck are you doing? We cannot rut her!"

Zeke shrugs. "My cock is not inside her," he points out.

Melody lies panting, slack-jawed, as she stares at Zeke's cock. I doubt she has seen one before. "Melody is untried, asshole," I growl, tightening my arms around her as if to pull her away.

Zeke scowls at me like I'm the asshole. "She is going to be seeing a lot more cock very soon. Best she gets used to it. I'm just going to come on her."

My dick jerks as though in approval. "Draven won't like

that," I say, only my inner voice is already coaching me that Draven did not expressly forbid this.

"Draven's not here, is he?" Zeke says, still jacking his cock while staring at Melody's pussy. A long trail of pre-cum leaks from the tip and creates a compelling sight as it connects with her slick pussy.

"Please," she says, spreading her legs wider, presenting herself perfectly to him.

My blood pounds in my temple, and my cock ejects an enthusiastic blob of pre-cum. "She wants it," I say in wonder.

"Melody is an omega," Zeke offers unnecessarily. "They were born to take cock... Maybe I'll slip just the tip in. Nobody will know."

"Draven will know," I say. "Melody will fucking know."

"Oh! Please." She lifts her hips, trying to get closer to his cock as he slides the head back and forth over her clit.

"This is not a good fucking idea," I growl, already sensing the slippery slope before us... And then he lowers his dick and thrusts the small way in.

"Oh!" She arches up.

I clap my hands over her to keep her still. "Zeke. Fuck's sake! Draven will wipe the fucking floor with you, and then *you* will be the one going last."

"Don't care," he grunts. His neck arched with his head tipped back, and his expression is one of abject bliss.

My mind blanks out, and sweat breaks out across the surface of my skin. It's almost like I feel what he does. Imagine how it would be to have my cock lodged a small way in.

He suddenly pulls out and smirks at me as Melody humps her hips up for more. I don't think, I act, fisting her hair and twisting her face around so we can share a lusty kiss. My tongue plunges into her mouth, tasting her, wanting to swallow her whole.

"Uff!" My lips pop off as firm hands grasp the waist of my pants and yank. "What the fuck!"

Zeke liberates me of my sleep pants. The action pulls my cock down and under her. Before I can work out what the hell he's doing, my pants are flying across the room to land somewhere far away.

I hiss a breath through my teeth as my dick, hardened to the point of pain, slaps against her wet folds.

"Please, please, please, please, please!"

Her begging clogs what little is left of my wits. Zeke only grins as I huff and teeter upon the brink of madness.

"There," he says. "Now I'm not the only one with a wet dick when Draven returns. He will want her first, believing it his right as first alpha. I say we even up the odds."

The odds are not fucking even when I have a cock covered in her slick and mere inches separate me from the hot tight place I have yet to inspect.

"I need to put my fucking pants on," I say, only my hips begin to thrust upwards of their own volition, coating my dick in her juices. She clamps her legs together and groans, creating a tight channel into which I begin to thrust. Rational thought eludes me. I'm trying to work out how the fuck I let her go long enough to put some clothing between us when Zeke draws her legs apart and closes his fist around my cock.

I jolt. "Get the fuck off!"

He grins, his tongue swiping back and forth over his lower lip before his eyes lower. Fisting her left thigh, he pulls her up and pushes my cock down, and as he lowers her, I snag at her entrance.

I buck, trying to dislodge his fucking hand, which isn't easy while her wings are wafting gold dust everywhere. Somehow, amid this chaos, my dick lodges deeper still.

"Gods," I mutter weakly, my hip jerking.

"Fuck yes!" Zeke says, staring at what I do. "You are near halfway inside her." He takes his cock in hand again, braces over us, and rubs the head over her clit.

She moans, and her pussy clenches over me.

"She feels good, doesn't she?" he says, enrapt by what we do to her and ignoring my muttered protests.

My body is no longer mine to command as my hips thrust upward from below. Palming her lower abdomen to hold her still, I get deeper.

Zeke leans back a little to watch me, still slowly jacking his cock. "It looks fucking obscene," he says. "Your fat dick thrusting into her tiny pussy hole, opening her up. Why don't you hold her legs up so I can better see what you do?"

I shouldn't encourage him—I shouldn't mind his suggestion, yet I brace my hands under her thighs, pull them lewdly up and out, and begin to piston into her from below.

"Fucking debauched," Zeke says. His fingers are on her pussy, sliding all over her slick folds and rimming my dick where it pounds in and out.

I don't even fucking care anymore. I'm too far gone... almost at the knot.

Then he leans right over, palms her throat, and pins her back against me. "Does that feel good, Melody, when Theron fucks his dick all up inside your tight pussy? Do you want him to come like that? Do you want him to fill you all up?"

"Please," she says, her head thrashing from side to side.

He begins to squeeze over her throat in time with my thrusts, choking her a little before allowing her to suck a breath in.

I blink furiously, trying to gain control of myself, trying to stop. Only my dick has a mind of its own, and I sink even deeper, slipping the burgeoning knot into her tightness.

"Gods, how does such a tiny body take so much?" Zeke says

as though to himself. "Fairies are ever a wonder. Magical beings who are Goddess-sent to bring pleasure to their warriors."

"I need to stop," I say. Only I'm not stopping, am I? I'm thrusting harder, holding her lewdly open as I pound into her from below.

My balls rise as my knot passes in and out.

His thumb grinds over her clit. She moans wildly, clamping all over my cock. "Let's get her off. I want to watch you filling her pussy all up."

"No. Fuck!" I grunt. I slam deep, and still, my knot is pounding with blood, *bulging*. I need to pull the fuck out.

Only I don't pull out. No fucking chance of stopping as her head tips back, and she comes with a squeal, pussy sucking down on my dick and compelling me to follow through or die.

I don't die, but my heart is pounding as my knot swells further. My balls reach, and a heady gush of come ejects into her spasming sheath.

I growl.

"Fucking amazing," Zeke mutters.

Not that I give a fuck what he does or says when I am busy emptying load after load into the thrashing omega I have just claimed as mine.

My lips find the juncture of her shoulder and throat, and my teeth, following instincts, sink into her flesh, and hot blood spills down my throat.

Her pussy spasms again, and I shoot another heady load.

"Fuck! I can see her contracting around you," Zeke says thickly.

I groan and eject another jet of cum.

Chapter Nineteen

Draven

I have just explained the situation to our warrior master, Cecil, and our patrols have been canceled. Now Aengus is full of vinegar and attitude as we stalk for the practice pit. Word must have already gotten around if the crowds gathering to watch are any indication.

This is not the first time Aengus and I have gone at one another; it probably won't be the last. He is a barbarian. It's fair to say Aengus has the skills and power to back it up, but he will never be first alpha.

No sooner do we find a place on the sandy floor amid the crowds than he slugs me in the face. My head swings around from the blow, and I welcome the bite of pain as I return an uppercut that lifts him off his feet and drops him on his ass. He roars and tackles me around the waist, sending us both crashing to the floor. Here we wrestle, trading blows, not one of which is very effective.

Around us, the crowd roars their encouragement—warriors

like nothing better than a leadership challenge for a shared mate. Not that mates are shared often, and it is unheard of for any to have four. We are drawing extra interest all around.

I finally grapple him into a headlock and get a few blows to his gut. He elbows my ribs.

"Yield, you big, brainless fucker!" I grunt.

He gains enough leverage to slam his head back into my nose.

I taste blood and see stars... the bastard gets free and staggers to his feet.

We go at one another, trading blows, splattering the sandy practice pit floor with blood. He is determined, but I am more so.

The crowd roars.

We lay into one another with grunts, growls, and the meaty thuds of firsts connecting with flesh.

Finally, when he is swaying on his knees as I stand over him (also swaying), he lifts a hand.

"Fuck it! I yield," he wheezes.

I punch him one more time, just to be absolutely sure.

He grunts and eyeballs me from the floor before rolling to his knees and staggering to his feet.

"You are a joyless bastard," he mutters, swiping the blood trickling from his busted lip.

"And you are thickheaded and will not fucking submit until I must beat you half to death."

He grunts, which is Aengus's acknowledgment. "I'm too fucking weak to rut the brat fairy now."

I smirk and raise a brow as the crowd begins to move on... nosy bastards.

He shrugs, and his smile is rueful. "Well, I could probably manage to rouse myself... plus there is her blood.

"Which I will be taking first."

"Fine. Have at it," he concedes, wary that I might thump him again.

We head back to our quarters. Now that my place is established, I am clear-headed, even if my blood is up, and eager to return to our mate.

Only matters have progressed in our absence.

"Fuck!" Aengus mutters gruffly as we enter Theron's room.

That simple expletive does not do justice to the rage that engulfs me.

Melody is spread out on the bed between them. Zeke is braced over her with his dick buried in her cunt to the root while Theron is kneeling beside her head. His dick is glistening, and her lips are puffy—I presume she was blowing him before we entered the room. Both males wear expressions of surprise which might be comical were I not ready to kill them.

Further, blood is smeared over her throat and tits, so they have both fucking fed!

"Oh," Melody says, her eyes glazing over as they land upon me. "I think I'm going to..." she trails off into a lusty moan that sets every hair on my body and my dick to attention.

"Off!" I growl, stalking toward the bed, which is nowhere near fucking adequate for what I have in mind.

Theron lurches away, catching his foot in the covers and pitching to the floor—a grunt follows as Aengus cuffs the whelp.

"I am knotted!" Zeke protests, eyes darting frantically between me and the omega, busy coming all over his dick.

I close my fist around his throat and squeeze. "Work it out, or I will."

"Fuck!" He tries to pull out. She moans and humps her hips up.

A hiss escapes his clenched teeth as I close my other fist

around the root of his dick and force one finger in until I can hook his knot.

"Shit! Don't! Fuck! Draven!" His knot and cock pop out, and a gush of cum splashes over the bed.

I shove Zeke aside, then I am momentarily stunned by the vision of her gaping cunt full of frothy cum. My fingers are inside her before I can gather wits, and I pump slowly into her. "What the fuck have you been doing to her?"

"It is not our fault that she needs cock—uff!" Theron's explanation of matters is cut off as Aengus thumps him for the second time.

🐌

Melody

"This will all need to come out," Draven says, getting a determined glint in his eyes.

I'm too far gone to care what he does to me so long as his hands are upon me in some satisfying way. "I need cock," I say, not even caring that both Zeke and Theron have already rutted me, and this statement is both bold and forward. I believe they have broken me with their attention, for I crave yet more.

My innocence has long flown out the window... were there any windows down here, which there are not. It is a metaphorical kind of window... either way, I have needs that must be met.

I watch Draven through hooded eyes. His nose is a little puffy, his cheek is bruised, so too is the line of his jaw. His hair is scruffy from where he and Aengus have fought over me. Establishing his place, Zeke called it, as if there was any doubt. He is the oldest of my brothers. He is dominant in every way.

As he explores my pussy with his fingers, I pant with need.

How I secretly craved his touch. How it is everything that he is finally here.

Then he does something with his fingertips, curving them up until they press on the front wall of my pussy just right, and the pleasure is so intense that my eyes cross. I arch up off the bed. "Oh, Goddess!" My wings turn rigid.

The look on Draven's face turns dark and possessive.

"Good girl," he says, circling his fingertips around the spot again and again.

It's too much—it's too sensitive. I squirm, gasp, shudder, and finally twitch uncontrollably, fingers closing over his wrists to try and pull him off. He plucks my hands away and pins them to the bed above my head before working the magic spot without mercy.

I thrash and try to kick. There is literally nowhere for me to go.

"Come," he commands. It's not quite a bark, but it is nevertheless an order that compels a climax from me. My pussy clamps over his fingers, and a great gush of slick and cum gushes out.

"That's my good girl," he says approvingly. "And again."

Again? What? He wants me to come again. I'm overstimulated. I've already come more times than I can count.

"Do not dare defy me, Melody," he says sternly. His eyes narrow on me, and he pets me.

He is so determined and handsome; and now he is all mine. I want to be good for him, to please him, to do as he asks, but I'm feverish, and all I can think about is the thick cock tenting his leather pants and how it would be far more satisfying than his fingers.

"That's my good little omega," he says. "You can do it. You can come one more time."

I can't stand the pressure building. I feel like I am bathed with fire, desperately wanting to come, yet stuck in limbo upon the cusp.

I court madness. I climb ever higher when I am sure there is nowhere higher to go. Heat bathes my skin, and I become convinced I will expire from this sweet, tormenting pleasure that is never quite enough.

"Come now!"

Sweat pops out across the surface of my skin, and my whole body turns rigid before sweet climactic waves rip through me. I grunt like an animal, lifting my hips toward his fingers like I might get even more. By the time my hips have done dancing around, I'm utterly drained and barely cognizant of anything save the debauched squelchy noises Draven's fingers make as he thrusts them in and out of me at a more leisurely pace.

"It will have to do," he says, and then he gathers me up in his arms and stalks past his brothers, through the central room, and across into his bedroom. I snuggle in his arms, aware of my other mates following.

The door clicks shut, and the lamp beside his bed is turned up.

His bed is huge compared to Theron's and of thick oak construction with four posts.

I am dropped into the center, where he tips me onto my belly.

He curses. I hear the jangle of buckle before he takes my hips in his hands and yanks my ass up.

Draven

My hands are shaking, I've got tunnel vision, and I'm so fucking hard and ready there's a danger I'll lose my load if I don't get my dick inside her now. This is not me. I have more fucking finesse.

Seeing Theron and Zeke fucking her, my sweet, innocent Melody getting railed by two alpha warriors has tipped me over the edge. Not only were they fucking her, but she was fucking loving it. I understand what this is, how the frenzy has come upon her, how her body, magical beyond our understanding, was made to take all an alpha's lust. Yet now the moment is upon me, I see it all through a new light.

I know I'm not going to last. I also know that it doesn't matter. How did I get so fucking lucky? How am I possibly worthy of this? *I'm not,* the voice inside my head reminds me. I'm nothing but a lowly warrior. I possess no magical blood, nor do I have portal skills worthy of a legend.

Melody is something extraordinary and destined for greatness. The four of us will dedicate our lives to keeping her safe from the dangers her existence presents.

But even though she is special, she is still an omega experiencing her first frenzy. She has chosen me. She has chosen all of us. It is my duty to tend to her however she needs.

Taking my cock in hand, I line up and sink slowly into her hot clenching cunt. I grit my teeth lest I come. My knot is already bulging, already sensitive beyond comparison. My need is too great, and I manage three good deep strokes before my knot blooms. The base of my spine tingles, and I shoot a heady gush of cum against the entrance to her womb.

My hips jerk. She mumbles something as she lays prone before me, held up by courtesy of my hands on her hips. With my knot locked, I fill her up, replacing all the cum Theron and Zeke left with my own.

But this is not enough. I need her to come too, and I reach around her to find her slick clit, strumming it lightly, for she is swollen and sensitive.

"Oh! Unmmmm!" Her pussy clamps over my cock and she jerks against my hold.

"Good girl," I say. "You can come for me. I know you can. Does that feel better now that you're all full up?"

She mumbles nonsense as her pussy falls into climactic waves that demand more cum from my cock. Like I'm hers to command, I come over again until, finally spent, I recover my wits.

I pet her slippery clit as she twitches and squeezes over me, but my eyes are drawn to her pretty wings that slowly waft.

They are a revelation, one that makes her impossibly more special than she already is. I gently trace the line of her right wing—she shudders, and her pussy fists my cock.

"They are very sensitive," Theron offers.

I glare across at the bastard. "And you would know?"

Aengus cuffs him, which I appreciate, given I'm busy.

With my cock and knot buried in my mate, I find my vexation with Aengus has softened. It would seem all of us are a little addled by our lusty sprite.

Chapter Twenty

Aengus

Today I learned a lesson in humility... and not to piss Draven off. I do not get to fuck the omega. But that is my punishment for toying with her.

Actually, I might have gotten away with that part if I'd reported to my brothers afterward.

I didn't—I kept my little secret and have paid the price.

My cock does not go inside her, where I might feel her perfect pussy clenching over me. Instead, I watch my brothers fuck her. Later, when they're done, I at least get to drain my balls all over her pretty tits.

I accept the consequence of my actions, just as I accept Draven's beating before he allowed me back in our quarters.

Draven's room is larger than the rest of ours. The bed is a sturdy four-poster construction that dominates the space, while an oak table with chairs sits opposite the door. A lamp is lit on the table beside me. Another is set low on the nightstand to the right of the bed.

I lean back into my chair, watching the bed where Melody lies sleeping between Draven and Zeke.

Theron has gone to rouse servants to bring us drinks and food.

I remain lost in the brooding darkness as I stare in wonder at the tiny, precious imp who has claimed my heart even before I taste the pleasures of her body or the potent blood in her veins.

It's fair to say I have a lot of issues. My childhood was character-building, and not for the good. There is no place for empathy and certainly no place for love or weakness when one must fight to survive.

I killed people for a crust of bread, and so I might live to see the next day.

I killed people I once cared about.

And I killed people I did not.

Afterward, as I stood over them, I offered a silent prayer to the Goddess, beseeching her to care for them in the ways they deserved.

There were times during the most brutal fights when I sensed my opponents possessed an equal will to survive. I wondered if it was my time and considered submitting to the allure of death and the blessed darkness.

Only the Goddess would not be waiting to welcome me. Eternal damnation would be my destination, given all I had done, and even so, some deep-rooted instinct drove me on to ever greater violence for the sake of living another day.

Time has a way of distancing us from the deeds of our past, yet we never truly disconnect. As I sit brooding upon the chair, staring at the sleeping beauty with her golden wings folded up neat and my two brothers covered in shimmering golden dust, I know I'm not worthy of her.

When I die, I'm going to hell, but between then and now,

and no matter if I'm unworthy, I shall avail myself of every lusty inch of her delectable body, every opportunity I can.

Heaven will never be for me, yet I will discover what it tastes like when I feast on her juicy cunt.

The danger I represent is significant. I shall ever need Draven to remind me why I'm second, and he is first, to be controlled lest I harm the precious omega for whom I must care. I need somebody pure of thought, body, and mind to keep me in check.

I was little more than a savage animal when Jacob liberated me from the orcs.

I cannot go back and undo my past. The Blighten molded me into a dark barbarian whose conscience is rarely roused and certainly not enough to give up my place with the omega. I don't give a shit that I am unworthy of her. I still want my fucking taste.

The door opens, and Theron enters carrying a laden tray. Beyond the open bedroom room, I hear the bustle of servants. He puts the tray on the table next to me.

Draven rouses himself from the bed, drawing Melody into his arms. Half out of it, Zeke mumbles a complaint and tries to hang onto her. Draven growls—Zeke awakens with a start and lets her go.

Draven strides directly toward me with our omega. I hasten to sit straight in the seat. As we share a look, her scent washes over me.

"You may feed her," he says. "See that she drinks plenty."

I nod, every muscle in my body turning rigid as he lowers the sleepy omega into my arms.

She blinks at me, her wings folding and shrinking before my eyes as a pretty blush covers her cheeks.

I've never been so fucking tense. My gaze shifts from Melody to Draven and back again.

"Don't fuck it up," he growls.

My nostrils flare. "I will not fuck it up!" Only my hands are shaking against her. She is naked, sticky with dried cum, along with the scent of fresh slick. My eyes lower to her tits, where a few bruises have formed from their enthusiastic rutting.

My throat works as I note the pale pink puncture wounds at her vein.

On the other side of the room, Zeke stumbles from the bed. My brothers gather around the table in various states of dress and pass out drinks and food. A cup of water is placed on the table beside me, and rouses me from my inspection. I take the cup and hold it to her lips. She goes to take it off me. I growl.

"I will hold it," I say.

Her golden brows pinch together—she is not pleased with this development. I couldn't give a fuck. The darkness inside me demands her utter dependence. She will drink by my hand, eat by my hand, and submit to my tending. I will accept no less.

She eyeballs me over the rim of the cup as I slowly tip it up —a little water spills over her chin and splashes against her chest. I don't mind it and tip it up some more. As she gulps, she glares at me.

When she has drained it, I put the cup down and swipe my thumb across her chin, gathering the water that has spilled before pressing it between her lips. Her eyes go wide—she sucks—a low rumbly purr emanates from my chest. I let her suck it for a little while and then slowly pull it out again, aware of the quietness that has descended upon the room.

I lift my head and pin each of my brothers with a look. Zeke looks hungry, Theron is intrigued, and Draven raises one eyebrow.

My lips tug up. He has not told me to fucking stop or taken Melody away from me so I consider that permission to carry on.

"You have made a little mess," I say, trailing my fingertips down her throat, over her collarbone, before cupping her right tit. I test the weight in my hand before pinching her nipple and giving a little tug.

She gasps, her chest arching into the touch. Her nipple is very hard and flushed with blood. "Such a pretty little fairy. Such a pretty little tit. Does that feel good?"

Her breathing turns a little choppy. For all her frenzy has passed, she is still needy.

"Feed her some fucking food, asshole," Draven grumbles, shoving a filled plate toward my end of the table.

I smirk and let go of her tit.

The plate holds cold meat, cheese, fruit, and a slab of buttered bread slathered with honey. I select a grape and hold it to her lips.

Her eyes flash to meet mine before she parts her lips and accepts the offering. As she bites down over it, her eyes darken, and she smiles as she chews.

And so I feed her, one morsel at a time. I hear the others talking, but I'm so enrapt by the omega in my arms that I don't hear a word. She relaxes into the feeding, taking what I offer her and submitting to her dependence on me for food. The ever-present malevolence inside me retreats a small way as I gentle the omega who will soon become my mate.

When she has finished eating and taken more water, she sighs and nestles against me, her eyes drooping and her hands tucking together under her chin.

I run my fingertip over her shoulder and down her arm until my hand encloses hers.

She is utterly precious.

I am entranced by the curves of her body and the gentle passage of the air in and out of her lungs, her beauty, her long strawberry-blonde locks, and the thick eyelashes that make a fan against her cheeks.

I need to toe the line with Draven because I might go on a fucking rampage if I don't have my turn at her soon.

I take a little food and drink as I watch Melody sleep, feeling myself soften as a lifetime of tension slowly eases its hold.

Chapter Twenty-One

Melody

After breakfast, Draven calls servants to prepare me a bath and fetch some suitable clothes. Two things dawn upon me as I sink into the warm water and wash off the sticky, crusted evidence of our coupling. One, I called the portal again, and the nightmare did not occur. And two, I'm an omega who has been claimed by four. The residents of Sanctum will soon be gossiping about me. Perhaps they already have been given Draven's consultation with the warrior master when this first began. Still, it's hard to keep the smile off my face when happiness consumes me.

After they took my blood during the frenzy, I sensed a burgeoning connection between me, Draven, Zeke, and Theron. Aengus has not taken my blood yet for his mischief, Draven having taken a firm line. I want to argue. I want to bond with Aengus too. But the power play between the alphas is something they must work through on their own.

The binding leash is thick, dark, and ugly.

The bonding thread presents like a delicate golden vine weaving around the binding leash. Whenever I think about them in a joyous way, it seems to thrum.

I feel shy when, bath complete, Draven escorts me to visit Shiloh. Like he needs the connection as much as I do, he takes my small hand in his as he leads me through the many levels of Sanctum. It feels so strange to walk beside him like this. He is handsome with thick, shaggy midnight hair, and intense green eyes. His beard is short and accents the strong line of his jaw. I am a little intimidated by the powerful warrior and blush near constantly as I remember all the things we did... the intimacy we shared. Perhaps the bond growing between us alerts him to my mood, for he glances down often during the walk to smile or gently squeeze my hand.

"You have a very pretty blush, Melody," he says. "Do I detect some naughty thoughts?"

I shake my head, but I'm confident he knows it for a lie when he chuckles and suddenly draws me abruptly off the main corridor.

"Where are we going?" I ask in a hushed whisper.

He only smirks before ducking into a room.

"Oh!" The word escapes me with a squeak, for I suddenly realize where we are.

"Someone's naughty thoughts were getting out of control," he says dryly. "Which has a predictable effect on me. I cannot take you to see our parents in this condition."

"Oh," I say again, this time in a breathy whisper, which feels woefully inadequate, given we are in one of the blood gifting rooms.

"Are you sore?"

I gulp and find avid interest in the floor until his fingertips gently tip my chin until I meet his eyes.

"Do you want me to use my mouth, fingers, or cock, Melody?"

"Cock," I blurt out before I can better consider that I am a little sore. "I want you to knot me."

I have never asked for something so scandalous and want to swallow my tongue. The events of the frenzy are blurred in my mind, but I'm sure I begged. Only now that I'm no longer subject to the effects, I have nowhere to hide.

This is all me.

"Hmm," he says, his voice a low purr. "I think I better judge what you can take."

My insides turn to a puddle of mush.

I'm carried to the long couch, where he spreads me out and lifts my skirt. He makes a tutting noise as he drags my ass to the edge of the couch. His fingers are gentle as they trace through the slick folds. My face is on fire as he caresses the sensitive place. I'm impatient for more... right up until he pushes a finger inside me—I wince.

He stills, one finger buried intimately. "Melody?"

Meeting his eyes makes me clench over him. It is a little sore, but it also feels nice, and this time I moan.

His pretty green eyes darken, and his nostrils flare. "I will take it slowly," he says. Tugging my bodice down, he cups my breast before rolling my nipple between his finger and thumb. "Give you my mouth until you come once or twice, and then we shall see if you still need more." He pumps his finger slowly into me as he toys with one breast and then the other. His eyes are on mine the whole time as my arousal floods, and soon the wet, squelchy noises show how well I like what he does. "That's my good girl." Then he lowers his head and circles the tip of his tongue around my clit as he continues to pump.

His beard is tickly against such a delicate place, and makes me all squirmy and urgent.

"Please, please, please!"

I go off like a celebration rocket, back arching, legs trying to jam shut around him, and body twitching and spasming as I grind myself onto his face.

He doubles down, pinning my legs open and back while lavishing my sensitive clit with the flat of his tongue.

It's too much.

It's also perfect, and my body soars directly for a higher peak before tumbling me straight over.

I blink my eyes open, chest heaving as Draven lifts his head. "More. Please more."

"You want my cock?"

He pulls one finger out and presses two back in.

The stretch is perfect, and there is not a bit of pain. "Yes!"

He forces a third finger in and curves the fingertips until they rub right over my slick gland—I nearly shoot off the couch. "And my knot?"

His deep growly voice and the way he pets the entrance of my slick gland make me wet and clenchy, and is a near unbearable kind of good. I'm panting—I want to come, but it's like I want it too much.

"Goddess, yes!"

"If I fuck you from behind, bend you over this nice couch, the head of my cock will rub over this magic place on the front wall of your pussy with every thrust... Is that what you want, Melody? Want me to put you on your knees and fuck you from behind? Fill your needy cunt with my cock, knot you until you're a panting mess of fairy stuffed full of my cock and cum?"

"Yes!" The word is ripped from me on a scream as I come, flooding around his fingers.

I'm still coming when he flips me onto my belly and lifts my skirt. The jangle of his buckle has me quivering with need, and then the thick head of his cock slides the length of my pussy before nestling at my entrance. He sinks a small way in. I wriggle and clench around him. He palms his hips to still me.

"Is that hurting?"

"No!"

He thrusts shallowly like the beast is intent upon driving me mad. "Are you sure? Maybe I should stop?"

I growl.

His chuckle is low and rumbly, and I love this playful side of him, even as I want to curse the alpha out.

"Fine then," he relents, sinking deeper and making me moan with joy. "But you are to tell me if it's too much."

My answer is to push my ass back for more.

He gives me more, building up slowly, making sure I feel only pleasure as I open around his cock, and then when he bottoms out and is buried to the root, he pounds me into the couch. Our flesh slaps together under the vigorous thrusts that set tingles of pleasure shooting through my core as the head of his cock rubs the sensitive entrance to my slick gland.

"That's my good girl," he rumbles. "Taking my cock so well. I can feel your pleasure through the bond. You like it rough and deep, don't you? You're getting off on me pounding your sweet cunt. Creaming all over my dick, fisting me to encourage me to knot."

I am, I really am.

"Come for me, Melody, and I shall give you my knot."

I do. The pleasure explodes through my core and doesn't stop as he keeps rutting me, his knot blooming, making me an insensible wreck of intense twitching pleasure as he thrusts the fat knot in one last time and stills.

I feel him pulse inside me, a hot flood filling me so well as my pussy squeezes lovingly over his thick length.

He helps me clean up and put myself back together before we continue to meet with Shiloh.

I don't know what I'm expecting, but Shiloh only hugs me. "I'm so happy for you, Melody," she says. "Your aura has changed yet again. It is one of deep content."

I smile as I catch Draven's eye—he returns a smirk.

He kisses Shiloh's cheek, then takes me in his arms for a chaste kiss that nevertheless leaves me breathless... and then he takes his leave.

I feel unexpectedly shy with my new change of status. I'm still young in fairy years, and it's unusual for one to mate so soon.

When you know, you know. I don't need to lay with another to know they are perfect for me, nor to explore my sensuality elsewhere.

The relationship is new, and there are sure to be challenges ahead—I'm not yet mated to Aengus, nor have I explored the darkness I sense within him.

But that is for later, and as I leave Shiloh after our tea and cake, my good mood carries me through my usually boring portal lore lessons.

Athena gives me a haughty glare and tips her nose in the air.

Isabelle grins as she playfully pinches my arm. "Is it true?" she demands in a hushed whisper. "Have you been claimed by all four?"

I nod.

Athena huffs out a breath, but I don't mind her or her bad mood.

The joyful episode ends when I enter Celeste's study, where she informs me I have a quest coming up at the end of the week. This time I will use a portal site to leave and return.

I worry that this means they no longer trust me after the

last disaster, when I disappeared through the portal and pretended I could not remember where I went.

It has been some time, and the horrible nightmare has been put aside, but today brings it all back.

This is the right thing to do, to overcome my fears and prove my usefulness to our community, but I hoped there would be more time with my mates first.

"I'm recommending you magically enhance the binding," Celeste says, surprising me from my inner turmoil.

Her office is luxurious, as befits an imperial omega charged with overseeing quests. I heard she is nearly as old as Winter and remembers the time before the portal keystone was lost and the endless war.

"W-what does that mean?" I stammer. I hate the binding and was determined to request its removal at the earliest opportunity. Shiloh and Herald have no binding because she is a former breeder.

Then there is Winter and Jacob. While the circumstances that led to Winter having the binding removed were clearly fraught, I see how happy they are now. Her words play upon my mind. I asked her about the time before the binding existed. *"Balanced,"* she said. *"It was surprisingly balanced."*

I want that balance. What's more, I want to submit to my mates fully. They already asked me when they took the strap to my bottom. I liked it *very* much. It is all about trust. They asked me to put my trust in them. I am safe with them. The binding feels like an abomination—a horrible lashing leash. I'm young and lack experience, yet I know my mind in this.

"I have some skills in binding magic," she explains. "It is a simple procedure. The king has already given his agreement."

Her words apply pressure to comply. She is older, experienced, and has discussed it with the king... although why the king would agree to this when he offers mated omegas the chance to remove the binding confuses me.

Is the king worried too?

Despite his approval, I have many doubts. "I would like to think about it?" I hedge.

Her smile lacks warmth. "Of course. This is recommended in cases with more than one mate, especially in a young omega like yourself. The effect of a single alpha can be overwhelming. Four, well, it is enough to fog even the most experienced minds. It could influence your decisions, make you complicit with acts you might ordinarily refuse."

Her lips curl as though in distaste before she smooths her expression out and offers a smile. "I seek only to protect you during this delicate time. Your free will is precious."

Those words rock me, and as she moves on to discuss my quest, my focus is split. I want to dismiss her suggestion, but I second-guess myself and my motives. Am I already under their influence? Is that why I submitted to them, even though I'm an imperial and should not?

The binding still feels twisted and ugly. It feels like *I* am taking their free will away, not vice versa.

I feel sick that I might have been deceived. Celeste has been my mentor since I first arrived as a young child. I'm so confused. I want to trust myself, but now I question everything.

Are Winter and Shiloh genuinely happy or subject to alpha glamor or mind control?

I don't have the answers, only Winter's words echoing in my mind, the omega who knew both before and after. Only Celeste was there before, too, and that only makes it harder to decide.

Chapter Twenty-Two

Melody

It has been two days since Celeste recommended I increase the binding, leaving me in a conundrum as instincts and logic war with one another.

It is a moot point when I don't see any of my mates for two days. They are busy making up for the time they lost while they tended me through my frenzy.

I miss them.

My decision on the binding cannot be made quickly, and life surges forward as new quarters are prepared with a proper nesting chamber and bedrooms for each of my mates. They are now elevated above other warriors since I'm an imperial omega —which I still don't believe myself to be when I have unremarkable blood and, further, my portal mastery is up in the air.

But I am distracted from these worries when I receive news that my new quarters are ready.

They are beautifully appointed with a day room offering views across the city, five bedrooms, and a nesting chamber.

213

There is no bed in the nesting chamber. It had to be refurbished to accommodate my number of mates, and instead, a dais centers the room with a bare mattress of substantial proportions. An elaborate assembly is attached to the ceiling from which hang swags of light silken gauze that can be lowered to surround the whole dais and form the perfect nest.

Nest. The last time I ventured to nest, I was a little girl. I made a nest in the corner of my bedroom, where I layered blankets and soft cushions. I have vague memories of my first mama praising my diligent work with a smile.

Then dark fae came and ripped me away, then came the Blighten. In all that time, I did not nest once. Then afterward, when I arrived at Sanctum, the urge to nest was gone.

Perhaps bonding with my alphas has triggered me to do so now, for as the sun sinks over the great city of Sanctum, I decide to make my nest.

First, I close the swags to lend a sense of intimacy before taking my time to place throws, pillows, and soft blankets to my liking.

I miss them so much, and it has only been two days. My heart softens with tenderness toward the alphas who claim my heart even as my body stirs with carnal interest as I remember what we did.

I rummage through my closet, where I find my most scandalous nightgown... a pretty shade of lilac, sheer and beautiful, it leaves little to the imagination while wrapping me up like a perfect little fairy treat.

In the privacy of my quarters, I need not worry about my wings. Although I more often keep them bound, tonight, I set them free, letting them scatter the room with dust.

Restless, I return to my nest and lay down in the center of it. Feeling needy, I place one hand on my right breast while the other dips between my thighs and plays. I close my eyes and let my mind wander, thinking about my mates and how it felt when they were inside me, filling me: their presence, their scent, their *dominance*.

I start, hearing a click and snatch my hands away. My nipple is hard and sensitive, while my pussy is wet and slick.

And then I hear the purring, two distinct rumbles, and my heart rate explodes anew even as my pussy clenches with need. How can I tell from the timbre of their purrs that it is Draven and Aengus?

I rush to straighten out my gown, a little flustered that they are about to see my nest. The footsteps draw closer until Draven moves aside the swags and peers inside.

"Someone has been very naughty," he says, planting his hands on his hips. In place of his usual armor, he wears plain pants tucked into serviceable boots, and a light cotton shirt. He smells fresh and clean... he smells *alpha*.

Then Aengus steps up beside him and makes a tutting noise. "This is what happens when you leave her alone for two days."

"So it would seem," Draven agrees. He kicks off his boots and plants his knee on my bed.

I yelp and dive for the other side, only to be snagged around the waist. He tumbles me onto my back and, closing his fingers over my wrist, brings my hand to his nose and sniffs.

My stomach performs a slow dip.

His eyes darken. "Somebody has been playing," he says. "Playing with her alphas' toys. Did you miss my cock?"

I respond to his scandalous question with an eager nod. My eyes shift to Aengus, who stands watching us. "I want Aengus, too."

Draven raises both brows. "Do you, now?"

"Yes, I do." Of all my mates, Aengus is the most complex. There is darkness and depth to him. Like a caged beast under his skin. He is huge and intimidating—a barbarian to the core. Yet beneath his fearsome exterior and the layers of darkness is a wounded part that calls to the nurturer within me.

I desire him, all of him, in the same all-consuming way I do Draven, Theron, and Zeke.

Draven shrugs, and his lips tug up. "It is always an omega's choice."

"Good," I say decisively, trying to take my wrist back so I might take off my gown.

"Uh, uh," Draven says. "You have gone to all this effort to put this pretty little gown on. It is only fair that we get a chance to"— he turns to Aengus, who finishes the sentence with a smirk— "savor the unwrapping."

Aengus

Catching Draven's nod, I kick off my boots and enter the nest. He draws her into his arms, and I crowd in behind her, getting my hands on her for the first time in many weeks.

That night she came to our former quarters, not even looking for me, but Zeke, and where I held her in my arms and ordered her to lift her nightgown, feels like forever ago.

During her frenzy, the best I did was watch and, toward the end, was granted permission to come on her pretty tits.

Tonight she shall be mine. Tonight I may fuck her and bond with her. By prior agreement, Theron and Zeke will not be here. I put my trust in Draven alone to keep me in check.

I'm an alpha and a barbarian. My ways are rough. It has ever been a battle to contain the coarse edge of my lust. But it is so much harder with Melody, who will become my mate.

My lips find the back of her neck, even as Draven cups her

cheeks and slants his mouth over hers. She wraps one arm around his neck and reaches back with the other to clutch at my side. Her hand on me is all the encouragement I need, and my hands slide up from her waist over her ribs. The material of her gown is sheer and offers a delicate barrier between us that makes my dick stone hard for the want to rip it off. I lean into her beautiful golden wings and cup her breasts from behind, feeling their weight, pinching the stiff little nipples. Her scent saturates the air. She has been playing with herself, petting her needy little pussy. Perhaps she was thinking about me... or Draven, or Zeke, or Theron.

Perhaps she was thinking about us all.

My lips trail down her throat, and when I pause with my lips over the claiming mark, she sucks in a sharp breath. I only kiss gently, feeling her shiver. I believe she is sensitive here, her claiming mark, the place where they have taken her blood, and where I, too, shall drink later. I deepen my kisses, sucking against her soft skin. Her wings tremble, and golden dust smothers me, creating a firestorm of sensitivity across my skin.

I kiss up the side of her throat until my lips can enclose her ear. I suck hard just as I squeeze her nipples roughly. She arches up, moaning into Draven's mouth, thrusting her ass back at me. She's so tiny between us, two towering walls of alpha, while she is all sweet and soft.

The potency of the moment wraps around me, the recognition of what I do, finally accepting my place in taking and sharing a mate. My unworthiness is like a canker, one I must purge from my mind. Not that I have a choice. I can either be with her or die a slow death.

Instead, I get to live and fuck my mate in her nest. I will make it filthy, smother it in my scent and cum. I will defile the sweet omega in it before this night is done.

Draven breaks away and reaches to pull his shirt over his

head before tossing it out of the nest. His pants come next, and he returns to take Melody from me so I might do the same.

I take my time, watching them kissing as I rid myself of my clothes. Then I fist my cock and slowly pump. His hands are all over her, caressing her delicate flesh, sliding over her breasts, between her legs, but not lingering in one place.

Like she senses my study, her lips wrench from his. She looks back and holds out her hand. "Please."

A growl bubbles up from my throat as I climb into the nest. I take her hand and bring it to my lips so I can suck her naughty fingers into my mouth and taste her. Her lips pop open, and her eyes go round. "What a filthy little omega," I rumble. "Did you get off before we turned up?"

She shakes her head.

"No? Are you sure?"

"I did not," she protests vehemently, eliciting a dark chuckle from Draven.

"It wasn't for the want of trying, was it?" Draven says.

She blushes. She is so beautiful. I'm a lucky bastard, beyond my rights, to be allowed to be part of this.

Once a delectable tease, her gown now feels like an unnecessary hindrance. My hand trembles as I gather the fine material between my hands and tear it clean in half.

Draven's nostrils flare, and his eyes light with approval. He nods to me and, cupping the back of her neck, gently lowers her back to the bed. He lays beside her, leaning in, closes his mouth over her nipple, and gently sucks.

Her steady gaze meets mine, watching me as her knees rise and then fall apart.

I am fucking lost, staring at the perfect slick little slit that hides her feminine treasure from me. And then Draven, the bastard, knowing I'm already teetering on the edge, lowers one hand and, using two fingers, spreads her open for me.

I swallow. My dick ejects an enthusiastic blob of pre-cum that she certainly doesn't need, given how drenched she is.

Draven lifts his head and stares down at me. "Why don't you have a taste?"

He goes back to her tit.

I growl and fall upon her with all the savagery I possess, closing my mouth over her juicy cunt, licking and sucking until she arches up on the bed. Her fingers fist my hair and she cries out as she gushes over my waiting tongue. I want to consume her and her pleasure. I feast and feast. She comes over and over again, and I can't get enough.

Some distant part of me cautions me to stop. Draven, my chaperone, is busy kissing her and playing with her tits and offers me no fucking caution at all. By the time I can drag myself from the temptation of her sweet slick, my face is numb, and I've lost all possession of my wits.

I stare down at her in a daze. Draven reaches down and thrusts three fingers into her cunt without a hint of preparation. She moans and pushes her hips up for more.

All my blood is in my dick, it is little wonder there is none left to support my brain.

He pumps slowly—the wet sticky sound captivating me.

I don't realize I've moved until I'm poised at her entrance. His hand is gone, and he's busy feeding her juices to her.

"Take her," Draven says, not even bothering to look at me. "It's what she wants. It's what she needs. It's always an omega's choice. And she has chosen you."

Before entering the room, I told myself I would be gentle with her.

I am not gentle. As I grasp her hips and slam deep in a single thrust, I am the quintessence of brutality. She is already coming and spasming around me, coaxing my knot to fullness with devastating speed. I knot on the third stroke, mind whiting out to the rapture of release as I spend hot cum right next to the entrance of her womb.

I'm half blind. I can't hear a thing beyond her wild moans. Then my vision tunnels on the claiming mark at her throat. I don't notice Draven move away, only realize she is all mine as my teeth pierce her throat.

She screams and her pussy fists my cock. My balls rise to deliver another scalding batch of hot cum. Her blood gushes, filling my mouth. I swallow, and it hits my stomach like a tornado. Pleasure rips through me like lightning, driving deep into the root of my cock, and my knot blooms thicker as yet more cum floods her slick cunt. As I drink deeply, her pussy spasms all over me. Her fingers are in my hair, gripping, holding me to her throat.

Mine! The roar echoes through my mind: the leash, that abhorrent mechanism of control, is wrapped in a golden thread that weaves around. I feel her pleasure like a mirror of my own. It pours into me, filling me in warmth and euphoria.

It takes me long moments before I remember to ease my lock on her throat, to soothe her wound with my tongue.

My heart is beating wildly in my chest. I can feel hers beating against mine. She trembles. Or I do. Maybe we both do.

It doesn't matter. Nothing matters. Not now.

I lift my head and look down at her in wonder before I slant my mouth over hers, pouring all the wildness I feel into the kiss as our tongues tangle. I taste her—I want to consume every part of her.

My knot barely softens before I take her hips and pull it out. She wails in protest—I bare my teeth and growl. Flipping her onto her belly, I yank her hips up and penetrate her from behind.

"Yes!"

Her pretty wings flutter as she thrusts her ass back for me.

"I think the brat needs something to keep her quiet."

Her clenching pussy tells me she likes the sound of that. When I glance across to where Draven lounges watching, he smirks. He doesn't hesitate and, rising with grace, fists her hair, and directs a hot little mouth toward his cock.

She sucks him deep, her gagging a pretty symphony to which I rut.

She is a fairy, not like humans, but made of magic and golden dust. I cannot hurt her in the way I might do a human lass. It is only now that I truly understand she can take me and my roughness.

The walls within me tumble. I take her in the way I need, pounding into her hot cunt, the perfect vessel for an alpha's cock and knot. We fuck her between us, enjoy her sweet body, filling her pussy and belly with cum even as we take her blood.

She comes. She doesn't stop fucking coming.

As dawn breaks, bringing light beyond the nest, the madness eases its stranglehold. She is above me, riding herself to completion. My saucy little imp, rising up and down on my cock, her pretty tits swaying until she finally coaxes my knot to fullness, and we come together, sharing a lingering kiss and gusty breaths.

She's sticky with sweat and cum... We are all covered in her dust. She collapses against my chest. I emit a deep rumbly purr, content to my very core. My knot is still locked as Draven collapses to the side of us, and I roll, pinning her between us, her beautiful wings folding and shrinking small.

As her breathing evens out, I look at Draven over her head.

He only offers me a lazy smirk before he closes his eyes.

I don't sleep. I draw the strawberry blonde hair back from her hot cheek and watch over my mate.

Chapter Twenty-Three

Draven

"So she has accepted Aengus?" the king asks.

We are in his study, a grand room where the leaded windows offer sweeping views across Sanctum. The wooden desk at which he sits is dark and ancient. The stone walls are lined with bookcases and cabinets holding thick leather-bound tomes and curious widgets whose purposes elude me. The fire is banked low, and a few lamps are lit to combat the dull and dreary day outside.

"Yes, my liege." Before the portal incident, where Melody came under attack, I had not met the king in person. Now, I am once more before him on account of taking Melody as a mate.

Jacob stands to my left while the king, dressed in a fine burgundy silk jacket with gold needlework on the lapels and cuffs, lounges in his desk chair, expression thoughtful. "Word will get around."

"I'm certain Sanctum is already buzzing with it," Jacob offers. "It's unheard of for an omega to take four mates."

"The binding is not meant for four," the king says, his expression distant as he turns to stare out the window.

I feel the prickling of unease. "What does that mean?"

Jacob quirks a brow at me that says I'm overly familiar with the king and too bold for my own good.

The king glances up. "The binding holds true for omegas against all alphas, just as it has always done. But the blood gift during mating is different, especially when it involves a psychic link."

"It feels like a golden thread wrapping around the leash," I say before I can consider the merits of revealing this.

"You can sense it already?" The king's brows pull together.

I internally curse my runaway mouth. Still, the damage is done—I nod.

"She has not gone through her heat, though?"

"A frenzy," I reply.

"And with Aengus? He bound her later, I heard."

"Yes, my liege. I was with him when he took her blood several days after the frenzy. It was certainly... enthusiastic." This is not a conversation I want to have with the king. A sense of unease rises in me, and I worry that he questions the binding and how it pertains to us and our unique circumstances. I fucking hate the binding to start with. But I don't want any reason for him to separate us.

"And do all the others sense it?" The king presses.

"I have not asked them," I offer honestly. I don't presume myself to be anything special. It makes sense that we should all feel it equally.

"I have been petitioned," the king says, "to enhance the binding in your particular case."

"What the fuck does that mean?" The words are out, and my tone is combative, but I will not take it back.

The king raises a brow at my impertinence but lets it pass.

"It means exactly what I said. Change brings suspicion and resistance. That I have removed the binding for some mated couples has rocked the foundations of Sanctum. If I had my time over, I would do things differently. Not introduced the binding at all—And I trust you to keep that insight private. Still, we cannot undo the past. We can only press forward from where we are. Historically, and on the few occasions when an omega took more than one mate, we would enhance the binding magic to ensure they still had full control. Melody is young. Unless she chooses to strengthen the binding, it will weaken over time. Hence her mentor came to me and recommended it be strengthened. Have you noticed any changes since taking her blood?"

I am reeling from this list of revelations and must take a moment to compose myself before I can answer. "Not yet." It is a small white lie. When his eyes narrow upon me, I rethink my wording lest I piss him off and encourage him to strengthen the damn binding without delay. "Nothing tangible. I feel... different." It sounds vague, and I sense Jacob's stillness. He has coached me to speak plainly to the king. I believe I have failed to follow this advice, have courted the line of disrespect, and further have fucked things up for my brothers as well as me. Now I have backed myself into a corner where I try to explain something deeply mystical that does not make any fucking sense.

"Strength? Increased stamina?" the king asks.

"No." I place my palm over my stomach. "It's a feeling here, like something grows within me—intangible as yet. I've tasted imperial blood before. There is a surge of adrenaline, a sense of power, alertness, and stamina that are obvious and instantaneous but which wears off over time. When I took Melody's blood, it felt more pervasive... core deep. Whatever her blood does, it has already begun and does not appear to manifest in obvious ways. There have been no physical changes either short or long-term."

"It will happen," Jacob says. "I'm confident of it."

"I don't want the binding to be strengthened—a thicker leash," I press. Nor do I want them to take her away from me. "She needs protection. The reasons behind the Blighten attack remain unclear. I will tear this fucking city apart if someone tries to separate us."

Jacob surprises me by chuckling. I level the bastard with a glare.

The king raises a hand. "Steady, warrior. I do not seek to separate you from your mate, nor did I intend to magically strengthen the binding for your pack—unless Melody asks me to, and then I would." He narrows his eyes upon me.

My gut roils with unease. I have left plain talking far behind and launched into foolhardy insubordination—the damn omega has broken my brain.

The king nods, seeming satisfied by something. "Fate is in motion. It is not our place to stand in its way. I had hoped her blood would offer the usual enhancements as benefits warriors charged with her protection. No matter. We shall see... Still, it has been months, and we are no closer to finding out who was behind the orc attack. Perhaps it was random and intended to incite fear. An omega on a new quest is an easy target, and perhaps it's no more complex than that. From now on, communications between you and Cecil will be direct and in person, so there can be no confusion."

I nod. "I heard that Melody is to resume her quests."

"Yes," he says.

Unease unfurls inside me. "And what about her disappearing through the portal and not remembering where she went? It happened again after she was back here. Shiloh found her chilled and her nightgown saturated after she used the portal to return from Zeke's room."

"If she remembers nothing," the king says, "or is choosing not to tell us, there is very little we can do. Have you asked her about it?"

"No," I admit.

"If you are concerned, then you should."

I swallow. I do not want to broach the subject with her. Instinct tells me she was deeply troubled by whatever happened. Her skills with the portal are beyond impressive. Perhaps she does this more often than we realize, yet instinct tells me whatever happened the night Shiloh found her was different and significant in some way. "I will."

"Do you think she lied?" Jacob asks bluntly.

My fist clenches. I experience a strong urge to punch him in the face for daring to doubt Melody, even as I doubt her myself.

"Peace, warrior," he mutters, lips tugging up briefly. "I meant no disrespect in questioning her response at the time. Her memories might have subsequently returned, but she doesn't know how or who to talk to about it. Or, perhaps, she did hide details from us for reasons we cannot begin to guess. But I agree, it's important. With hindsight, we should have pressed her at the time. She is the only omega who can call portals at will. Who knows where she goes and how often she uses them? Even her portal scholar was troubled to learn she was porting about Sanctum."

"She understands portal lore instinctively and in ways even the Chosen do not," the king says. "Whether she understands the seriousness of what has transpired or not, better if she is guided through quests of our choice than further unsanctioned portal trips occur. The keystone is once more on the move. I want Melody close to it.

My instincts tell me she will not need many interactions before she latches. Cecil will inform you directly when the warriors have returned and the path is confirmed clear. This time you have a dozen warriors under your command to accompany you with Melody. Further, Zeke, Theron, and Aengus will accompany the earlier patrols, ensuring no opportunity for miscommunication."

I nod, my earlier dread easing, knowing my brothers will have my back. The king has his reasons—we are all pawns in a broader scheme to keep Sanctum safe.

"Report to Jacob directly when you return," the king says. Dismissed, I take my leave, mind already on the coming quest... but also, although I fucking hate the binding, I cannot help but anticipate the gift of blood that must happen before.

Chapter Twenty-Four

Draven

We meet in the warrior hall to discuss tomorrow's quest. My three brothers have their orders. Each will accompany a different patrol, responsible for scouting the area ahead of Melody and me. A path is mapped out for them to ensure our destination is clear of enemies, save the single party we are tasked with tracking. Given what happened last time, Melody and I will be accompanied by an entire patrol. Perhaps it's overkill. There are benefits to traveling as a pair, making it easier to remain undetected. There are also disadvantages, as Theron found out last time.

"Are you going to take her blood again?" Zeke asks, as a serving lass delivers a round of ale to our table.

"It is customary," I say.

"It will make the binding stronger," Aengus points out, "when we take it that way."

I believe he is trying to put me off taking her blood.

I smirk.

He scowls at me and lifts his beer to his lips. He understands well that even at the risk of it strengthening the leash around my neck, I will take her blood any opportunity I can because we all know she'll be begging for my cock from the first pull.

"Did the king say anything about the binding?" Zeke asks.

The king said a great deal about the binding, but we are not in our private quarters and, even there, risks exist in such troubling times. "He said only that it would fade over time unless strengthened."

"What the fuck is that about?" Theron demands.

"If Melody requests it, the king can increase the binding between us. If she does not, it will gradually fade, given we have formed a pack."

"Pack?" Aengus grins. "I like that. Is that what we are, then?"

"According to the scholar, that is the usual term when there are more than two mates."

"I like it too," Zeke says. "It feels right."

"It does," Theron agrees. "So, how long will it take to wear off?"

"Years, decades possibly."

Scowl forming, Theron takes a swing of beer before the tankard hits the table with a thud. "I hope she behaves better for you than she did for me."

"She will," I say confidently... perhaps more confidently than I feel.

"I'm glad we're part of the patrols," Aengus says. "They still don't know what happened to that last one, which makes me uneasy. Six good men lost."

"It won't happen to us," Theron says. "We are part of this

and connected. I can sense you, all of you, through Melody. It's very fucking weird but also comforting."

I nod. "It takes some getting used to. Perhaps that's why they call it a pack, like what happens between shifters when they hear each other's thoughts."

"Do you think that will happen to us?" Zeke asks.

I shrug. "I didn't get a chance to speak to the scholar myself. But pair bonds, especially with high-ranking omegas, have a psychic connection... one rarely discussed with lowly warriors."

"I felt when she was coming," Aengus says gruffly. "It was like an amplifier to my lust."

"It was very fucking trippy," Zeke says, with a dreamy expression.

Theron cuffs him.

"What?" Zeke scowls at his brother.

"I don't want to discuss this," Theron says. "Especially when we cannot go to her."

"Why can't we go to her?" I ask.

"Are you saying we can?" Theron raises his brows and all eyes swing my way.

"No one said that we could not," I point out. "Her new quarters are our quarters now. Or so I was told."

"Fuck!" Zeke says, as his eyes take on a wicked gleam.

I chuckle at his enthusiasm. "I dare say there might be a bit of that going on."

Melody

There are four strapping warriors in my new quarters—*our* quarters, I amend.

All of them look hungry.

One of them holds a small bottle of oil. I wonder what that is for... *Goodness!*

"It's time to make a fairy sandwich," Draven announces in a seductive purr.

I gulp, and my pussy clenches so fiercely with arousal that it is like a mini climax going off.

Aengus' chuckle is positively devious.

"How does that work?" Zeke asks. "There are two pieces of bread in the sandwich, and there are" —he turns to his brothers as if verifying they are all here— "four of us."

"Well noted," Aengus says, striding for me. "Run."

Run? *Run!*

I run.

I run from Aengus straight into Zeke's arms.

"Got you!"

As his arms band around me, heat shoots like lightning to my core—I groan.

"I guess Zeke is part of the first sandwich," Draven says. "Heads or tails, and you get first dibs on using the oil."

"Tails and oil," he says without the briefest hesitation.

I glance up—a big mistake when I find him smirking down at me. How did I ever mistake him for sweet? I know what the oil is for. I have heard other omegas talk about warriors taking the dark place and how it is the wickedest, most depraved kind of pleasure... how it fulfills the need to be dominated some omegas secretly crave.

A shiver ripples through me as I stare into Zeke's eyes.

"Do you trust me, Melody?"

"I do." My breathing is unsteady, and the words come out on a breathy pant.

"Good." He traces his fingertips over my cheeks, then winks. "Something tells me you will take well to this. I'm going to take good care of you. We all are. If you want us to stop, you need only ask."

I already know I won't want him to stop, and he knows it too.

He grins and tosses me over the shoulder.

❧

Zeke

I'm going to be the first to take her ass—to pop that cherry.

It is well known that I am partial to such deviant acts. I believe Draven already knew my answer, even as he asked. For whatever reason, he is entrusting me with her first time. I fucking love ass-rutting. It is dark and delicious. It makes omegas quiver and plead. It is a supremely dominant act and perhaps the only time an omega fully submits and is mastered to their limitations.

I stride toward her bedroom door, through new quarters that I have never entered before, which, as Draven pointed out, are ours. They are fancy, as befits an imperial omega of her standing—the stone walls prevalent in the warrior quarters are lined with beautiful wood paneling. The room even boasts leaded windows that offer views across Sanctum. The furnishing is of the best quality, and when I enter her nesting chamber with her draped over my shoulder, I can only stare in wonder at the bed.

Nest, I correct myself. This creation of soft cushions and pretty shimmering swags is assuredly a nest. "Fuck!"

"That is one hell of a nest," Theron mutters gruffly.

"There are four of us," Aengus points out.

Draven strides off to collect a chair which he then places to

235

offer a good view of the dais—I can assume from this that he had decided he will not be part of the first sandwich.

"Who gets heads?" Theron asks.

"I do," Aengus says, in an I-will-kick-your-ass-if-you-challenge-me kind of tone.

"Aengus," Draven confirms, and I can hear the smile in his voice.

"Fine then," Theron mutters as he stalks off to fetch a chair.

I'm not used to an audience when I fuck, although I suppose there has not been a lot of thought as to who might be around when I have. I have witnessed many warriors complete their trials and I have taken part alongside them in the debauchery that follows, rutting sweet omegas for our pleasure and theirs. Only this is different. This is with my mate. She is the mate to all four of us.

As I look around me at my brothers and our mate, another thing that strikes me as different is that no one before has pulled up a fucking chair like they are getting ready for a show!

Aengus takes the oil from Draven and nods his head to me. "Put her in the nest so we can get her out of these cursed clothes."

I drop her into the center of the massive mattress and follow straight down after her, dispensing with the little buttons and liberating her of her dress with a complete lack of finesse. Her dress lands with a *woosh* on the other side of the room as Aengus places the stoppered bottle on the nightstand, kicks off his boots, and proceeds to undress.

Her hands get in the fucking way as she tries to help me remove her underclothes—it would seem she is as enthusiastic about this as I am.

"Please hurry!" she mutters.

My pleasure. I strip her down to her wing band, stockings, and cute little boots. She fumbles with the buckle on her boots until I take over, slipping them off and tossing them out of the nest. Staring at her pussy half the time, which is very fucking distracting, I peel her stockings down.

Finally comes the thick cloth band that covers her wings. As the last of the material unravels, they spring open amid a shower of golden dust.

I blink, mesmerized by this omega who holds my heart, caught by how beautiful she is, outside and in. Our brave mate has endured so much in her young life, overcome dangers and survived. She is so delicate yet incredibly strong.

My heart softens with love for her even as my dick grows hard.

"Best strip, runt," Aengus says, taking Melody into his arms and rousing me from my lusty stupor. "Not going do a lot of ass-fucking while you've still got your pants on." And then he slants his mouth over hers and swallows up her needy whimper.

They share a lusty kiss, lying side by side. I undress, staring at them the whole time. He is a big burly alpha, and she is tiny beside him. I always wondered how it would feel to be part of something like this, to form a pack, as Draven calls it, sharing a single mate, and whether I would feel jealous.

She has always been closest to me, and perhaps I deluded myself into believing we shared a special bond and that the others would be merely side characters in our play.

Except I am discovering that it's not like that at all, but so much better. It's not jealousy I experience as I reach for the bottle on the nightstand but a heightened sense of arousal and belonging. Aengus' big hands touch her with surety, his lips against her throat, his kisses moving down one breast until he encloses the stiff peak of her nipple. He sucks hard—she arches into him.

I fucking love watching my lusty omega being pleasured in this way.

His hand skims over her hip before sliding between her thighs, and she gasps as he pushes up. His wrist works as he pumps his fingers into her, and her legs fall apart, giving me the perfect view of what he does—opening her slick pussy, teasing, and stoking her pleasure.

Time to take control of the situation. In this, I am in charge.

I slide into the nest behind her, and her eyes flash around to meet mine.

"Come," Aengus growls.

Her body turns rigid, and she emits a deep, breathy groan, coming, staring at me as Aengus sucks on her pretty tit and fingers her cunt.

Fuck! I nearly fucking come in response!

"Gods," Theron mutters weakly from the other side of the room.

I'm not the only one nearly spilling my load.

Aengus smirks at me over her head. The bastard knows what he's doing as he pulls his fingers from her with a sticky pop and shoves them in his mouth with a groan.

I take her by the hips and roll her over him. He rolls with it, laying beneath her and fisting her hair to pull her down for a heated kiss.

But now her ass, her perfect peach-shaped ass, is directly in front of me. I place one hand on her hip to steady her as she twitches, her hips moving erratically as she rubs her pussy against Aengus' cock.

"Eyes on me, Melody," Aengus says as he plays with both breasts now, pinching her nipples to get her attention. "It's time for Zeke to open you all up."

Cursing him and his words that seek to unman me, I uncap the oil and trickle some over her ass. She jolts. I pour more over my fingertips, circling that puckered little entrance and ensuring she is well covered before I ease my thumb inside.

Her ass clenches over me, tight and compelling. I imagine how this hot tight passage will feel around my cock.

"Oh!" She glances back at me, trying to pull away.

"Eyes on me," Aengus barks, and her head whips around. "You can take this. You can be a good girl for us, can't you? Zeke needs to work the oil in if he's to get his dick inside you."

Her breathing turns choppy as I slide my thumb in and out, stretching her. Opening her, circling the little hole, and then pushing in, watching my thumb disappear inside her and pop back out again. I know the exact moment where it passes from confused tolerance to pleasure. She clenches tightly around my thumb and then groans and pushes back for more.

"Fuck. She's enjoying it," Aengus says roughly.

Hell, yes.

I add a little more oil and replace my thumb with a finger, taking my time, teasing her with it before I work up to two.

"Oh! Oh! Oh!"

She is close. Sweat breaks across the surface of my skin, and my dick spits an enthusiastic blob of pre-cum onto her nest. I need to get inside her before we both fucking come.

Melody

I know what is coming, and the only feeling I experience is fierce arousal. There is no fear here. I trust them with my life, heart, and body.

I am an omega and a fairy, unfettered by earthly constraints, a vessel for pleasure.

"That's my filthy little omega," Aengus purrs beside my ear.

I moan, pushing back on Zeke as Aengus shoves three fingers deep into my mouth until I gag.

"How about I give you something to suck on? It looks like you might need a distraction."

I moan helplessly around his fingers. The truth is I don't care what they do to me. They are everything I dreamed of. To have their hands on me, and be the center of their pack, makes my heart swell and my body sing.

Zeke's fingers are replaced by something thicker and he palms my hip to hold me still. Aengus rises to his knees and, leaning down, cups my cheek to watch my face.

There is momentary panic as Zeke presses—the girth is considerable, and the stretch is alarming. But he is also slippery and my body gives, allowing the head of his cock to pop inside. There he holds still, so intimate, as my ass burns and pulses around his thickness.

Instinct tells me clenching is a bad idea, even before my body seeks to squeeze his cock out. Like he senses my intention, Zeke presses forward, and his slippery length surges deeper still.

"Fuck! Don't do that," he grunts.

My wings waft slowly as a deep, wanton moan rises from the pit of my stomach. I can feel the blood pounding in my ass, dark and twisty pleasure lurking on the periphery.

Goddess help me, I did not expect to feel so full, so possessed, so thoroughly mastered.

"You like that," Aengus says, watching me as shock and pleasure contort my face. "Don't you?"

I nod helplessly.

"Fuck, I'm going to nut," Zeke grunts. "And I'm not halfway in."

"Hold it, runt," Aengus growls. "I'll give her something else to think about."

My eyes clash with those belonging to my barbarian, and then I lower them to where a thick cock is presented to my lips. I fall onto him enthusiastically, sucking him straight back into my throat, gagging a little but not caring because I need him so much.

"Good girl," Aengus says. "Take what you need."

And then Zeke begins to move in slow, shallow thrusts, and more tormented pleasure blooms the length of my back passage. I'm so very *dominated*. The burning pressure in my ass clashes with the fat cock surging into my throat. I ache where they take me, yet I would be devastated were they to stop. The sounds I make are the dreadful hoarse sounds of denied breath. Pre-cum and saliva soon drips down my chin. This is not Aengus' doing but mine. Although his fingers twist my hair, he applies no pressure.

I'm wild, barely contained. The steady pumping, going deeper, filling me, has me high. I'm going to come. I can't stop it, and the fluttery pleasure rises and then tips over into fierce contractions the length of my ass that have me humping back with wild abandon even as I suck Aengus to the back of my throat.

Zeke groans, taking my hips in his hands and setting up a fast, pounding rhythm that has me twitching and sparking as another twisty climax tears through me... it does not stop. And now I understand those whispered conversations, how I feel ravished in the best kind of way.

How I never want this to end.

They take me, pushing and pulling me on and off their cocks, driving a fever through my veins until I lose command of my muscles and spasms rock my whole body. A fiery bliss consumes me from the follicles of my hair to the tips of my fingers and toes.

They come with me, a flood filling my throat and another

hot pulse in my ass.

We hang out of time and reality, floating in the hazy glow of hot cum, quivering wings, and spasming muscles.

Then they ease from me, and I fall limp like they have cut the strings on a puppet.

"Good girl," Aengus praises, gathering me into his arms as Zeke stumbles from the bed to clean up. My barbarian purrs for me, and I sink into the sweet sound as Zeke returns and a hot, damp cloth is applied to my bottom. "I'm so proud of you."

The heady glow still holds me captive when other hands come as Draven and Theron replace Aengus and Zeke. My body is still tender, and I bemoan as much even as I'm guided to straddle Draven's lap. I willingly take his cock in my hand, putting it where I need it. As it nocks at my slick entrance, he takes my hips in his big hands and slams me onto him, filling me to the root in a single, savage thrust.

He sits up, wrapping one arm around my waist and fisting my hair with the other before slanting his mouth over mine. We share a kiss full of breathy gasps and tongues. My pussy quakes around his thick length and burgeoning knot. It's only belatedly that I realize Theron is behind me, sweeping my hair aside as he kisses the back of my neck. He places one hand on my hip to steady me as the other plays with my slippery, tender ass.

His intentions are clear. I ask myself if I want this... if I can take this. Only they are both still kissing me, and the pleasure rises and makes its demands—I want more.

Tearing my lips from Draven's, I glance back at Theron. "More."

Our eyes meet—his handsome face is flushed, his pupils so dark, I can barely see the color. Then he smirks, and his slippery, oiled cock lines up and applies pressure until the head pops past my puckered entrance.

My jaw hangs slack as Draven kisses up my throat, his

hands on my breasts. "That's my good omega. How beautiful you are. I loved watching my brothers take you, fuck your sweet body between them. And now, it is my turn. I want you to enjoy this, to feel pleasure and only pleasure as we fill you all up."

Theron thrusts and it is so slippery there that he surges in with alarming and rapturous ease. I make a sound that is somewhere between a wounded animal and a cat in heat and all visceral pleasure. I'm sore, well used, but this is so perfect.

It is almost too much. The fire within me barely lowers before they ignite it again. "More."

Draven rolls back onto the nest, taking me with him, his hands shifting to my waist. His cock slides almost out, allowing Theron to slide all the way in.

I moan, head tipped back, lost to the sweet rippling sensation that sets sensitive nerves to light.

Then Theron takes my hips, and they begin to move. One in. One out. Over and over.

I am so perfectly full. There is no space inside me that is not taken. As if I am not already high on them and the pleasure they wrest from me, they begin to move in time, filling me together, increasing speed, pounding my smaller body between theirs until the starburst explodes behind my eyes and I pitch into a climax that never finds an end.

It seems I pass out without knowing it; for when I rouse, I am locked on Draven's knot, sprawled out over him. To my right is Theron, and to his left is Zeke. Beyond him is Aengus. We are a sleepy tangle of limbs.

I feel perfectly loved.

"Are you sore?" Draven asks, stroking his fingers through my hair. The motion is soothing in contrast to his rough rutting so short a time ago.

"A little," I say. "But I liked it very much."

Zeke chuckles. "I knew you would."

Chapter Twenty-Five

Melody

I fall asleep surrounded by four alphas and wake up with only two, but even that does not last as Aengus presses his lips to my forehead and rises from the nest, leaving me alone with Draven.

He lays behind me, and as I turn to glance back at him, he tightens his arm around me and pulls me into the curve of his big warm body. Their scent covers the nest and me. I like it very much. I'm still a little achy between my legs and ass, a reminder of what we shared.

"I've always known fairies were magical"— Draven's voice is a sleepy rumble beside my ear— "but seeing your wings shrink and expand is messing with my mind. I thought they would be absent or there all the time."

"I think it's to do with the portal," I say.

His head lifts, and he leans on his elbow, rolling me onto my back to face him.

"How does that work?"

"When we pass through the portal, we cease to exist and reform on the other side. I think portals are the domain of fairies because that's how we work. The fairies created the first portals, although it was a long time ago. That's what the orc portal scholar told me, and when I asked about it here, they agreed it was the most likely theory. When I was little, there were many fairies with wings, along with shapeshifters who would disappear into dust and return as a wolf or a bear. Some had no shape but would form dust and then pop up elsewhere. My childhood memories of Estoria are vague, as I was very young at the time. But I remember how a cousin a few years older would disappear and reappear on the other side of the room when we played chase. No one thought it was strange, that I can recall. I think that is what I do with portals. Maybe it was common to my people. Maybe some fairy races never needed a portal site or keystone at all."

His frown makes me wish I'd never brought it up. I wish I could tell what was going on behind my first alpha's green eyes.

"Can you take on other forms?"

I shake my head. "The portal just happened when I was little. I think if I could change shape, it would have happened too. I've always been able to make my wings shrink. They are very large when open and get in the way."

He chuckles. It is a deep happy sound that makes me feel all warm inside.

"Your wings are beautiful, Melody, whether they are these cute little ones or the larger version that scatters dust all over the place." Draven leans down to kiss me.

My belly takes that slow tumble, and neediness kicks off between my legs. I open my mouth with a sigh as my hand reaches up to cup his cheek. The faint stubble is prickly under my fingertips, and I pet him as we kiss.

When he lifts his head, he smirks at me. "Is someone having naughty thoughts? You know I can feel it through the bond."

I blush, my fingers slipping from his cheek. The bond is like a seedling growing. It sets down roots in the binding leash and wraps light around the darkness.

I wish the binding were gone, but I also feel unsettled whenever I remember what Celeste said. We are not yet fully bonded until I go into heat. I want to ask the king to remove the binding, but I'm also unsure of myself. My trust would lie with Winter over Celeste, yet it is far more complex than simple trust.

I question myself and my opinions. I love and trust my mates, though I also acknowledge I lack maturity in many ways.

I'm to go on another quest. What if I put Draven in danger by disobeying him today, as I did with Theron?

What if the binding is gone, and I'm compelled to obey, and then I lose them?

While I disobeyed an order from Theron, I believe I saved him in doing so, for he could not have killed five orcs. But I may have misunderstood the situation. Perhaps he would not have engaged them if I had made it safely through the portal.

Trust is complex; both trust in others and ourselves, and tied directly to trust is that little thing known as confidence, which has wavered in me in recent times regarding portals.

"Where did you go?"

Draven's words stir me from my ruminations. I know instinctively what he speaks of. Did he sense me touching upon the memory through the bond? I don't know how this bond works, only that I believe they sometimes shield from me.

My brows pull together. He can read me, yet I'm only faintly aware of my four mates, like they are choosing to project certain things... like there is a wall between us.

A lingering effect of the binding?

He cups my chin and traces his thumb over my cheek in a gentle caress. It turns firm as he directs me to face him in a move I'm sure is intentional, and which reminds me he is an alpha, my first alpha, and that, despite the binding, he holds power over me, power that is soul deep—power that reaches back to the fundamental at play between alphas and omegas. "Melody, where did you go?"

I swallow. He is not going to let this go nor will he allow me to retreat or hide. As I reflect on it, I am amazed no one has pressed me on the matter before.

"I would like a bath and to dress first," I say, hedging for some space and time to better formulate what to say. One might think I would have already done so, given how much time has passed, yet my thoughts scatter, and the only story I can find is the truth.

He shakes his head and, seeing right through me, says, "Not a chance."

I have been avoiding this for too long. Now Draven has me at a disadvantage in my nest, naked and smelling of sex, and while this is, in part, a gentle inquiry from my lover, it is also a command for an answer from my first alpha responsible for my protection.

I still hold back.

"Melody, if you saw something, tell me what it was. If you went somewhere and it frightened you, it's important I know about it. I am not an old alpha, but I am also not young. My experience tells me that understanding your trauma is important to keeping you safe. You are so courageous, and it breaks my heart that you have had to be. I wish I could shelter you from danger for the rest of your life. That option is not available to me while Sanctum exists in precarious balance with the

Blighten. That you must go on these quests gives me the gravest concerns. Yet I acknowledge, too, that you have within you powers that could change the landscape of many lives for the better. I want a safer life for you, one where we can shut the Blighten out if we recover the missing keystone, but I need to know the risks. I need to know how to protect you, and I can only do that if you talk to me... if you trust me."

There it is again, that word, *trust*. I have trusted Draven since I met him, only if it feels very different now. Fairies who have suffered trauma must attend counseling, which I have done for many years with Celeste.

"I experienced a waking nightmare—one I know is not true."

His brows knit together. "A waking nightmare? You were trapped inside the portal? How do you return cold and wet? What did you see?"

I swallow. My throat is tight and dry. His questions are pertinent. I have asked myself the same ones many times. "The first time it happened, I was with Theron as he battled the orcs. I had opened a portal, back to Sanctum, or so I believed. Only I didn't want to go through it and leave him alone there. I was terrified I would never see him again." My voice breaks as the fear comes crashing back.

He purrs. "Please go on."

"My horse reared. It tossed me through the portal. Except I wasn't back at Sanctum but in a forest path much like the one where I had just been with Theron. It was the same yet different. Theron was not here, and there were subtle differences in the landscape. Grass was showing between the snow, like it was later in the year, or somewhere perhaps sheltered from the weather."

"And what happened there?"

Tears spill down my cheeks, and my chest heaves. I had banished myself from talking about this, from thinking about it to some extent, with limited success.

"I saw Zeke die."

Chapter Twenty-Six

Draven

I am caught in a riptide of emotions as Melody tells me what she saw. That she has been carrying this burden around for months fills me with a deep well of shame. I should have pressed the matter sooner. Had I known, I could have comforted her, and shared the burden with her.

Although the little voice inside tells me she was not ready to talk about this before.

I have questions, yet these are overridden as my gut instinct urges me to abort this mission. It is already too late to some extent. My brothers have left. They will complete their tasks and not return until done.

It feels like a complex puzzle has been thrust upon me; one I do not have the skills or acumen to fit together into sense. While I accept what she is saying and what she thought she saw, we both know she could not have seen Zeke die when he remains alive.

Yet I believe she went somewhere. Especially the second time when she came back in her nightgown, cold and wet.

I don't claim to know the complexities of the human mind, nor that of fairies, who must be different to some extent. Her childhood trauma, the death of her parents, the dark fae, and the Blighten have all played a part in her young life, and then she came here where she has been indoctrinated into Sanctum culture, where we live in a state of perpetual war, and alphas are kept subservient.

I was born here, yet the day I came of age and took blood for the first time, my misconception of freedom was destroyed. Some bear the burden easier than others. Some mate the lesser omegas, the breeders and the feeders, where the binding does not cut so deep.

The way of things in Sanctum is to compel alphas to obey when we would give our loyalty freely, but for the asking.

We are all prisoners here, of some kind or another, caught on an eternal wheel and not knowing how to escape.

I consider all this not out of self-pity, but because it hamstrings my ability to protect my mate. My instincts tell me this quest must be aborted, but when it comes down to it, I could yet be forced to take actions not of my choosing—I could be compelled to take Melody out on this quest.

I could be compelled, by her command, to put her at fucking risk.

I want to shelter her from dangers past and present, from hurts of all kinds, whether they are real or of the mind. She believes she saw Zeke die even if reality proved this memory false. Perhaps she overlaid one image with another in a confused state of terror.

My heart breaks as I pull her into my arms and offer my sweet sobbing omega whatever comfort I can. "Hush, love." She trembles, and I draw her closer, trying to meld her tiny body with mine as if to liberate her of this nightmare.

I cannot.

My purr doesn't calm her. I feel helpless, *impotent*, like I have failed her in letting this happen, although I have no idea how I might have anticipated or stopped it.

I draw her face from my chest and brush the tears from her cheeks with the pads of my thumbs. "You had another bad experience in the portal after you left Zeke's room." I hate pressing this, but my gut tells me it is important.

"It was the s-same," she sobs. "Exactly the same. I went to the same place, arriving on a forest path. I feel a distant rumble under the soles of my feet, parties approaching from ahead and behind. I scramble from the path, slipping and sliding down a slope, hiding behind a sturdy tree just in time as the two sides clash. They battle, and the sounds fill my ears. When I look, I find a confused jumble of soldiers, half in Sanctum uniform, and half that of the Blighten, but they're human warriors, and not orcs.... The fight is vicious. Their numbers are equal, and it could go either way... H-his helmet is knocked off. I'm no more than twenty paces away—there can be no mistake. He fights a soldier at the front as another cuts him down from behind."

She breaks down into tears. "Both occasions were identical. I don't know how that is possible, only what I saw."

My mind is moving fast and slow, racing in one direction, even as it wallows in another.

She is so tiny and precious in my arms. I would erase her past and pain in a heartbeat if I could. I wish she'd talked to me earlier. I want to scold her for not doing so. I might have gone blindly into this if I had not pushed the matter today. She might have slipped into the portal again, been snatched from me, and thrust into this terrible place alone. I need to comfort the omega in my arms—I also need to speak to Jacob for I believe this is important in ways a mere warrior cannot hope to understand.

"We need to discuss this with Winter and Jacob."

"I don't want to think about it," she sobs.

"We must," I press, even though doing so makes me feel like a bastard.

"Do you? Do you think it can be true? Did I go to some parallel universe? Like the ones the scholar talks about."

I know nothing of parallel universes and don't claim to understand this one well. I am a blunt tool who uses his fist and sword to follow instructions given by those of a better mind. "I don't know, Melody. Perhaps it is. Either way, this is too important for us to try to manage on our own. I also believe you should not go on the quest today. Not while you are upset. The patrols have already gone, but they will return, and when they do, we must share this with them too."

She heaves a breath and scrubs the tears from her cheeks. I can see she is relieved by my recommendation to abort the quest. "Okay."

We dress. She is shaking, and I must help her with this task. Her cheeks are pink, and her eyes are red-rimmed and ravaged by tears. I wear my armor and sword. Once we are ready, I take her hand in mine. Whether it is a manifestation of her mind, someplace between, or a parallel universe, it doesn't matter. I don't want her ever to go there again. If she steps into a portal, her hand will be in mine, and we shall go together.

We share a look. There is something amiss here, *danger* lurks both inside Sanctum and out. "Are you ready?"

I see the wary enter her eyes.

"No one will be cross with you. I will be right with you, whatever happens."

She nods. "I'm ready.

Her small hand squeezes over mine, and my throat becomes tight as I feel her trust in that simple touch.

❧

It is a short walk to Winter and Jacob's quarters, and early enough that I'm hoping one of them will likely be there.

We find Winter standing before her window—her smile drops as she takes in Melody's tear-stained cheeks and my grim expression.

"Goodness!"

"Apologies, my lady, for our visit so early, but we need to talk."

Winter's eyes dart from me to Melody, and her whole countenance softens. "Of course." She hastens to draw Melody into her arms for a hug before guiding her over to the ornate couch and encouraging her to sit. "Jacob is on his way."

As if on cue, the door bursts open, and Jacob strides in, doubtless sensing Winter's emotions through their pair bond.

"What has happened?" he demands.

Before we can answer, another knock sounds on the door.

"Do-don't open it," Melody says.

I suck in a sharp breath. My entire body coils as her fear surges through the bond. "What's there?"

She doesn't answer. I draw my sword. Jacob nods to me and likewise draws his sword before opening the door.

A messenger stands there. "I have news, my lord," he stammers, eyeballing our weapons.

Jacob takes a letter with a nod, checks the seal, and rips it open.

I sheath my sword, trying to swallow down the sickly, dizzy feeling that might come from Melody or me. I sway.

Jacob lifts his head. His face is ashen, and his throat works

259

like he is trying to get the words out. His eyes land on me and then shift to Melody.

I stumble forward as Melody admits a gut-wrenching sob. Falling to my knees before her, I drag her into my arms, rocking her as she makes a high, keening wail that I know will haunt me for the rest of my life. "Zeke!"

I try to swallow down the lump in my throat, and my chest works like bellows before I can find my purr. It does not help. Nothing can help.

My eyes meet Jacobs over Melody's head. He nods once. "Lost in a skirmish."

Another mournful cry escapes Melody, and I pull her closer, her pain wrapping around mine.

Somehow and someway, Melody had a premonition.

One we failed to act upon.

Chapter Twenty-Seven

Melody

I am lost in my grief. Inconsolable. I cling to Draven only to try and shove him away. "I don't want you. I want Zeke!"

My words are cruel as my grief lashes out like a wounded animal.

He doesn't give me space. Nor let me go. He holds me until the rage seeps out of me, and I fall to sobbing once again.

Last night, Zeke was inside me, bringing pleasure to my body. I still feel the faint ache of where he has been, can almost smell his scent, feel his hands, his caresses, and see his smile, but they are only memories now.

The door is opened and closed many times. People come in and out. First, Shiloh and Herald. I cling to the mother of my heart, and we both weep anew.

Then Aengus and Theron arrive, bloody and bruised. I don't need words to know they fought for their lives.

I hear voices from a great distance as I sit on Theron's lap, his purr a low rumble under my cheek as I cling to Aengus' hand as he sits beside us on Winter's couch. My sorrow is raw and malevolent and batters me until I am one big ball of tender and sore emotions.

Cecil is already here. The king and the portal scholar soon arrive, making the day room crowded. My head hurts as they all talk at once.

"I've never heard of this before," Winter is saying. She stands opposite the couch in her mate's arms.

I believe she addresses a point made by the portal scholar, but I have missed that part.

Why can they not all leave me to my grief? Why must they all be here when nothing they do or say can bring Zeke back?

"I have," the king says, turning to Draven. "How many times did she go there?"

I do not know the king well enough to judge his character, yet I still hate him because it was under his direction that Zeke went to his death.

"Twice," Draven replies. I fret a little, realizing they are discussing me.

"I don't believe this was a premonition," the scholar says.

"I saw him die." My voice quavers. I'm arguing a point that is pointless now.

"You did, my love," Winter says. "But from what we have just learned, you may have really been there."

I wipe the tears from my eyes, so puffy that I can barely open them. "What do you mean? I thought it was a premonition." Fresh tears well in my eyes. "Only I didn't tell anyone. And now Zeke is gone."

She comes and crouches down beside me, taking my hands in hers. "When you opened the portal, did it feel like the journey was longer than usual? Like when we travel to other worlds, but perhaps even longer than that."

It was several months ago, and my shattered mind is struggling, but now that she mentions it, it does seem like that was how it happened. "Yes," I say.

She glances back at the scholar, who nods. "We believe you may have passed through time," she says.

Her words astound me. I glance around the room finding all eyes on me.

"It's true some omegas have the gift, or curse, of foresight, but these manifest during dreams. Draven has explained that you saw this scene twice, and on both occasions, you had passed through the portal. You were not dreaming when you saw this."

Fresh tears spill down my cheeks as I try to make sense of his words. Could I really have passed through time? Does that mean I could... My hope surges. I really went there. I traveled forward in time and saw Zeke die. "If I went there once... I can go there again."

A stretched silence greets my words before Winter finally asks, "Is it possible? Could we?"

"A dangerous undertaking," the king says.

Draven's eyes search mine. I see the sorrow there. They are red-rimmed like mine, and his face seems to have aged. "Do you think you could open it again, Melody? Do you think you could guide us to that place?"

I scrub the tears from my cheeks. Could I? I cannot bear the thought of putting Draven in danger and losing another mate. Yet we are all echoes of ourselves while Zeke is gone. Where I have lost a mate. They have lost a brother.

"I would need to go with you."

"Not a fucking chance," Draven growls.

My lips tremble, but I hold my line. "We go together. I have been there twice. I know what happens and can guide you."

Aengus curses. "I don't like it either. But she has a point."

"Can this be done?" the king asks, turning to the portal scholar.

"As Melody has pointed out, she has been there twice, my liege. Has a clear reference point. That she was drawn to this event suggests it was for this very purpose. All this aside, it assuredly carries risks."

"If there is a chance, I will take it," Draven says.

The king, after a long pause, concedes.

And out of hopelessness comes hope.

My tears dry up, and a nervous tension settles in the pit of my stomach. I want to go immediately. Under the king's command, caution dictates that we plan.

Painful though it is, I must go over the details time and time again, all the while clinging to the burgeoning hope that I will see Zeke again but this time it will not be to watch him die.

A team is assembled. Draven, Theron, Aengus, and Jacob will be accompanied by Jacob's elite forces. There will be little time once we arrive, so everything hangs on us assembling swiftly once we exit the portal.

In the midst of these preparations, the door opens, and a newcomer arrives. He wears a fine silk jacket covered in intricate gold needlework and has cold, blue eyes and strange, sinuous grace. His face is compelling and ageless, and it is hard to look away.

"He is one of the Chosen," Winter offers quietly for my ears only. "No one knows their names, but I long ago nicknamed him Blue. Your ability has drawn attention. It would seem his endorsement is required."

I scarcely breathe as I watch him converse with the king. Around the table, the warriors have likewise fallen silent.

Blue's steady gaze briefly touches me. He nods to the king before approaching me.

Both Winter and Shiloh, who stand at my side, bow deeply. I do not.

His thin lips curl up the tiniest amount. This close, I can see his eyes are the palest shade of winter blue.

"You have been given a great gift, young fairy who hides her wings. Know that you are seen by us and by our enemies. You will save your warrior, but it will come at a cost."

"I will pay any price," I say boldly.

Winter's gasp suggests I am treading a fine line.

Blue only smiles. "I foresee many quests ahead, young fairy, with your four warriors at your side."

With those parting words, he turns and takes his leave.

"You have wings," the king says, unnecessarily, as the door shuts again.

I nod.

"Are there any more surprises we should know about?"

"No."

He's looking at me like he's trying to work out where they are.

"They shrink," Draven offers dryly. His smile is fleeting. "We got quite a surprise when we unwrapped her for the first time."

His words feel natural, like those he might offer if Zeke were still here. They make me want to believe that we will save Zeke, steer our lives to a different path, one free of this terrible pain. However, there is a great deal of uncertainty between then and now.

I sway a little on my feet.

"Time to rest, love," Shiloh says.

Winter shows me to her bedroom. "I expect they shall be in discussions for some time," she says, setting a lamp low beside the bed before drawing the heavy drapes across the window.

"I should go to my room," I mumble.

"Nonsense," Winter says as Shiloh helps me out of my shoes and gown. "Our mates are busy. Goddess willing, Zeke will be with you again. If they need you, I will fetch you straight away."

She hugs me, and I feel all her love in that simple touch. It nearly has me weeping again but I blink back all but a few stray tears.

"There." She brushes them from my cheeks. "The best thing you can do for Zeke is rest, so that you are ready when they call you."

"You're exhausted, love," Shiloh adds. "Just take a few moments. I will sit here with you."

I tell myself I won't sleep, but I must do, for the next thing I know is that I'm being lifted into strong arms. Roused from my slumber, but still disorientated, I recognize that it is Aengus who has me. My eyes crack open even as I seek to linger in sleep. For a brief moment, the world is normal, and then memory floods back, and I burst into fresh tears.

He purrs. "Be at ease, Melody. We shall get Zeke back. But first, we all need to rest."

He carries me the short distance back to our quarters, with Theron and Draven at our side. Once inside, they strip me and release the binding around my wings. Then we settle together on the vast bed, missing one vital presence.

I dream fitfully of Zeke, happy memories all jumbled up with that dreadful moment when I saw him fall.

I awake with a start, the violence of my movement rousing my mates.

I awake to a revelation.

"I have just realized how we can do this safely."

"Go on," Draven says.

Theron suddenly chuckles—he catches on to what I am thinking.

"What?" Aengus demands.

"We need to call another meeting," I say. "Right now. I do not want to delay another moment. It's time to bring Zeke back."

Chapter Twenty-Eight

Draven

It has been the longest morning of my life. After Melody roused us, we called another meeting, and swift consensus followed.

Now, the waiting is over as warriors gather in the great vaulted portal chamber, dressed for war with sturdy leather armor, weapons sharp and ready.

Since we lost Zeke, I've been trying to be strong, yet feeling broken inside, not only for myself but also for my mate, my brothers, and my parents.

Discovering that Melody can portal through time has been quite the revelation. It gave us hope when we had none. Now, also thanks to Melody, we have more than hope, although there is still danger here.

It's not until you lose someone that you understand the magnitude of the hole they leave behind. Zeke will always be our runt, the youngest who struggled the most to become a warrior. The one who fucking fought with grit and blood and heart to claim his rank and his mate... only to have his life snatched away.

What we attempt to do today is outside the bounds of reality... We are about to travel back in time.

The warriors who line the circular wall do not know the details of what will transpire, only that they must be ready. That we travel through time will not remain a secret long. I wish I could erase the dangers Melody's capability represents, but all I can do is dedicate my life to keeping her safe. I can admit to being unnerved. Yet I can hold my fears in check when Melody has done it twice, witnessing a man she loves die in the most brutal and horrifying way.

I look down to my right, where Melody stands and, as though she senses my study, her eyes lift to meet mine. She wears functional leathers with her red-gold hair in a long plait over her shoulder. She is beautiful in anything and nothing, but the coarse attire contrasts against her pretty face... and the stunning wings she chooses not to hide anymore. I swear everyone in the portal chamber is now staring at her—some with admiration, some with longing, some with disbelief.

Her smile is small and too brief—I hate that her eyes are puffy and her face has been ravaged by tears. I pray her joy will return before this day is done.

Jacob stands before us, Theron and Aengus at his side. He turns to Melody. "Are you ready?"

"I am," she says.

"Seal the doors," Jacob calls, and the grand double doors of the portal chamber close with a *boom* leaving us ensconced in darkness save for the torches that line the walls.

I take Melody's hand in mine—she begins the chant. The air crackles, and the portal sparks to life, a black, star-filled ocean waiting to take us through the fabric of time.

I put my trust in the omega at my side.

Then Jacob, Theron, and Aengus turn to face the portal. Weapons are drawn, and we step forward as one into its oily embrace.

❧

Sharp, cold air greets us, our breath making vapor clouds. We are on a path, a snowy forest to either side. Beneath the soles of my feet, I feel the vibrations of the yet-unheard rumble of approaching horses' hooves.

"We are here," she says, a tremble in her voice.

Collectively, we move from the path and into the cover of the trees. Jacob and Aengus to one side. I lead Theron and Melody to the other.

My heart rate elevates as adrenaline courses through my body, and I will my senses to remain open and alert. The rumble manifests into the rhythmic drum of hooves as friend and foe draw nearer to us until they finally come into view.

"Now!"

She chants, lips moving fast and urgent, eyes closed, and brows knitted in concentration.

The drum rises to a roar. I can hear the clank of weapons and horse tack and then the battle horn.

A shimmering portal pops into place right before the charging Blighten patrol.

They spill into it, horses screaming as they try to pull up.

Three do.

Our patrol, a greater distance from the portal, turn their horses away from it.

The portal winks out.

"Zeke!"

At Melody's scream, he wheels his horse back around.

"Fuck!" I mutter. Theron manages to snag her around the waist before she can throw herself into the path of danger.

"Take them prisoner!" Jacob calls as he and Aengus charge into the melee on the path. Swords clash, horses rear and men battle in a short, ugly fight. The Blighten scum are torn from their steeds and subdued with fists until they can be bound.

"What the fuck is happening?" Zeke's patrol leader demands as, breath heaving, he wrestles a Blighten warrior to his belly.

Theron releases Melody and she charges at Zeke before he has fully dismounted his horse—the beast side steps, and Zeke staggers to right himself as our sweet omega launches into his arms where she peppers him with kisses.

Her wings beat wildly, sending golden dust scattering across the snow. The sight brings a momentary collective still-ness to the clearing.

"It is a long story," Jacob offers, breaking the silence while grinning from ear to ear—we are all fucking grinning. "And one better discussed back inside the safety of Sanctum. Melody, it's time to take us home."

Zeke

It is a confronting moment to be told that you have died. That your family and loved ones grieved for you. And even more confounding to discover that then a miracle happened, and a different path opened up.

Melody won't stop clinging to me. Her legs are wrapped around my waist, and her arms are around my neck. She has her nose buried against the side of my throat, her small teeth nipping the flesh and refusing to let go.

I don't mind. I'm shaken, truth be told.

We are all fucking shaken. We rode into an ambush that, but for Melody, would have left half of us dead.

I fucking hate that she had to deal with this terrible burden alone. Watching me die—twice—being subjected to a living nightmare, only to find out it was real. And not only for Melody to discover this, but my brothers, and Shiloh and Herald.

Then she saved me.

There was a debrief with the king before I was given leave to reunite with Shiloh and Herald, the mother and father of my heart.

After that, we return to our quarters, where we have the privacy to come to terms with what happened. An electric kind of tension envelops us all. Stress is etched into the lines of my brothers' faces and manifests in the ways Melody still clings to me, nestling on my lap in the day room of our quarters.

"When did you decide to show your wings?" I ask.

"I met one of the Chosen," she says. "He told me it was time."

I chuckle. "Well, it's hard to refuse a Chosen. I'm glad that you are finally showing yourself, Melody."

"She was already a target," Draven says solemnly. "This will make her more of one."

"I don't care," she says.

"Well, I fucking do care," I say. "I hate that you had to do this for me. But I swear if I'd have been at the Goddess's side, I would have had words with her and demanded she send me back to you."

"That is a very bold statement," she says, only there is a smile in her voice.

"It's true," I say, cupping her face. I kiss her—a gentle kiss before I tuck her head against my chest.

We are all exhausted. Yet I feel the toll it has taken upon them in ways more than words courtesy of the bond.

Melody

We retire to the nest, where we have space and time to process all that has happened, how close we came to losing Zeke, and the relief now that he is back.

But I am restless, moving between my mates for cuddles, needing to touch them all, and frustrated when it is near impossible with four of them.

Finally, with a growl, Draven pins me between him and Zeke, closes his teeth over the claiming mark, and bites down as he purrs.

It creates a strange, compelling heaviness, and I submit to sleep.

Chapter Twenty-Nine

Draven

Aknock sounds on the door early the next morning—I'm surprised we have been given this much time. It is a message from Jacob looking for me.

Leaving Aengus and Zeke to care for Melody, Theron and I report to the summons, joining Jacob in the lower chambers of Sanctum.

The dark stone cells offer an ambiance of foreboding. Here, the beaten and bloody Blighten prisoners are chained against the walls of a long narrow room. Fresh dark stains cover the floor—blood. A drainage trough runs through the middle to take the excess away.

It is a room designed for torture.

I walk the length, eyeing each man, wondering which one of them dealt the killing blow to Zeke in that other iteration of the game we call life. We will never know, and I'm not asking Melody to relive the nightmare to identify the bastard.

It doesn't matter now.

They all deserve to die slowly... once we have our answers.

"What have you found?" I bring my inspection to a halt on reaching Jacob and Theron.

"Very little yet." Jacob's smile is without humor. "But the Chosen's questioners will be arriving soon, and they always get their answers."

୫

Melody

We snuggle in the nest after Draven and Theron leave until I force myself to rise at the risk of spending all day there. The wound of almost losing Zeke is sore. It will take time for me to put events into perspective.

Still, it has made me realize how precious life is, how joy can be snatched away from you, and how quickly everything can change.

I am young, and so are my mates, but my decision has been made where the binding is concerned. Whether life is measured in human or fairy years, I see now how precious and fragile it is. I don't want to spend more of it with this leash between us.

We eat a late breakfast in the day room, where Aengus insists I sit on his lap so he can feed me from his hand.

"Is that a barbarian thing?" Zeke asks, gesturing toward us. He cannot take his eyes off us and barely touches his food the whole time.

I smile, thinking that it will soon be an all-my-alphas thing.

"What the fuck is wrong with you even to ask?" Aengus mutters, reaching for a dried apricot and offering it to me. He cups my breast as I chew, brushing his thumb across the stiff peak he has already roused with his attention. "Why would I not feed her? Why would I let her sit in a chair when I prefer her to be on my lap where I can pet her at my leisure while she eats?"

Zeke's throat works before he can drag his gaze back to his plate. Aengus kisses me while I am still chewing and selects a grape next.

"Maybe I should have her for a bit... while you have breakfast," Zeke offers gruffly.

"No need," Aengus replies easily. "I'm having fairy for breakfast."

I swallow the grape as Zeke spits tea across the table.

Aengus chuckles. "Don't overeat, runt. She has a filthy pussy, and there will be plenty to go around."

A knock on the door interrupts us—Celeste's alpha, Jonas, informs us his mistress requires our presence. A reminder that life goes on. The high omega has been present in my life since I arrived at Sanctum, mentoring me and influencing my training in consultation with the king. She will have reservations about my decision to revoke the binding, but that is none of her business.

I dress swiftly, wanting to get the meeting over with.

"I'll come with you," Zeke says. "Draven said one of us should be with you, at least for now, given what happened with the portal... and your wings."

"We'll both go," Aengus says.

He collects his sword, as does Zeke, and we follow Jonas to the lesser portal room, where Celeste has requested my presence. It's not unheard of for us to meet here, although reasonably rare.

"Nosy omega probably wants to grill you on your newfound time-hopping skills," Aengus mutters. "Don't let her persuade you to open a portal. She can await the king's approval."

I glance across at the stern alpha of my heart. "I sense you don't like her?"

"I've accompanied her on a few quests. She likes her power over warriors too much for my comfort." Aengus shudders. "I'd sooner gnaw my own arm off than take her blood."

A hiss escapes my lips, and I come to a stop. "You have rutted her?" The white-hot rage that consumes me is near enough to render me blind. I am no fool. I know my mates have been with other omegas before me, yet I feel betrayed that they might have shared such intimacy with Celeste.

Jonas has come to a stop a small distance ahead, where he folds his arms and looks impatient.

Aengus goes to touch me. I bat his hand away. He growls and lifts me, pinning me against the nearby stone wall with his big body between my spread legs. My wings beat uselessly against the stone, sending a shower of dust in my agitation.

"Unhand me, barbarian!"

Zeke chuckles. Oh, he finds this funny, does he? I will have words with him just as soon as Aengus puts me down.

"I'm a barbarian now, am I?" There is amusement in Aengus' voice, and I thrash helplessly in his hold. "Foolish omega. I have not rutted her. I took the blood from her wrist. Were you not listening to the bit about me preferring to gnaw my own arm off?"

I *was* listening, but the words did not sink in. I peep at him under my lashes. The beast is grinning. I had forgotten alphas enjoy possessiveness in a mate. He will probably be boasting to the others later about my little show.

He lowers me to the ground slowly, still grinning, and then takes my hand in his. Zeke takes the other one, and they hold them all the way to the lesser portal room. I don't mind it. I find it a comfort. It also makes me all squirmy inside, remembering how they missed their breakfast. I believe it is my duty to make it up to them later.

We arrive at the lesser portal room while I am still lost in happy thoughts. With one look at Celeste's frosty expression, my joy disappears—Jonas takes up a position beside his mistress.

"You may leave," she says to Aengus and Zeke. "I expect to be here most of the day. I'll send Jonas for you when we're done."

My heart sinks at the mention of the 'all day' part.

Aengus folds his arms and takes up a position beside the door. Zeke joins him. "Draven ordered one of us to remain with her."

"And you always do what Draven says over an imperial," Celeste snaps.

Aengus shrugs. "We are mated. He is first alpha, so yes."

I bite back a smile at his boldness, even though he will likely be bored witless long before Celeste is done with me. He will end up as joyless as Jonas.

"So be it," Celeste says. "One of you may remain."

"I'll go let Draven know," Zeke says and, winking at me, shows himself out of the room.

"You were reckless, risking yourself by going back to save Zeke," Celeste says coolly as the door closes. "Did your other mates persuade you to do this?"

Aengus growls lowly.

"I—no. Why would I not save him if I could? No one persuaded me. I wanted to."

"I believe it's time you strengthened the binding." Her narrowed eyes rest on Aengus.

I don't turn to look at him, but I can feel vexation through the bond.

"I'm not going to do that," I say. I've already decided to

remove it. Her words only make me want to double down on that decision. I think about telling her but decide that she will find out soon enough, assuming the king agrees.

She huffs out a breath. "Stupid child."

Aengus growls again, but Celeste barely spares a glance toward him as, to my confusion, she takes the portal keystone from around her neck and says the words of calling.

The portal springs to life, a shimmering black surface that sparks with light.

"You have so much potential but no matter; better you serve a sympathetic cause than the wrong one."

I'm slow to react, not realizing her intent until she fists my arm.

Aengus snarls and surges forward, drawing his sword.

"Stand down, warrior!" Her words crack like a whip. I feel them reverberate through the binding, and the leash tightens like a noose around my mate's neck. Aengus crashes to his knees with a roar.

"Don't think your other mates will sense you from here," Celeste says, lips curling in a sneer. "The chamber is muted. It would take something far more extreme."

"No!" I plant my feet, trying to peel her cruel fingers away. My mind whirls as the magnitude of her betrayal dawns. "It was you, wasn't it? You tried to have me taken that day the orcs attacked and when Theron was nearly killed. Then again, with Zeke!"

Jonas closes behind me, forcing a strap between my teeth. Only now does it dawn on me that I could have tried to close the portal. Aengus' growl echoes off the walls of the small chamber as he fights and rails against Celeste's command, straining to rise. Jonas tosses me to the floor and drags my arms behind my back, quickly binding my wrists before dragging me to my feet.

Celeste smiles.

The portal looms.

I know not what is on the other side, only that it represents my doom, perhaps Aengus' too.

Jonas hands me off to Celeste before taking another rope from his pocket and stalking to Aengus.... Aengus who snarls and turns the sword on himself.

I scream behind my gag as the sharp blade plunges into his stomach.

His pain savages me through the bond—it might as well be my own.

"I'm sorry," Aengus pushes past gritted teeth, his face turning a sickly shade of gray. "It was the only way."

They are the last words I hear as my eyes roll into the back of my head, and I collapse toward the ground.

Aengus

The room is muted as all portal chambers are, layers of stone that shield Sanctum from the power. If I want to make a connection with Draven, Theron, and Zeke, for them to feel my terror at what Celeste intends to do, I need to take drastic steps. The binding holds firm. I could no more raise my hand toward the bitch fairy than I could hurt the sweet omega who claims my heart.

Only I have to make an impossible choice—I have to hurt Melody if I hope to save her life.

I cannot strike out at my adversaries, but I can strike at myself.

The pain explodes through my gut. I feel the echo of it slam through the ether as it hits Melody and then my brothers.

They are coming.

As I watch Melody's eyes roll back and she crashes to the stone floor in a dead faint, I pray they will be fast enough.

Celeste was right when she said the binding should be strengthened. It's already weakening as the golden thread Melody formed with her love chips at the leash.

I cannot harm Celeste. In my pain-addled state, I suffer no such restraint toward the bastard alpha who does her bidding. Yanking the blade from my guts, I slam my hand over the wound and stab upward into the alpha who comes for me. His eyes go wide. I'm one-handed and maddened by pain, so I dig deep to twist the blade, thinking about what will happen to Melody if I don't do this. Thinking about Draven, Theron, and Zeke, rushing here even now. I just need to slow him down and give them a chance. Celeste is dragging Melody to the portal, but she has fainted dead away, and it is not an easy task.

A fist comes for my face, one I cannot hope to evade. I crash to my side, head cracking against the stone floor, blinking the sparking dots away, trying to rise only for my feet to slip in blood pooling across the floor.

My vision swims in and out of darkness. Blood turns my hand slick where it presses to the wound in my gut.

Jonas stumbles forward, lurches, and rights himself again.

I cannot let him get to Melody. If she's taken through the portal, she will be lost. The wound is of little consequence now in the face of this threat. I have only one purpose: to give Melody and my brothers more time. Heaving myself to my knees, I throw myself at Jonas' feet, knocking him to the ground.

Then the door behind me bursts open just as the blackness comes for me.

§⁂

Draven

I race along the corridors with Theron, Zeke, and Jacob at my side toward the source of pain. I brace myself, not knowing what lies ahead, only that it will be bad. Sweat pops across the surface of my skin—the echo of the pain through the bond is near debilitating.

Aengus, what have you done?

As our race brings us to the lesser portal room, my mind clears on my purpose.

I slam through the door.

It takes the barest moment to take in the scene. Celeste drags Melody's limp body toward the portal that sparks with life. Aengus appears unconscious as he weighs down Jonas's feet.

Blood is everywhere, smearing the floor around the two warriors and forming a pool.

Jonas grunts as he tries to rise, kicking Aengus to gain freedom.

Theron and Zeke roar, charging Celeste.

I'm on Jonas. My sword slashes down as I put all my force behind it. His arm raises too slowly. My blade severs his fingers and cleaves into his throat.

On the other side of the room, Theron slams into Celeste, knocking her away from Melody.

Zeke is on Melody, but I sense only quiet from her side of the bond, unconscious—her life is not under threat.

For once, Aengus, the giant barbarian who seems the epitome of indestructible, demands my focus.

He lives. But as I gently roll him over, I see his wound.

"Fuck!" I press my palm down over the gash, blood pooling around my fingers.

He must have done this to call us when Celeste, the traitor, sought to drag Melody into the portal. With the binding in place, Aengus was defenseless, even to protect his mate.

I push down the sorrow and focus on the man who is my brother in all ways that matter, whom I have fought with so often, but for whom I have always held the deepest respect. It is not an easy thing to take a blade upon yourself. It takes courage and strength of will to overcome deep-rooted human instincts.

He did this for Melody.

He did this to give us time.

Warriors and fairies crowd into the room around us. The portal winks out.

Winter drops to our side, her wrist already sliced through and dripping blood as she holds it over Aengus' mouth. Another omega kneels beside me, removing my hand from the wound and tearing clothing away so she can get to the gash. She takes the tiny healer dagger from a sheath at her hip and slices through her wrist before holding it over his wound.

Come back to us, Aengus. Open your eyes and take the blood. Come back. Melody needs you. We all need you.

I sense the moment Melody rouses. "Aengus!"

Her cry pierces my heart.

It is broken.

It is devastation.

It is everything I feel.

Theron snags her around the waist lest she interferes.

Come back to us, Aengus. Come back to us.

He swallows, and it is the sweetest sound I've heard.

Chapter Thirty

Draven

It has been a week, and Aengus has made a full recovery. He is indeed a tough bastard.

He saved Melody's life.

Today, we will learn more about why he needed to.

Jacob nods his head in the direction of the closed door. "In here."

Aengus and I follow him inside.

Celeste hangs in chains, filthy and naked, her body littered with cuts and crusted blood. My fist clenches. I've never harmed a woman, but I must battle the urge to take her by the throat and squeeze until life leaves her eyes.

She spits on the floor at Aengus' feet and rattles the chains holding her wrists.

His snarl is feral, and his rage for her batters the bond.

"Her binding has been stripped," Aengus says, drawing my attention to the strange lightness in her presence even as my unease cranks up to the max.

Jacob nods. "The king stripped her of the binding before the Chosen oversaw her questioning."

I shudder. The Chosen's questioners are as brutal as they are efficient. No one holds out against them for long.

"There have been murmurs of discontent since Winter was released from the binding. It has worsened since a few mated couples similarly chose to revoke the curse."

"That is what this is about? Resistance to change?" I cannot keep the disgust from my voice.

Celeste curls her lips back to bare her teeth. Making her fingers into claws, she lunges at Jacob. "You started this. You broke her!"

The fight abandons her as swiftly as it arrived, and she falls limp against the chains.

"A fairy of high standing with centuries of life and the ear of the king, and she throws it away for what—bitterness that a few have chosen to free themselves from the binding?" Aengus' calm exterior does not reflect the maelstrom lashing our bond. "She cannot be working alone."

"Unlikely," Jacob says. His eyes turn hard as they rest on the pitiful woman. "The questioners will be back. The king will turn his focus to those most vocal in discontent, although it does not follow that they are treasonous simply because they hold different views. Celeste was in contact with another kingdom with ties to the Blighten. The full extent of their collaboration is yet to be uncovered. The questioners will wring what they can from her over the coming months and years. I foresee she will soon lose her defiance and be praying for death."

"Good," Aengus said. "A quick death is too good for the bitch. Her warrior?"

"To be hung," Jacob confirms.

Aengus nods. "I have seen enough."

We leave the cells and walk up to the more civilized levels of Sanctum. Only I know now that they are not so civilized, and I wonder what other threats lurk.

"What will happen now?" I ask as we come to the place where we will go our separate ways.

"You will need to keep a close watch on Melody," Jacob says. "Her powers are considerable. Even without us discovering Celeste's plot, your mate was bound to be the subject of envy and fear. More so as her potential is revealed."

"The king means to use her," Aengus growls.

"The king means to use us all," Jacob says honestly. "Don't delude yourself otherwise. You have claimed her and been gifted the right to protect her. Be grateful you get that much."

Chapter Thirty-One

Melody

Aweek has passed since I traveled through time to save Zeke. The very next day, Celeste tried to kidnap me through the portal. The horror of what happened to Aengus, my brave barbarian, is still fresh in my mind. It is a small consolation that he received blood from two of the highest imperials and recovered swiftly.

I still wish it were my blood that had healed him.

While I am grateful to Winter, I want to scratch out the eyes of the other omega, even though I am grateful to her too.

Jealousy is not a rational beast. I have made Aengus take my blood frequently ever since, and this despite him walking around in glowing health.

He only chuckles at my possessive displays. As do all my mates who purr approvingly when I bite or mark them and insist they take my blood.

It's fair to say that everything has changed for all of us.

I no longer attend the portal lore lessons with the other

young imperial omegas. I still meet with the portal scholar, only now I work researching forgotten tomes for clues on this lost skill.

In Sanctum, where change is slow, I have unwittingly achieved a state of notoriety due to those things that mark me as different: my wings, taking four mates, and my ability to bend space and time.

Celeste's betrayal runs deep, and I must live with the fresh scars from what she tried to do.

It is amidst this backdrop, and against Winter's advice to let the dust settle, that I seek an audience with the king.

His royal blue tunic is embroidered in gold stitching. He cuts an imposing figure as he rises to greet me.

"Let us take a seat." With my hand over his arm, he walks me to an inlaid mahogany table before the window, where he offers me a seat.

He sits opposite, his eyes shifting to my wings. There is a little dust escaping, and I quickly call it back.

"Mesmerizing," he says. "Do they shed often?"

I blush. They shed more often when I'm aroused, although there is always a little fallout unless I'm perfectly still. "A little, my liege. I can gather it so that it does not make a mess."

His smile is predatory. It reminds me he is a warrior with magical blood and only slightly below the Chosen.

"Don't mind it," he says. "Sanctum will grow used to a little gold dust in a century or two."

Is he joking? I offer a weak smile.

He moves on without any preamble. "You wish the binding to be removed."

I gasp. Having lamented how to broach the subject for many hours, it is a little anticlimactic when he anticipates my request. "Did Winter tell you?"

He shakes his head and smiles—it is less predatory this time. "Call it intuition."

"Will you?" I want to swallow my tongue for my outburst, which lacks formal address—at least he does not appear offended.

He leans back in his chair, head tilted to the side, eyes deeply assessing to the point of unnerving. "If your mates agree."

"Why wouldn't they?"

"Have you asked them?"

"Well, no..." I trail off, feeling somewhat foolish for missing this step. "I thought you might—you know—remove it, and then I could surprise them."

He throws his head back and laughs.

I tell myself this is a good sign, but I'm not entirely sure.

"And where are your mates now?"

"They are with Jacob. Zeke left to join them after escorting me here."

"Elwund." I blink in confusion when a servant materializes out of a shadowy corner and makes a deep, formal bow. "Collect Melody's mates and bring them here."

The servant bows again and hastens to do the king's bidding.

This is not quite how I expected things to go, and I'm suddenly very nervous. The king stares at me. I find avid interest in the intricate inlay of his tabletop.

"How is your research going?"

"Well, my liege. It's going really well."

Goodness, this is awkward. I'm so relieved when the door opens to admit my mates that I leap from the seat and nearly knock it over. My heart is racing a mile a minute. I feel strangely guilty. Worse, their mere presence has a predictable effect, and my wings start shedding dust quicker than I can gather it up.

"I—um."

Draven frowns. Zeke smirks. Aengus and Theron just look confused.

The king rises slowly, indicating I should go and join my mates. As I reach them, I see questions, but I slip between Zeke and Theron and wait for the king to speak.

"Melody has something to ask you," the king says.

It would appear the king has a questionable sense of humor, the wicked beast!

"Melody?" Draven asks.

A small growl escapes me, and my head snaps around. "I want to remove the binding." The words tumble out—I am not winning any awards for finesse today.

"Why did you not mention this?" Draven asks, his frown deepening.

When we are in our quarters, and I am nestled in his arms, I can convince myself that he is not a veritable giant with a menacing air that makes me a little nervous even as it makes me all fluttery with love inside. "I wanted to surprise you."

"Well," Aengus mutters. "That would have been quite a surprise. Also, we need to be present."

"Oh." I had not realized this.

"Do you know what you are asking for, Melody?" Draven asks, coming to stand before me and taking my hand in his, which is very distracting, and I blush. "Are you sure you wish to do this now? That you would not rather wait a little while? It will fade over time, either way."

My eyes meet his, then shift to each of my mates before returning to Draven. "I don't think any omega can understand how it feels to lift the binding until it is done. Celeste tried to coach me to have it strengthened. Winter only said that it was balanced before the binding came, and she felt relief when it was gone again."

"I believe Winter speaks true. I also know that you are young, and Celeste's actions might have left scars," Draven says.

I'm confused that he appears to be persuading me to keep it. "Do you not wish me to remove the binding?"

He brings my small hand to his lips. "Every warrior under the control of the binding dreams of its removal. I would love the binding to be gone, to be aware of you fully, but not at the cost of your peace of mind. Not after everything you endured so short a time ago. Not unless you're certain beyond doubt. Once it has been removed, there is no going back."

"Your words serve only to make me more certain," I say honestly, and I love how his face softens, and his eyes spark with desire and love. "I love and trust you all. I truly have no doubts."

Draven

I move aside.

The king begins to speak.

From the very first word, I feel a quickening in the air. It reaches out like tendrils of awareness and crawls under my skin, seeking, finding, and unraveling a long-buried part of me and rousing it to awareness.

The words fall like delicate hooks that sink deep and tug the leash wrapped around my throat.

I breathe: it feels like the first true breath I have ever taken.

Balance. There should be a balance between alphas and omegas. It is time that it was restored.

The words float towards me, wrapping me in yet more hooks that gently untether me from the binding. My skin breaks out in goosebumps. I hear Melody gasp. She is closest to Theron and leans on him for support. I sense even if we wished to stop this now, it is already too late.

Her distressed whimper is a catalyst for action. I move to comfort her, my hand settling on the back of her neck, finding her skin hot and clammy. We crowd around her as the melodic words of unbinding abruptly cease.

The hooks, deeply embedded, tear the last of a leash away.

I growl, my chest heaves—

Gone. The binding, the terrible pressure, the sense of oppression. My system floods with fresh awareness bathing my mind in blinding light. I have lived an echo of my life, been kept in servitude, but now I am free.

We are unbound. So too, is Melody.

Her scent slams into me.

My body reacts instantly, coiling tight, arousal sharp and insistent. Gods, has she always scented this good?

Instinctively I know she will taste even better in the hot, slick place between her thighs. I swallow. My fingers stroke the back of her neck in a caress. My teeth ache. I want to bite her. I want to spread her thighs and feast... and I will.

She moans, sweet and needy, finally ours in the way she was always meant to be.

Ours to be claimed.

Ours to dominate, in the way an omega needs.

"Please!" She reaches out blindly, raking at the nearest male, tearing streaks of red into Zeke's throat.

His hiss shifts to an approving purr.

"If I might encourage you," the king says, "to adjourn to your quarters."

"Hot," Melody says, clinging to Theron. "Please, I'm so hot."

My ears ring. A prickling awareness settles at the base of my skull as I understand what is transpiring.

Heat. Our sweet omega, our mate, is going into heat.

҈

Melody

The shock as the binding is released shoots arousal straight to my core. Scents bombard me, complex, unique, one for each of my mates. I have never experienced their full potency before, and they overwhelm my awakened system and set my body adrift at sea.

I thought the binding only worked one way, compelling an alpha to obey omega commands.

Now I see it works on omegas, too, shielding us from the full potency of an alpha.

Heat bathes my skin, and blood pounds through the veins at my throat. I am flushing not only with arousal but blood. A womb-deep contraction tears a cry from my lips. My legs lose their ability to support me, and I would surely collapse but for the strong arms that sweep me up.

As though they pass at a distance, I'm aware of sconces flickering on the stone walls, the opening and closing of doors, the familiar scent of my nest, and my frustration at the bothersome clothes in the way of the skin-to-skin contact I crave.

"Strip her," Draven barks.

They grunt and growl over their prize, although their touch is surprisingly gentle as they divest me of my dress and undergarments.

The binding is gone. They are free. They can do with me

whatever they wish, and I cannot compel them to stop. That right is no longer mine.

But there is no fear here as I accept my place and submit. There is only joyful recognition that these are my mates, for how could I ever fear them when they gift me so much love? In the privacy of our room, in the nest which I have made, it is not only they who are free. I too am burdenless now, *unfettered,* unworried.

They will take good care of me.

They will rut me through my heat.

I am still Melody, their Melody, but now, I am unbound.

๛

Aengus

Theron and Zeke are being too fucking gentle with her as they divest Melody of her clothes, her wings beating slowly and scattering her fairy dust.

But I don't miss the way her body arches... how she kicks out her feet, making cute little angry noises as though what they're doing is not entirely to her taste.

The binding is gone, and in its place is a chaotic bombardment of rushing senses and clamoring instincts. I sway a little as comprehension dawns.

I kick off my boots and yank my shirt over my head. "She needs it rough."

"She has been through a lot," Draven says from where he stands at my side, sounding calmer than any alpha has the right to be, given there is an omega in heat close enough to touch.

Both of us stare down at the nest. On her side, she faces Zeke, who kisses her, fingers already making sticky noises between her thighs, doubtless playing with her slick gland.

Theron is behind her, a little hampered by her wings, although he is doing an admirable job of working around them, and sliding his hand over her hip begins to thrust his fingers erratically beside Zeke.

"Oh!"

"She likes that," Draven says thickly.

"She will like it rough more."

We share a look. I'm closer to my animal side than he is, and perhaps that gives me an edge in this, one that dictates I should lead here. He will always be first alpha, even if I am a big bastard. "I need you to ensure I don't go too far."

"Fuck!" He swipes a hand through his hair. "I am fucking close to my rut. I don't know how much control I will have once I get my dick in her."

"More than me," I say dryly.

His chuckle is dark. We know what's about to go down. She's sinking into heat. Zeke and Theron are thrusting their cocks erratically against her as Melody grows ever more restless.

We will all be too far gone soon. Draven has the mettle above and beyond the rest of us. He will keep us in line —even me.

My cock is hard to the point of pain and being strangled behind my pants, the knot aching for the need for somewhere to plug. "We know what she needs. She will not settle until she is mastered. Until she has been forced to submit."

Draven nods. "I trust you, Aengus. I know we go at one another. But that is between us. I don't believe you will need me to hold you back, but know that if you do, I shall."

"That is all I fucking need." I kick off my pants. "Out of the way, runts." I growl to back up my command as I plant my knee on the bed.

Zeke's head pops up first. He takes one look at me and rolls away. Theron is a bit slower but soon rouses to what's going on when I take him by the throat. My growl is aggressive. He growls right back.

"Theron!" Draven's bark snaps the younger alpha's head around.

Melody is cooing with interest at our aggressions, her thighs rubbing together. She may be an imperial omega, but here she is no more or less than an omega in heat.

Theron grunts and rolls away. "I'm not a fucking runt."

I smirk. It fades as I turn back to Melody. She peeks up at me through lidded eyes as she nips coquettishly on her lower lip.

"Hands and knees, brat."

She shakes her head. My grin is all teeth as I flip her into position.

"Oh!" A breathy gasp is accompanied by her thrusting her hips back... but as I line my cock up, she dips her hips out of the way.

"Do you not want my cock anymore?" I taunt.

She huffs and wriggles her ass at me again; her giggle is pure joy.

"Never mind," I say more calmly than I feel. "If I come over you, it will satisfy me just as well."

Her screech is predictable. My cock spits an enthusiastic blob of pre-cum on the nest when she rakes her nails down my arm. "You will not waste your seed!"

I hear somebody chuckle. It might be Zeke. He's a deviant bastard, and this is right up his street.

"Present," I bark. "Present your pussy for ravishment. Or know that the four of us will leave you to simmer a bit until you can be better behaved."

She twists to glare at me, and I see the conflict inside her.

She very much wants to submit, but she also wants me to make her, to show her I am a worthy male.

Leaning down, I grab a fistful of her red-gold hair and tug. "Do you want to play a game?" I growl beside her ear.

Her breath shifts to a pant. She nods her head. "Yes."

"And what game do you want to play?"

"I want... I need.... I need to be forced."

"What happens if we are too rough and hurt our omega?"

"You won't," she says. "I trust you. But I will lose my mind if you do not give me more. And if... and if I should happen to want you to stop... well then, I will... say honey cake."

"What if you're too far gone to remember your words?"

"If I'm too far gone, then we both know I won't want you to stop. Please. I feel so empty. I want to be set free, to embrace my heat, and know you will be there to catch me."

What is a male to do in the face of this unwavering trust? I line my cock up with her dripping cunt and slam to the root.

She groans, and her pussy clamps over me like she never wants to let me go.

I take her by the hips and pound into her softness, deep hefts that make our flesh slap together as otherworldly pleasure sparks.

Melody

My body rocks as Aengus ruts me. Except he is no longer simply Aengus but a savage alpha who is giving me what I need.

My body climbs, soaring straight for that high. My breath stutters, and then everything locks up. I tip my head back and squeal.

But he is not done with me and keeps rutting me through the shattering climax. His knot swells as it slides over the entrance to my slick gland, and I pitch into those sweet, heavenly contractions again.

His teeth lock at my throat, and I moan as blood rushes, showing me how dangerously flushed I am. And there he holds me, a thick arm around my waist, his fingers petting my slippery clit as he pumps his cum deep into me and sucks down my blood.

My pussy squeezes, and I groan. The sensation of fullness is utterly sublime.

But I'm sinking into a feral headspace, one that makes me do reckless things. I dare to try to pull away from him. He tightens his hold, stirring another round of sweet spasms deep in my pussy.

I love this.

I love being trapped inside and out, his cum filling me until it leaks and drips to the nest. I wanted to be dominated, to be shown how it can be between us without the binding.

I love him, the alpha who fought to survive. Of all my mates, Aengus is the most complex. He rails against Draven, even though they are different sides of the same coin. His character is morally gray, and his heart troubled, but his flaws only make me love him more.

He rocks his hips, and my stuffed pussy clenches in the most arresting way. Heat bathes my body. The surface of my skin is damp with perspiration.

Breathe.

His teeth disengage, blood trickles down my chest and drips from my nipple onto the nest.

I throb.

They think that they know me.

But they don't understand my dark side.

They will.

I have tasted death and fear.

I have survived.

Their carnality does not scare me.

I crave it.

I want to be used.

No words are needed except one. "More."

His hips shift, and the knot slips out. He begins to thrust anew, and all the delicious sensations rise.

Soon he is pounding me into the nest.

In my mind, I see stars collide.

🐍

Theron

I have an out-of-body experience as Aengus takes Melody. I don't blink. I don't breathe anywhere near enough, and the lack of oxygen makes me dizzy.

Or maybe that is her unfiltered scent slamming into me.

I don't realize I've moved until I feel her hair under my fingers and her lips slam against mine. My hand shifts to her throat, my thumb sinking into her pulse point as we share a lusty kiss that is all nipping teeth and tongues. Her nails rake at me, trying to pull me closer.

I drag my mouth from hers and suck in air, taking in where I am, kneeling on the nest with her between Aengus and me. Getting inside her is imperative. I direct her legs to wrap around my waist. She has moved on to kissing up my neck, lighting a fire inside me. I line up my cock... only to find her plugged.

I snarl at Aengus over her shoulder. "You need to fucking share."

He growls back.

I don't care if he's bigger. I'm going to fuck him up if he doesn't fuck off.

"Aengus!"

His head swings around at Draven's bark.

"Fine," Aengus purrs. "There is plenty of room for two."

He shifts his hips back, and when he thrusts them forward again, Melody moans and clamps her teeth over my throat. The pain shoots straight to my cock. My hips jerk forward. There is nothing in my way this time, and my dick wedges a small way inside her hot, wet pussy.

I curse, and my eyes cross from the pleasure of Melody's too-tight cunt as she savages my throat.

Gods, I'm not going to last. With Aengus wedged deep in her ass, her pussy is crushing me, but her slick is copious, and my next thrust sees me seated deeper despite the constricted space. My hands clamp over her hips, trying to push her down as I thrust up.

She moans, her small teeth worrying my throat, claiming me. "Be our good girl, Melody. Try to relax for me. I'll have no choice but to take you roughly if you don't."

Her pussy has a lock on me, and her arms and legs wrap around me tighter as if to drive me deeper.

"What the fuck are you waiting for?" Aengus grunts. "The brat is greedy for it. It's not like she needs further lubrication. Fuck her already."

"I need some fucking space," I snarl back.

"If I move, I will fucking come," he pitches back.

"You think I give a fuck about your pleasure when you have already fucked her twice?!"

We both growl. Melody groans, and her inner muscles fist me, redirecting my focus.

Sparkling dots form behind my eyes, and sweat pops out

from every pore on my body as I make a series of short sharp thrusts that see her yield to take me to the knot.

Just as I convince myself she cannot possibly take me deeper, Aengus pulls a small way out of her ass, and I slip all the way home.

Compelled by a slippery heat, my body decides that one good thrust was enough, and blood pounds into my knot with alarming speed. I grunt. I can't pull out, even when Aengus rams back in... and takes her ass in a pounding rhythm.

I blink, my palms turning slick against her skin. She has moved her teeth to new ground and is savaging me again. I try to stave off my climax, but my spine tingles, and my balls rise.

It's too much—I feel like the top of my head blows off. Her arms and legs squeeze, and her pussy begins that sweet fisting that compels me to eject my seed. Her squeal is muffled against my throat. Aengus thrusts once, twice more, and stills with a grunt.

My head is pounding. My cock is pounding, too, as more and more cum jets against her womb.

We crush her soft, lush body between us and fill her all up.

Zeke

I have been forced to watch Aengus and Theron fuck Melody into a limp fairy puddle. Draven must be made of stone. Other than when he barked at Aengus for not playing well with Theron, he appears relaxed.

I have no such restraints. It is only Draven's arm banded around my shoulders, holding me back as we stand at the foot of the bed-come-nest, that has stopped me from wading in... especially when Aengus takes her ass, and she fucking loves it.

I am the youngest and the weakest among our pack. I understand my place. That doesn't mean I have to like it.

"It will be worth the wait," Draven says—I am as yet unconvinced of this. "Once she is well-rutted, we can take her together. Something tells me she will enjoy two cocks in her cunt."

Fuck!

It is like he has reached inside me, found my darkest, most depraved desire, and slapped me with it. I jerk against him—he tightens his hold. And I like that he controls me. It makes my dick weep pre-cum... even my teeth fucking ache.

"She is going to be wrecked," I say, words a soft groan. "All open and softened—*defenseless*—for whatever we want to do."

He growls lowly as though in appreciation.

"I want Zeke!"

Those words are music to my ears, and as Aengus and Theron move aside, I wade into the nest.

Melody

I cling to Zeke as he claims me in the nest. His mouth moves over mine, lips hungry, and his hands shake as they skim over my body. Then Draven comes down over me and tumbles us over so that Zeke is on his back, and I am straddling his waist.

Looking back, I see a dark gleam in Draven's eyes that makes my breath hitch.

His attention is fixed on where his hand moves below me— Zeke grunts—I turn my attention to look down, trying to work out what he is doing when he barks out, "Sit!"

I am not given a choice when he clamps his other arm to encircle my waist and push me. Zeke's hands are on my hips, and together they direct me down. My eyes clash with Zeke's and my jaw pops as two thick cocks, mashed together, seek entrance to my most intimate part.

My moan rises from the pit of my belly as my flesh is forced to yield.

Goddess help me, do they seek to kill me with pleasure and their cocks?

"Tell me what you need," Draven purrs, lips beside my ear. "Tell us to fuck you together like this, to ruin your hot, filthy little cunt, to open you all up so we can rut you how you need."

The pressure is intense, and the pleasure becomes thick, dark, throbbing, blissful waves I need more than my next breath. "More," I say. "Deeper. Please. Oh, Goddess, I'm going to come."

They hold me pinned between them as they begin to thrust up into me, slow and steady, forcing me to stretch to take them. They are unstoppable forces acting on me, and I cannot get enough.

I begin to shake, heat flushes the surface of my skin, and I arch my neck, offering my body and blood to them.

Zeke rises from the bed, his lips latching to one side.

Draven takes the other.

The brief and sharp pain is followed by a halo of light. My pussy pitches into spasms that tear a guttural cry from my lips. "Oh, oh, oh!" I twitch and thrash. One hand reaches back to press and clasp Draven's neck, my other fists Zeke's hair as I hold him close. The steady pull as they feed shoots pleasure to my womb—a kaleidoscope of color dances behind my eyes.

Zeke

When she is done dancing and thrashing on our cocks, we put her between us in the nest. Aengus lays down behind her as Draven staggers off to get a drink. Theron moves in close eager for his turn at our mate. It is a spacious nest, so we all manage to fit.

My chest is heaving, and my dick has no fucking chance of going down.

Also, I need to see. I spread her legs—Aengus obliges me by holding her leg up as I scoot down the nest.

"What the fuck is the runt doing?" Aengus grumbles, peering down over her shoulder to see what I do.

"I'm obsessed with her pussy," I say. "She is nicely softened. All open for us." I pump my finger in, reveling in the sticky wet noises her pussy makes, her soft moans, and the way her hips undulate as she seeks more.

"Fuck's sake," Theron mutters.

Draven chuckles from the other side of the room.

"I don't like it," she whines.

I smirk. "Can you hear that? Can you feel how open you are? Your pussy is gaping after what Draven and I have done. You will only feel better with a dick in here, filling you all up again. You are ruined such that we could fuck our knots in and out of you without too much discomfort. Well" —I grin— "there might be some. But you could take it, couldn't you, Melody?"

"Please!"

She begs so sweetly, humping her hips back at Aengus, who pushes his cock into the gap, sliding it over her slick pussy and coating his length in our combined cum. "Our filthy little omega will take well to a good deep fucking with a fully formed knot."

He is not joking about the knot being fully formed. It is like he is broken or something. I can't help myself—I need to see, and the next time he thrusts forward, I push his cock, and the tip slips in.

Fuck, I think his cock is even thicker than usual too.

She moans as he rolls his hips, filling her to the knot, and my eyes flash to hers, watching the pleasure contort her face.

"Work the knot in," I say. Returning my attention to her ruined pussy I become riveted as he flattens his palm over her abdomen and, with the next thrust, pushes deep. There is a moment of resistance—she thrashes and strains—before the knot nestles inside. "Gods, that looks fucking amazing. Work it in and out. She can take it. Look at how flushed she is."

"She is getting off on it," Theron says. Fisting her hair, he leans in to kiss her, swallowing her little mewling cries as Aengus fucks her.

Heat. It is a strange mystical event that few warriors as young as I get to experience, and fewer still with a mate.

As time passes, I come to understand that what I thought was heat was merely the prelude. A veil comes down over the human side of me and the animal within rises. We fuck her, one then the other, together, the hours blending into days. There is only her scent, and her begged demands for *more*. A call we are compelled to answer.

Our bodies become littered with scratches and bites as she claims each of us and marks us as hers. Scars we will wear with pride for the rest of our lives.

Life?

Mine was already forfeit. Although I have no recollection of it, I have visited the Goddess's side. Now, my life is Melody's, and I, her humble servant, will love and dedicate it to her in any way she chooses.

Her heat pulls us ever deeper into our rut. We come on her, in her, and over her once beautiful nest. I teeter on the brink of exhaustion, yet am insatiable and can find no peace when I am not touching her or tending her in some way.

Finally, as the sun rises for the third day, and much to my relief, she finally collapses over Theron, knotted, and mutters, "No more."

"Thank the Gods," Aengus grunts.

Draven staggers off to fetch water which he forces her to drink. She complains bitterly, which makes me chuckle, even as I pitch face first into the nest at her feet.

"Drink some water, runt." Draven lifts my hand and wraps it around the neck of the bottle. "I'm not letting you sleep until you do, so best get on with it."

"He's an annoying bastard," Aengus grumbles. "You can take him at his word."

I manage to lift my head and gulp half of it down before Draven is satisfied and takes the bottle from me.

Sleep pulls me under, and when I finally rouse myself, it is morning once again.

Chapter Thirty-Two

Melody

After the experience of rescuing Zeke, I spend a lot of time thinking about my ability to travel through time. I think about my parents.

Whether I could save them.

If I could use it to find Bard.

The portal scholar, having consulted many books on the subject, confirms what I instinctively know—that long time jumps are dangerous, that it would be impossible for me to have a clear reference point to an event that happened when I was a child, that fairies were lost when they attempted such, and that opening a portal through time is a gift to be wielded with caution.

I resume my quests, although it is no longer a lone warrior who accompanies me but my four mates. There is still the keystone to monitor, a duty which the king hopes to pass on to me. As I have discovered, questing involves a lot of snowy forests, cold fingers and toes, and trekking around. Occasionally, I manage to get close enough that I can feel the portal key. After several such quests, I'm able to pinpoint the direction and distance from us with ease.

But no quest is without danger, even with my four brave alphas at my side. And when we come under attack from a band of villainous raiders I discover that my blood is not, in fact, impotent, as I had believed.

As Draven raises his sword to strike down the nearest raider scum, a mighty crack rents the air. Lightning zaps from the sword, shattering the raider's skull. Zeke wheels his horse around to engage a man of his own. His blow lands with the same devastating force, sending the raider flying from his horse and crashing into a nearby tree.

The remaining raiders turn and flee.

"Well, that is an impressive trick," Aengus says, eyeballing his sword as though it is not merely a weapon but the instrument of a god.

"Wow," Zeke says.

"Impressive," Theron says dryly. "The power came through my sword, but it was assuredly coming from within me."

"Melody's blood," Draven says, turning to look at me.

I gulp. "I don't think," I stammer. "I don't know... Is it possible?"

"I have felt the changes for some time," Theron says. "An awareness of power. I nearly took Kirk's head off in our sparring session a few days ago. I suggest we reserve sparring for our... for within our pack, lest we inadvertently harm a fellow warrior."

"A good call," Aengus agrees. He indicates the fallen raider. "Exploded his head clean off like a ripe melon."

"Please, I do not need the details," I say, trying not to look at the dead body minus the head.

"The king will be pleased," Draven says.

"The king will be fucking ecstatic," Aengus replies.

"One of them struck me," Zeke says. "But the wound has already healed." He holds up his arm. There is a distinct slash in his leather armor and a bloody stain, although beneath is only clear skin.

"Very impressive," Aengus says.

"It can't be my blood," I say.

"Why not?" Draven asks, grinning. "Did you not realize you were an imperial omega? Did you not have lessons with other imperial omegas?"

"Well, I know that," I say, feeling a little cross about his teasing. "But it never did anything before, and the other girls— well, one of them—used to taunt me and say I wasn't an imperial omega at all."

"Who the fuck was that?" Zeke demands, bristling indignation.

"It doesn't matter anymore," I say. "They allocated her to a mature warrior. The other girls mentioned he was very strict. I think his name is Kain."

Theron chuckles. "Kain will keep her in hand."

"Indeed," Draven says, grinning broadly. "I heard the king is set to strip him of the binding under special circumstances. It was Athena, I am guessing, for I heard Kain mention she was a brat in need of correction. I foresee a very sorry omega."

I might take a moment to gloat a little. It is only what she deserves, given she sabotaged my homework and put glue in my hair.

A familiar quickening distracts me from Athena's demise. I still and turn my head to the north. "I sense the keystone— moving swiftly." I close my eyes, allowing myself to center upon it. "Five miles. Maybe a little less, due north of here, and moving east."

"We should try to get closer," Theron says.

"Agreed." Draven wheels his horse around. "We ride."

We track the keystone for the rest of the day until we near Gailey's crossroads, where we spot them in the distance turning south toward the Blighten stronghold. The sun has dipped low on the horizon, bathing the sky in pink streaks. The temperature feels as though it drops swiftly.

"I have an idea," I say, frowning in the direction of the retreating Blighten.

"Why does that make me nervous?" Zeke asks.

"You have good intuition," Draven says. "Last time she said that we opened a portal through time to save your ass."

"Fuck!" Zeke says gruffly.

"No," Aengus says.

"It might just work," Theron says reasonably.

"I agree," Draven says.

"With who?" Zeke demands.

"With all of you," Draven says. "Not without approval, but yes, it might just work. They were an unusually small party traveling at high speed. Hard for them to stop if you open a portal. Easy for us to subdue on the other side. A risk, for sure, since we cannot know who is in the group. But if it does work, well, fuck, that's a game changer. Open a portal back to Sanctum, Melody. We'll talk to Jacob first."

We talk to Jacob and then the king.

We return back in time; only instead of tracking the Blighten, we cut a path through the forest directly for the crossroad. Draven and Theron dismount and take up a position under cover a little closer to the tree line.

I feel the keystone approaching from far away, drawing ever close and building tension within me.

As they are finally near, and I can hear the thunder of hooves, I know the moment is upon me.

"Now!" Draven calls.

Melody Unbound

I say the words of calling, my eyes trained on the cross-roads. There is a spark, and then a flare as a shimmering portal pops into existence.

A horse rears as they try to pull up.

Too late.

They tumble into the portal to where Jacob and his elite warriors are waiting, and then it winks out.

By the time Draven and Theron join us and we portal back to Sanctum, it is the start of a new era.

The keystone is once more ours.

We have finally severed the Blighten connection, not only to our world but many more.

Chapter Thirty-Three

Melody

Firdst it was the scented bath oil from Zeke that he insisted would only deliver the full benefit if he tended me through the bath, which he did... while I was blindfolded and spoiled blissfully and lovingly until I was a limp puddle of sated omega that he carried to the nest.

Then there was the decadently soft lambswool blanket from Theron. He explained that it could only be integrated into the nest correctly if he spread me out on it as he lavished my pussy with attention. And Goddess, Theron is a thorough kind of alpha who knows how to make me tremble and quake with pleasure.

Next there was the honey cake from Aengus. Baked, with a little assistance from Shiloh, and which melted me in an instant because what omega could resist a big, gruff barbarian, looking unusually bashful as he presented you with a misshapen honey cake that he had made with love? I nestled upon his lap as he fed it to me and teased me until I was begging for him to rut me on the pretty day room couch… which he did, the deep, rough kind of rutting, which Aengus does best.

My mates have taken it upon themselves to woo me, even though I have already accepted them. Aengus has bemoaned that this is all the wrong way around. In the barbarian clans, when a man wants to catch a woman's eyes, he gives her gifts and might entreat her to walk with him in the evening after work is done. After they are mated, it is a man's duty to ensure the home is well provided for his mate and children and that his mate is rutted often among the furs so she never doubts his dedication and love.

In Sanctum, things are done a little differently, especially when imperial omegas are the mistresses and alphas are subservient. Here, it is always an omega's choice, and even for the lower breeders and feeders, alphas pride themselves on satisfying an omega, on gifting them carnal attention so they might pick them again, and even, one day, accept them as a mate.

My heart is filled with joy and happiness simply by having my four mates. That they love me as I love them is a blessing, one I feel to my very soul. The bond between us, now unfettered by the binding, has strengthened from that gold thread to a golden vine that grows ever stronger with each passing day.

I do not need gifts. Their loving attention is all I ever wanted. I gift my love back to them with equal enthusiasm and passion, mindful that there are four of them. They are all very different in their life journeys but united as they came together as a family, and that later encompassed mating me.

"What is this about?" Draven says as he enters the day room.

I'm on Zeke's lap at our dining table, where he feeds me from a plate. After watching and learning from Aengus, he has mastered the art of taunting during this otherwise functional meal. It's not like I want for their attention at any other time. My thin nightgown does little to shield me from their hands or eyes.

It's almost like they cannot help themselves.

Not that I mind. Far from it. I find myself rising enthusiastically, knowing one of them will take a turn to feed me.

Well, except for Draven. He is still my first alpha, but is now working closely with Jacob, and rarely present for breakfast.

"It is an important part of bonding," Zeke says, quoting Aengus from two mornings ago.

Draven frowns—it is only now that I notice the beautiful lilac scarf he holds in one rough hand. "Her face is flushed, her nipples are hard, and she smells like fresh slick."

My face heats further under his cool assessment, which is not wrong... also the scarf is very pretty, and I'm already certain it is silk. For all I deny my need for gifts, my fingers twitch with interest.

Draven turns toward Aengus, who is eating his breakfast with a smirk. "I believe it's time I started attending breakfast."

"About fucking time," Aengus mutters. "The brat is needy of a morning if she doesn't get dick. It is a joy to watch her squirm as she approaches the table, wondering which one of us will claim her first. Sometimes I even let her take a seat for a few minutes just to let her stew."

Theron chuckles. "She does not take well to sitting in her own chair anymore. You would think we never rutted her for the sour look on her face."

I growl, ready to box the wicked alphas' ears.

"Enough," Draven mutters as though exasperated with all of us.

A squeak escapes my lips as he plucks me from Zeke's arms

and drops my ass on the edge of the table. He draws my thighs open and, pulling up a chair, sits between them.

He captures my chin between his fingers and thumb and presses his lips to mine in a sweet kiss that steals my breath while his big body wedged between my thighs makes me feel vulnerable and needy all at once.

"Are you making a little mess, Melody? Is that how this goes down? Does one of my brothers tend to your sweet pussy during breakfast?"

I nod, drawing my lower lip between my teeth as his thumb brushes lightly over my cheek. My eyes are drawn to the pretty lilac scarf he holds casually in his other hand. They know well I like pretty things. I am already imagining it in my nest.

"Hmm," he says. "It would appear I'm missing out." His gaze trails over my body, over quivering breasts past my belly, until he settles on the juncture of my thighs. He presses a kiss to my cheek before leaning back a little. "Lift the hem of your nightgown, Melody. Let me see what they have done to you."

I groan helplessly, only too eager to do as he requests.

He makes a tutting noise. "Now, put your hands behind your back."

My tummy takes a slow tumble, and my pussy clenches. I am swift to obey, scarcely breathing as he traces the silk scarf over my quivering breasts, down over my belly, and feathers it against my pussy.

"I think I might use this pretty scrap of silk to bind your wrists," he says casually as he tugs my neckline down on one side to expose my breast. He cups the weight in a decidedly proprietary way, his eyes totally focused on his handiwork. My pussy clenches and weeps for his attention. My chest thrusts out in encouragement for him to pet me. "Do you like the sound of that, Melody? Do you wish me to bind your wrists while I eat this naughty pussy out?"

I nod enthusiastically. "Please!"

His dark chuckle is a promise.

I know he will deliver.

And he does, binding my hands at the small of my back, ensuring they are secure, but not too tight, before he carefully lays me back. How vulnerable I feel like this, spread out, opened, and bound, my back arched and my wings wide and fluttering against the table, shedding golden dust as my arousal spikes.

"Good girl," he praises. "What a perfect little omega, all bound for her alpha's pleasure so that he can eat out her sweet cunt at his leisure."

Oh my. He has not yet put his lips upon me, and I'm a quivering mess of need and already near to coming.

He hooks his hands under my thighs and spreads me wide and vulnerable, exposing my most intimate place to his lustful gaze. He can see all of me... how shamelessly wet I am.

Then he lowers his head and slides the tip of his nose up the length of my thigh until he reaches the needy place between my legs.

Here he feasts, closing his mouth over me, licking and lapping, kissing up the weeping slick, spreading me wider, and lavishing my clit with his tongue until my body explodes into a fiery climax that sets off a starburst behind my eyes.

He doesn't stop. Only growls, low and long, as he slips one hand around, thrusting two fingers into my pussy and finding that sensitive entrance to my slick gland where he pets without mercy.

I thrash against the silk bounds, made impossibly more aroused by my helpless state, coming again, groaning, humping my hips up for more.

He gives me more, surging up, still licking me from his lips as he frees his buckle and shucks his pants down far enough to free his cock.

I groan at the first rough thrust that sees him seated to the root. The glorious fullness blissful against the post-climax daze and setting nerves the length of my channel sparking to life.

There he ruts me, deep, hefty thrusts that rattle the things on the table and make our bodies slap wetly together.

"Beg me for my seed."

That command, the savage lines of his face, his dominance... his love.

"Please come in me. Please!"

I am nothing but the recipient of his pounding cock, and the vessel for his lust.

I am an omega who has found heaven while still grounded in life.

"I'm coming," I pant. Truth be told, I have not stopped coming, but the breath-stealing high that side-swipes me is a form of carnal intoxication, one I cannot get enough of.

He stills as my pussy quakes and spasms around his thick length and knot, and I sigh, heart racing, as a hot flood bathes the entrance to my womb.

I blink up at him as I rouse myself from my lusty stupor.

He quirks one brow.

"She has taken well to bondage," Zeke says thickly, reminding me that my other mates are all still here and have watched me come apart. "Perhaps we should try this some more."

I blush—it is hard to dispute this amid the overwhelming evidence.

Reaching behind me, Draven releases my wrists with a single tug, then he gathers me from the table and sits down heavily in the sturdy chair where he gently massages my wrists.

I fall limp against his chest, well stated as we wait for the knot to soften.

"It is customary to hand the fairy over, so we can all have a go," Aengus says.

"I have missed several mornings," Draven replies. "I believe I will be the one having another go, and you can all fucking wait."

Theron chuckles. "He has a point."

Epilogue

Melody

S anctum's library is a beautiful stone room with high vaulted ceilings and pillars, intricately carved with woodland scenes, gargoyles, and other creatures that reach toward the glass dome high above. A central circle is dedicated to desks, from which rows of shelves that lead out like spokes from a wheel.

Within this room lies all Sanctum's knowledge, some recent and some of it stretching back to the very beginnings of this fairy race. I spend my days studying portal lore, for although much of it is instinctive to me, there is yet much more to learn to uncover.

My wings waft slowly as I carefully read through the book that lies open before me. I sprinkle only a little dust, having gained some mastery of my wings now they are free.

My wings are accepted now, mostly, although some people do still stare on occasion when I pass by. One might also presume some of the interest is on account of me taking four mates.

I know what they whisper, how they think I am scandalous. Not that I mind when I am so blissfully happy.

Then there are other, hushed conversations that speculate on how I led the patrol that recovered the lost keystone. I have liberated Sanctum from the dark shadow of the Blighten. Not only Sanctum but all the other worlds that were subject to tyranny and raiding by the orc war machine.

There are many Blighten troops that yet linger in our lands, cut off from their masters. Over time we will find a way to subjugate them should they continue their warring ways. I pray they might take this opportunity to change, to learn the ways of the Goddess so we might live in peace with them.

I have come a long way through an eventful life journey. A fairy child who lost her parents under such terrible circumstances, who inadvertently helped the Blighten to conquer new worlds, and who finally played a role in freeing this fairy race and many others from centuries of war.

At the sound of footsteps, I lift my head from my book and glance over my shoulder. Happiness lights up my face as I see Draven approaching.

"It is time for a break," he says, a mysterious smile on his face, which, for once, does not take my naughty mind toward images of rutting.

"I have not been here long," I say.

"No matter." He places the marker for my place in the book and folds it shut in a way that says this is not open to discussion. "I promise the interruption will be worthwhile."

I raise a brow.

He only offers another enigmatic smile and, drawing back my chair, takes my hand in his and leads me from the library.

This is very curious, but I decide to play along. He is

masking his side of the bond and his emotions. An alpha trick I have gotten used to, but have failed to master myself.

No matter, I will find out what this is about when he is ready.

Our route takes us up several floors, out into the area where the highest imperial omegas live, until we arrive at Winter and Jacob's door.

I look at him enquiringly.

He lifts my hand to his lips and kisses the back... then, with only a cursory knock, he opens the door.

The first thing I see is Winter, the glistening in her eyes, and her joyful smile.

Then my head turns, and it is as though time stops.

I am cast backward like a bowstring being drawn tight before I am shot forward again to the unexpected, wondrous now.

My hand presses to my lips as a sob bubbles up.

I cannot quite believe what my eyes tell me. I cannot quite dare to hope that this is real and not some trick.

"Bard."

One word and a short but eventful lifetime between the last time I uttered it and now. A child, confused and feeling alone, realizing an adventure was upon me, one that would tear me away from the only connection to my former family and home.

I take the steps to him and hold his old, gnarled hand in mine.

"Indeed, child, it is your old Bard."

Another sob bubbles up. I share a look with Winter and Draven and see their love reflected back at me before I forgo all decorum and throw my small arms around Bard's neck.

I sob and mutter all manner of nonsense as he murmurs soothing words and pats my back.

"There," he says. "Anyone would think you have missed me. All I did was order you to behave all the time, and you were only a sweet young fairy full of mischief as all young fairies should be. How it broke me to chastise you, even as I prayed I could keep you safe."

"Oh, Bard, I never thought I would see you again. I always wondered. I always hoped. But where have you been?"

"Well," he says, drawing back and taking my hand in his again. "It is no small business to find a portal scholar willing to take you from one world and into another. I have traveled far, from the forests close to Kung, through Hydornia, and all the way to the capital and the library there where I'd heard a portal scholar from your former home could be found.... He had left some years earlier. And so I trekked to Dires End and the home of the Fallen Centaurs, where I was told a portal was linked to our former home, Citadel, now liberated from the dark fae by a powerful stag shifter. I passed through the worlds with the blessing of the centaur herd leader. Our former home is much changed and joyous again under a new fairy queen, her king, and five other mates."

I gasp at this part.

"Once they learned of my story and that I was seeking you, a former fairy child, they tasked their scholars with researching a pathway to Sanctum... It has been a long journey. It has taken me many years, through many towns and villages, where I played my songs for money and told tales of a young fairy girl I once knew. My many patrons thought it was a story, but I alone knew it was true. I never gave up on my quest to find you. I made a promise to your mother a long time ago. I had to let you go for a time, but I find peace knowing I fulfilled her dying wish. Seeing you all grown up, and hearing of what you have done here in liberating the people of Sanctum, is all the reward I desire... Your mother and father would have been so proud."

I burst out crying again.

Winter offers me a clean handkerchief, for I am a mess of tears, before she calls for tea and honey cake.

I feel a connection to my lost parents through Bard, a man who was once a simple bard but who became a hero.

Today, I realize that heroes come in many guises.

Some are brave warriors like my mates. Draven, my dominant warrior, who is like a steady rock against the current, holding our pack together. Aengus, who fought to survive amid darkness and despair. Theron, who would have given his life to save me when we came under attack. And Zeke, my final mate, sweet, yet wicked, who overcame the odds to become a warrior, and who fought bravely and fell, only to be reunited after we opened a portal through time.

And then there are some heroes who are simply ordinary people who do extraordinary things.

As I take a seat on the couch with Bard's hand in mine, asking him a million and one questions about his travels and barely giving him a chance to speak as servants bustle in with tea, I recognize that Bard is one such hero.

"Do you know what happened to Jasmine and her mate Doug?" I remember well the pretty and patient bondservant who would let me plait her hair, and her mate, a fearsome white orc-wolf shifter, who transformed into a fantastical beast the day they fled.

Bard's smile is broad. "I do. A story worthy of a bard's tale, which I believe I am. Now, where should I begin..."

Draven kisses my cheek and takes his leave with a smile.

Winter pours tea and passes us both a generous slab of honey cake. "One needs sustenance when journeying on adventures weaved by a skilled bard," she says with a smile.

"At the beginning," I say, grinning, taken back to that

precious, innocent time when Bard was a bard. "You must always start at the beginning."

He sips his tea, sets it down on the table, leans back in his chair, and begins.

Spellbound, I am taken on a new adventure. I sigh and gasp, and sometimes I even laugh.

"That is quite a story," I say, smiling and wiping fresh happy tears from my cheeks as he reaches the end.

"Indeed," he says. "Now that all my adventuring days are finally over, I have a mind to write it down."

About the Author

Thanks for reading *Melody Unbound*. Want to read more? Check out the rest of my *Coveted Prey* series and my other books!
Amazon: https://www.amazon.com/author/lvlane

Where to find me...
Website: https://authorlvlane.com
Blog: https://authorlvlane.wixsite.com/controllers/blog
Facebook: https://www.facebook.com/LVLaneAuthor/
Facebook Page: https://www.facebook.com/LVLaneAuthor/
Facebook reader group: https://www.facebook.com/groups/LVLane/
Twitter: https://twitter.com/AuthorLVLane
Goodreads: https://www.goodreads.com/LVLane

Also by L.V. Lane

Prey

I am prey.

This is not pity talking, this is an acknowledgment of a fact.

I am small and weak; I am an Omega. I am a prize that men war over.

For a year I have hidden in the distant corner of the Empire.

But I am running out of food, and I am running out of options.

That I must leave soon is not a decision for today, though, but a decision for tomorrow.

Only tomorrow's choices never come.

For tonight brings strangers who remind me that I am prey.

Prey is a fantasy reverse harem Omegaverse with three stern Alphas, an Alpha wolf-shifter, and a stubborn Omega prey.

Printed in Great Britain
by Amazon